How to Teach
Filthy Rich
Girls

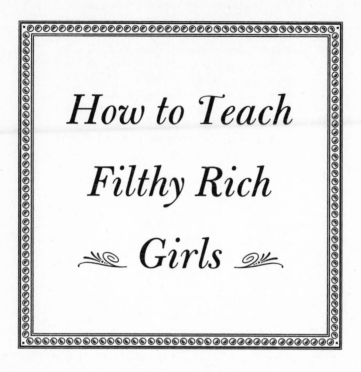

How to Teach
Filthy Rich
Girls

Zoey Dean

WARNER BOOKS

NEW YORK   BOSTON

Produced by Alloy Entertainment, 15 West 26th Street,
New York NY 10001.

Warner Books
Hachette Book Group USA
237 Park Avenue
New York, NY 10017

Visit our Web site at www.Hachette BookGroupUSA.com.
Book design by Fearn Cutler de Vicq
Printed in the United States of America

First Edition: July 2007
10 9 8 7 6 5 4 3 2 1

Library of Congress Cataloging-in-Publication Data
Dean, Zoey.
   How to teach filthy rich girls / Zoey Dean. — 1st ed.
      p.   cm.
   Summary: "If Megan Smith can tutor two heiresses with a combined
GPA of roughly 0.2 and get them into Duke University, their grandmother
will pay off Megan's college loans in full."—Provided by publisher.
   ISBN-13: 978-0-446-69718-7
   ISBN-10: 0-446-69718-4
 1. Children of the rich—Fiction. 2. Twins—Fiction. 3. Tutors and
tutoring—Fiction. 4. College attendance—Fiction. 5. Grandmothers—
Fiction. 6. Palm Beach (Fla.)—Fiction. I. Title.
   PS3604.E1547H69 2007   2007006030
   813'.6—dc22

To the A-list gang on West 26th Street,
and to the evil boy genius of my dreams.

How to Teach Filthy Rich Girls

The rich are very different from you and me.
　　　　　　—F. Scott Fitzgerald, *The Great Gatsby*

Choose the letter that would best fill in the blank spaces in the following sentence:

Exchanging family heirlooms and occasional sexual favors for _____ financial security is _____.

    (a) marginal; justifiable
    (b) complete; commonplace in Beverly Hills
    (c) a promise of; *so* 1990, circa *Pretty Woman*
    (d) reasonable; unforgivable
    (e) concert tickets and; totally legit

chapter one

Snatching my receipt from the bodega ATM, I already knew the bad news. I'd just withdrawn two hundred dollars, and my account balance was hovering a little over zero. So I stashed the cash and receipt in my battered backpack and asked what any recent Yale graduate whose student loans had left her seventy-five thousand bucks in debt would wonder:

"If I were to charge for sex, how much could I get?"

"Depends," answered my best friend, Charma Abrams, flatly. Her nasal monotone had been influenced heavily by too many girlhood hours spent with MTV's Daria. "Do you get to pick and choose your clientele?"

"Let's say I'm going for maximum cash."

"Hard to say. Let's go find you a pimp in Tompkins Square

Park." Charma examined her reflection in the anti-shoplifting mirror above the limp-looking green vegetables. "Or we could ask your sister."

My sister. Lily. As Charma well knew, Lily was playing a rich-girl-turned-hooker-turned-pimp in *Streets*, Doris Egan's new off-Broadway play. Lily's photo had graced the cover of last week's *Time Out:* "The New Season's Must-See Young Thesp."

My sister had been must-see her whole life. Drop-dead gorgeous, talented singer and dancer, Brown University grad, Lily had been born to be stared at. As I took in my own reflection in the warped deli mirror—medium height and weight, size eight on the top and size ten on the bottom on a good day, long brown hair exceptionally prone to frizz, a heart-shaped face with nice enough hazel eyes, a thin nose, and lips like the "before" photo on a lip-plumper ad—I wondered for the zillionth time how Lily and I shared a gene pool.

The chief reason I'd chosen to attend Yale was so I could do one thing in my life that was more impressive than what she had.

The immaturity of this is not lost on me, by the way.

"Come on," I told Charma. "I don't want to miss him."

We headed out of the bodega and crossed East Seventh, dodging a couple of joggers and a bag lady carrying on a one-sided conversation with the president: "You call that a foreign policy, you asshole?" It was one of those crystalline Indian-summer days when nature puts on a last-ditch floor show—the stubborn final leaves of autumn danced on their branches as the low November sun bathed them in ocher light. I wore my usual no-name jeans, a white Hanes T-shirt, and an ancient navy cardigan that my favorite of our family's three dogs, Galbraith, used to sleep on when he was a puppy.

"Where are you meeting this guy?" Charma asked.

"Southwest corner." I scanned the crowded benches lining the walkway to the center of the park. Everyone was enjoying the mild weather that surely wouldn't last longer than a day or two.

"Did he tell you what he looks like?"

"Tall, thin, dark hair cut short, soul patch, right ear pierced with a rhinestone stud," I rattled off. "He'll be wearing a red flannel shirt and Levi's, loose-fit."

"Boxers or briefs?" Charma asked.

I raised an eyebrow.

"I just wondered. Since you've got every other detail down."

"When I told him I was twenty-two, he said he was twenty-nine, which probably means he's mid-thirties and trying to pass. So I'd guess boxer-briefs." I made a beeline for an empty bench to our right. Too late. Three old Polish ladies had spotted it first.

Charma shook her blond curls out of her eyes. "About the whole sex-for-money thing? Waste of your brain. And I don't think your customers want to be remembered in that kind of detail. Stick with the magazine."

"Oh, like *that*'s not killing my brain cells on a daily basis."

I had a magna cum laude degree with a double major in English and American history and had been features editor of the *Yale Daily News*. So you can't say I arrived in Manhattan with the wrong credentials. I thought I'd have no problem finding a job writing in-depth stories at an important but left-leaning periodical like *The New Yorker*, or *Rolling Stone*, or hell, even *Esquire*—which only shows that a girl can be twenty-two years old, ridiculously well educated, and still as dumb as a bag of hair.

As it turned out, every other graduate from every other Ivy

League school had come to New York the day after graduation, and we all wanted the exact same jobs. Many of them, however, had something that I lacked. Connections.

My dad is a professor in the economics department at the University of New Hampshire, and my mom is a nurse-practitioner at campus health services. Lily and I had grown up in an old farmhouse filled with books, intelligent conversation, and excessive pet fur. My folks lived an ecological life. Theirs had been voted Best Compost Heap by *Earth Lovers*, the local greenie newspaper. It is a little-known fact that parents who win Best Compost Heap cannot help their daughter find a job at a hot-shit New York City magazine.

June morphed into July, which morphed into the hothouse of August, and I still was ridiculously unemployed. Then, right after Labor Day, I got my first and only job offer. Since I owed Charma the September rent and felt it would behoove me to sustain my body on something other than ramen noodles and canned tuna, it was either become an editorial assistant at *Scoop* or learn to intone "May I run through our specials this evening?" with a perky smile on my face. Walking gracefully while carrying hot food is not my strong suit. Nor is perkiness. The choice was made.

You know *Scoop*, though you may not admit to actually purchasing it. It's one step up from *Star* and two steps down from *People*. A few of my highlights to date included captioning such photo spreads as "Did Jessica Get Implants?" and "Lindsay's Wild Mexican Vacation!" Yes, I'd found it necessary to lower my journalistic aspirations a standard deviation. Or ten.

As Charma and I ambled along, a guy with short blond hair, a day's worth of stubble, and a ratty Wolfmother T-shirt smiled at us. Well, her. Charma turned to watch him pass, letting out a low, appreciative whistle. She's a much better flirt than I am.

I looked around, trying to find my mark. There was a junkie looking to score at ten o'clock. At high noon were two teenage schoolgirls with too much everything—makeup, hair, boobs, skin, stiletto boots—who apparently felt the need to shriek every other word at each other. Then I spotted a guy in jeans and a flannel shirt cutting through a stand of trees at two o'clock. Bingo. I waved.

"Megan?" He held out a hand with slightly dirty fingernails, but I was in no position to turn down a shake. He had something I really, really wanted.

"Yeah, hi, thanks for coming. Pete, right?"

"Yeah."

A couple with a baby stroller vacated a bench to our left. I sat down and motioned for Pete to join me. Meanwhile, I noticed Charma chatting with Wolfmother, who'd circled back to make actual contact. Who could blame him? Charma had the kind of natural curves women pay a small fortune for and even then have to settle for saline.

"You got it?" Pete asked, drumming his fingers on his jeans impatiently.

"Right here." My heart hammered as I unzipped my back-pack, taking out the white T-shirt that had, until an hour before, hung inside a frame on the exposed brick wall of our living room (whose futon also doubled as my bed). The front of the shirt featured a bird sitting on the neck of a guitar and the inscription WOODSTOCK: THREE DAYS OF PEACE AND MUSIC. Not only was it the real deal from the greatest rock concert of all time, it was also signed by Jimi Hendrix. Two Cornell students, who would later become my parents, had stuck it out until Hendrix's set on Monday morning. My father had managed to get the shirt signed by the guitar god himself and gave it to my mother as a sign of his love and devotion.

Now, as a sign of *my* love and devotion, I was passing it on. To what's-his-name. Right. Pete.

"Like I said on Craigslist, it's in mint condition," I told him.

He held out a callused hand. "Let's see."

I hesitated. "I'd like to see the tickets first."

Out came his wallet, and then there they were: two front-row seats to the Strokes at Webster Hall for that very night. The show had sold out within minutes last month. I'd tried everything to get tickets, but *nada*. Until now.

I should tell you, to be perfectly candid, the Strokes are not my favorite band. But my boyfriend, James, worships them. James—of the dazzling intellect and shining prose, a guy who considers Doris Lessing light reading—would blast "Heart in a Cage" and dance naked in his dorm room playing air guitar like a twelve-year-old. How can you not love a guy like that?

We'd met in a senior writing seminar where James quickly established himself as the most articulate student in the room, thinking nothing of arguing—and doing it well—with a professor who just happened to have written the preface to the latest edition of *The Elements of Style*.

I noticed James, of course. From my seat in the back, I was wowed both by his intellect and by his swagger as he walked to his rightful place in the front row. It was amazing what you could see when you weren't worrying about people watching you.

Take, for example, Cassie Crockett. She had a *Maxim* body and fabulous blond hair. But on the first day of class, I noticed two fingers sneak under what I quickly realized was a fantastic wig. Her fingers reemerged holding a few strands of dung-brown hair, which she covertly dropped to the ground. Then she did it again. And again. Trichotillomania—the obsessive-compulsive need to pull out your own hair. I spent whole seminars wondering what it was like for Cassie to go out with one of the guys constantly circling her. Maybe she never had sex. Maybe she had a No Above the Neck rule, instead of a Below the Waist one.

This is the kind of thing that goes around in my brain.

Anyway, back to James. A few weeks into the semester, I wrote a five-thousand-word piece for the *Daily News* about a New Haven intersection where businessmen pick up transvestite hookers. I'd spend an entire week blending in at a nearby coffee shop, observing the girls and their customers, memorizing every detail. Our writing professor read aloud a section of my article to illustrate the kind of specificity he sought from us. Then he nodded in my direction.

Every head craned around to look at me. I could see their reaction all over their faces: Her? *Really?*

James corralled me after class. I was too shocked to be nervous, and then I was too at ease to remember why I would have been nervous. We went for coffee and agreed on everything and everyone from Jonathan Safran Foer (loved *Everything Is Illuminated*) to Donna Tartt (loathed *The Secret History*). Lily, oracle of all romantic wisdom, had cautioned me to never, ever, *ever* have sex on dates one through three. I suppose you could say that I took her advice, in that my first meeting with James wasn't really a date. I was in his loft bed within five hours of "Want to grab a cup of coffee?"

We'd come to New York together after graduation, though

not so together that we shared an apartment. His parents owned an excruciatingly chic white-on-white pied-à-terre in a Donald Trump Upper West Side development, though their three-million-dollar mansion in Tenafly, New Jersey, was actually home. Dr. and Mrs. Ladeen—he was an intensely anxious but gifted cardiologist, she was a senior editor at the *New York Review of Books*—offered James the condo rent-free while he began what would surely be his meteoric rise to literary fame. Their expectation was based not only on the fact that he was truly talented, but also on the fact that his mother had used *her* connections to snag James a junior editor job at *East Coast. East Coast* is kind of like *The New Yorker*, except with even more of a focus on fiction.

Alas, James's parents had never warmed up to me. I'd tried, I really had, but there was no question they harbored hope James would get back together with his former girlfriend, Heather van der Meer, the youngest daughter of their longtime family friends. And thus the offer of lodging did not extend to me.

That was okay. There was plenty of time. James and I were happy. And tonight was his twenty-third birthday. I wanted it to be memorable, which was why I'd cut my bank account in half: first, dinner and a fabulous bottle of wine at the restaurant Prune. During dessert, I would casually break out the concert tickets, which would cause him to whoop with delight and lavish upon me the kind of public display of affection to which he was normally allergic. After the concert, we'd go back to his place for the best part of the evening. And morning.

To finalize my plan, all I had to do was trade my dad's Woodstock T-shirt for the tickets.

"We doing this or not?" Pete tapped his coffee-colored loafer against the sidewalk.

I bit my lower lip. My parents would understand. Of course they would. Or at least that was what I told myself. We made the swap. God, James was going to be so surprised.

I stuck the tickets in my backpack and then rose to wish Pete a pleasant life. A kid with a shaved head—he couldn't have been older than fourteen—wheeled toward us on one of those delivery-boy bicycles. He was swerving from side to side, taking pleasure in scaring the little old Polish ladies nearby.

"Thanks," I told Pete. "Take good care of my—Hey!"

The kid on the bicycle sped past me, snatching my backpack before I could sling it over my shoulder.

"Stop! Stop that kid!" I bellowed.

I gave chase, Pete gave chase, and a lot of other people did, too. But the kid cut off the path and through the trees, pumping for all he was worth. A few seconds later, he was speeding down Avenue A with my backpack swaying from a handlebar.

It was almost as if the concert tickets and my two hundred dollars were waving goodbye.

Choose the analogy that best expresses the relationship of the words in
the following example:
                    EAST VILLAGE WALK-UP : *SCOOP*

   (a) classic six on the Upper West Side : *The New Yorker*
   (b) condo in Panama City : *USA Today*
   (c) Hollywood Hills bungalow : *Daily Variety*
   (d) flat in Camden, London : *Blender*
   (e) SoHo loft : *Us Weekly*

c h a p t e r   t w o

A skinny white kid with a shaved head, combat boots,
baggy green shorts, black sweatshirt, and a tattoo on
the knuckles of his right hand," I reported, forking the larger
of the two filet mignons I'd just broiled in my apartment's ancient stove onto James's plate. "Also, one of his handlebars was
dented. So I told all that to the cop."

"Wow, that smells amazing." James inhaled appreciatively.
He tucked his dark hair behind his ears and blinked his gorgeous
gray eyes at me. "So what did the cop say?"

I slid the second steak onto my plate and headed back to the
counter where I'd left the side dishes. "He said it was the most
detailed description of a perp he'd ever heard and that I should
consider a career in law enforcement."

"Either that or you've been watching too much *CSI*."

James was sitting on a folding chair at the wooden table in my apartment's pathetic excuse for a kitchen. Charma had salvaged it from the street, found furniture being one of New York City's greatest shopping perks for the salary-challenged. It had various profanities carved into its surface—EAT SHIT AND DIE was my favorite. I liked to think the former owner had Tourette's and a fetish for sharp objects.

The rest of the kitchen was similarly déclassé: warped black and white linoleum, appliances from the middle of a former century, a sink permanently stained by antibiotic-resistant life forms. It was a long, long way from Prune.

Still, when I brought the mashed potatoes and braised asparagus to the table, James gave me a huge smile. I had remembered his all-time favorite meal. It was still a piss-poor excuse for a surprise, but what choice did I have? After the cop had complimented me on my powers of observation, he'd cheerfully added that the odds of finding the kid who had ripped me off weren't great, and even if they did find him, my backpack and its contents would be long gone. Meanwhile, Craigslist Pete insisted that a deal was a deal, refused to return my T-shirt, and took off before I gave the cop my statement.

I'd decided not to tell James that I'd lost both the money for dinner at Prune and the front-row tickets to the Strokes. Why make him feel guilty? Instead, I withdrew forty more bucks from my calamitously low bank account and bought the makings of a great dinner. As birthday surprises went, it pretty much sucked, but I figured I could liven things up with dessert.

"Oh, man, that's perfect." James closed his eyes in rapture

as he chewed the medium-rare steak. "You canceled your credit cards, all that?" he asked.

"Credit card, singular," I reminded him. Not that the kid could have used it anyway—my Visa had a two-thousand-dollar limit that I was already over. I tasted my steak. Delish. It was one of the few things I could cook well. "What did your parents give you?"

The night before, his parents had taken him to Bouley. I hadn't been invited, despite the fact that last year Heather the Perfect had joined them at Five Hundred Blake Street, arguably the best restaurant in New Haven.

Truthfully, I didn't know Heather very well, but I had of course looked her up on Facebook. She was the youngest daughter of a rich Rhode Island family that traced its roots back to Roger Williams, and she was currently a first-year law student at Harvard. Not only did Heather have a brain, she had straight blond hair, a swanlike neck, and the kind of pouty lips I longed to have. A mere mortal who writes photo captions for a living and is a size larger on the bottom than on the top could not possibly compete.

"My present?" James's voice pulled me out of my musings. "My mom got John Updike to sign first editions of all the Rabbit novels for me."

I took a bite of steak and tried to smile. The only collectible I *used* to have was the Woodstock T-shirt.

For the next few minutes, I ate while James regaled me with tales from *East Coast*. He'd been assigned to edit the short stories of a half-dozen well-known young singer-songwriters. According to James, they all sucked, and he'd had to rewrite every word while they got the credit.

"I *hate* it when that happens," I teased, refilling our glasses with an Australian Shiraz that I'd found in the bargain bin. "Like, why don't *I* get credit for what I rewrote about Jessica and Ashley's dueling lip injections?"

He reached across the table for my hand. "You won't be stuck there for long."

Easy for a guy working at *East Coast* to say. I made little circles with my fork in what was left of my mashed potatoes. "If I could just pitch one really great idea that Debra would like..."

Debra Wurtzel was my editor in chief. She knew pop culture the way James knew Salinger. Editorial meetings were Monday mornings, and assistants like me attended only at the mercurial behest of an immediate boss—in my case, Latoya Lincoln, who'd invited me exactly twice. The first time Debra hadn't even glanced in my direction. But the second time she'd fixed her gaze on me and asked, "Megan? Your ideas?"

When Debra looked at me, everyone else did, too. I think I've already established that the center of attention is not my favorite place to be. For one thing, I blush. Seriously. The conference room fell silent as my face turned the color of an overripe tomato. Finally, I pitched a piece about a new study correlating celebrities' weights with dips and spikes in the average weight of sixteen-to-twenty-year-old women.

Debra's assistant, Jemma Lithgow, a recent Oxford grad in size-nothing Seven jeans, reminded the room that we had recently done a cover story on diet secrets of the stars, so we couldn't very well turn around and rip that which we had just lauded. She didn't need to add "you size-ten asshole" because, really, her look said it all.

Ever since that meeting, I'd been relegated to *Scoop* purgatory. Ambitious peers no longer sat with me for lunch in the fourth-floor commissary, clearly afraid of being tainted by my loser status. At least the risk of being asked back to the Monday editorial meeting was slim. I was okay avoiding further public humiliation for a while, thanks very much.

When James and I had finished eating, I piled the dishes in the sink, put in the stopper, and added water and dish soap. My prewar—meaning, pre–World War I—building had not come with plumbing fixtures suitable for a dishwasher. James came up behind me and lifted my hair to kiss the back of my neck.

"Hey," he murmured as he nuzzled. "I was just thinking about the holidays."

This was an interesting development. Thanksgiving and Christmas were practically upon us, and we'd spoken about them only in passing. "Yeah?"

He kissed me again, then his hands snaked around my waist. "My parents want us to go to Florida, to our place in Gulf Stream."

Us?

"So I thought...maybe you'd like to come?" James asked. "For Thanksgiving?"

Thanksgiving was only ten days away. It wasn't what you would call a lot of notice. Still, I felt like pumping my fist in the air.

I cocked my head back far enough so that I could see his eyes. "Your parents invited me?"

"Well, not yet," he hedged. "I wanted to check with you first."

Not good. Wasn't this kind of invitation supposed to work the other way around?

"What do you think?" James prodded, sneaking a forefinger under the bottom of my T-shirt. He kissed me again, then pulled my T-shirt up over my head.

"I think..." I said, trying to concentrate on what it would be like to miss Thanksgiving with my own family. But then James slid his hand into my jeans, and all I could say was "Oh" and then "Okay" and then "*Yes.*"

I reached for James's pants, unbuttoning them with one hand and tugging them to his knees with the other. I should mention here that in addition to writing, I do have one other talent—at least that's what I've been told. Let's just say growing up on the dark side of my sister's celestial glow made me try harder.

I whispered to James that he should go wait for me in bed, I had a birthday surprise for him. He was only too eager to oblige.

I opened the fridge and pulled out a chocolate cake with mocha frosting from the Edelweiss pastry shop on Second Avenue. Maybe I didn't have front-row Strokes tickets anymore, but I was hoping that frosting some of his favorites of my body parts would make up for it.

"Hey, where's your Woodstock T-shirt?" he called from the living room/bedroom.

Shit. "I decided to store it at my parents' house," I called back, anointing myself with mocha frosting.

You might ask yourself at this point if I felt even slightly ridiculous. The answer is yes. Frankly, I had never frosted my nipples before. Nor any other body parts. But I was determined, in spite of everything, to make this a birthday that James would remember.

I was just putting the finishing touches on the lower portion of my anatomy and kind of wishing that his favorite flavor were vanilla or strawberry, because mocha brown is not really the most becoming color for a nude and edible seduction, when I smelled smoke.

I checked the broiler, but I'd turned it off. Yet the smell was getting stronger. I cautiously padded to the front door and peered through the peephole. The hallway was black. A split second later, the old-fashioned fire alarm above my head began to clang loudly.

"Fire!" I ran into the bedroom, completely forgetting my nudity and the frosting. "Fire! There's a fire! The hallway is full of smoke!"

James sprang from the bed, his enthusiasm deflating, his eyes wide with fright. He grabbed his boxers.

"The fire escape!" I commanded, knowing we couldn't get through the smoke to the stairs.

I grabbed the first thing I saw—a bed sheet—and wrapped it around myself. As it turned out, frosting serves as a reasonable adhesive. Who knew? It took precious seconds for James to manhandle the window that opened to the fire escape. When he was finally able to shove it upward, he pushed me through, then followed. I could already hear fire engines in the distance.

Did I mention that physical education was never my strong suit? Well, it turns out that if I'm highly motivated, I can really haul ass. Down and down and down we went. By the time we reached the base of the escape at the second floor, a huge crowd had gathered, staring straight up at us.

It was then that the realization hit me: I was draped in a white sheet stuck to me with brown frosting; I was not wearing anything underneath; and I still had to climb down the rungs of a ladder to the sidewalk. I looked back at James for guidance.

"Go, baby," he ordered. "Just go."

And so I went. But climbing down a ladder wearing nothing but a frosting-spackled sheet, all while keeping my legs together in a ladylike fashion, proved . . . impossible.

Which is how I ended up beavering the entire East Village.

Not wishing to appear _____, the junior magazine staffer kept her _____ well concealed.

    (a) unsophisticated; ignorance
    (b) desperate; trembling hands
    (c) cocky; brilliant ideas
    (d) fat; size-ten booty
    (e) overqualified; pedigree

c h a p t e r   t h r e e

*E*arly Monday morning found me sipping coffee and enjoying my second jelly doughnut at a small cafeteria table across from my sister, Lily, who daintily spooned a bite of fat-free yogurt into her pouty-lipped mouth. Of course, that's what *I* should have been eating. But I figured that the events of the weekend entitled me to a full-fledged sugar infusion.

My apartment was uninhabitable. According to our barely decipherable Serbian landlord, Charma and I wouldn't be able to return for quite a while—three weeks, at least. We were allowed one trip inside after the blaze to salvage a few personal effects but had to don mouth-and-nose masks that made us look like invading aliens from a C-grade horror flick. The masks proved necessary, because everything in our apartment was covered in a layer of soot.

During that salvage mission, I shed my sheet and donned the first things I found in my closet—jeans, a sweatshirt, and chunky black loafers that hadn't been stylish even when I'd bought them freshman year. I took my iBook—praying that it had survived—and a garbage bag of clothes, plus the twenty emergency bucks I kept stashed inside a copy of *A Brief History of Time,* knowing that even if a junkie wedged his way under our kitchen-window security grate, he'd never steal that book.

Saturday night I slept at James's place and didn't attempt a return to birthday-seduction mode. Trust me, if you had an army of sidewalk strangers give you a visual gynecological exam, you'd lose your sex drive, too. His parents' condo had a mini washer and dryer discreetly placed behind accordion doors, but my attempts to wash the soot and fumes from the clothes I'd salvaged proved fruitless.

Sunday afternoon, James lent me his smallest jeans, an old sweatshirt, and a hundred bucks. I went straight to the 70-percent-off clearance rack at Century 21. This being mid-November, it held nothing but summer clothes and a handful of items clearly left over from last winter because they were too hideous to be purchased by anyone who could actually see.

My hundred dollars bought a gauzy lavender and purple prairie skirt, a white cotton shirt, navy stretch pants with pockets over both hips that pretty much screamed WIDE LOAD, a brown sweater, and two summer T-shirts in the oh-so-palatable shades of vomit yellow and puke green. Sweet. I couldn't enlist even Lily in this mission—she had a matinee and then a photo shoot for the Gap; they were doing a Stars of the Future ad campaign that would launch the following spring. The shoot went well into the night, which was why my sister had met me for coffee at my corporate cafeteria before her Monday-morning spinning class. Even without makeup and in gym clothes, she looked depressingly flawless.

"When can you get back into your apartment?" Lily asked.

My landlord had left another update on my cell voice mail. "Christmas. Maybe the week after."

Lily swallowed another baby-size mouthful of yogurt. "I'm sure you want to stay with James, but you can always stay with me if you want."

I had never actually informed Lily that living with James long-term was not an option due to his parents' mandate. It just seemed too pathetic.

See, here's the thing about my sister. I knew she'd offer to share her airy brownstone apartment on West Seventy-fifth near Amsterdam Avenue, and I knew she'd do it with grace. One of the worst things about Lily is that in addition to being stunning and disgustingly accomplished, she is also genuinely nice. If she were a self-centered asshole, I could loathe her. But since she isn't an asshole and I still detest her for all the things she is that I'm not, being around her kind of makes me hate myself.

"Oh, I'll work something out," I said breezily, then polished off the second jam-filled doughnut.

"Umm...you've got a little..."

Lily motioned to her chest. I looked down. My new white shirt was smeared with strawberry jam between buttons three and four. I dabbed at it with a napkin, which only expanded the pinkish stain. Swell.

We walked to the elevators. *Scoop* occupied floors seven and eight of a magnificently renovated fifteen-story building on East Twenty-third Street, overlooking Madison Square Park.

Other magazines owned by the same European publishing con-glomerate—including *Rockit,* a new *Rolling Stone* competitor I desperately wanted to write for but couldn't even get an inter-view with—took up the rest of the building, except for the sleek floor-through cafeteria where we stood. I pushed both the up and the down buttons. Guess which one came first.

"If you change your mind, just call me." Lily gave me a little hug and stepped into the empty down elevator.

A minute later, I stepped out of a jammed one heading up to *Scoop* and beyond. I waved to Brianna, the receptionist who had started only the week before. The walk to my cubicle took me past Latoya's open office door.

"Megan!" she called. "Editorial meeting in ten minutes."

I hoped the horror of her announcement didn't show on my face. I'd been a bit too preoccupied with the smoked-out-no-place-to-live-purse-ripped-off-no-money thing to plan a pitch for a meeting to which I'd been entirely positive I would not be invited again.

Ha.

Debra Wurtzel, my editor in chief, managed to be both totally cool and completely intimidating at the same time. She was in her early forties, with jet-black blunt-cut hair that fell just above her shoulders. Her severe bangs drew attention to her pierc-ing blue eyes, which were, as usual, rimmed in blue-black kohl. There were five tiny platinum loop earrings lining her right ear and one in her left. Today she wore black wool trousers, a fitted black blazer, and layered black tees. When the last straggler ar-rived for the editorial meeting—thank God it wasn't me—she took off her cat's-eye reading glasses. I'd figured out at my first meeting that this was her signal to begin.

We were in the eighth-floor conference room, whose windows overlooked Twenty-third Street. I sat between Debra's assistant, Jemma, and Latoya. Always stylish, Jemma sported a gossamer white blouse under a black Betsy Johnson corset top, a red-and-white-checked miniskirt, and round-toed heels that reminded me of Minnie Mouse. The only suggestion that she wasn't as perfect as she looked were the raggedy cuticles lining her ballet-slipper-pink manicure. Evidently pressure got to her, too.

Latoya wore a thick gray cashmere sweater, a straight black skirt, and piles of oversize black beads around her neck. She looked like Debra's style protégée, which of course she was. In my own jelly-stained shirt and absurdly out-of-season skirt, I looked like the protégée of a bag lady.

"Let's start with Hooking Up/Breaking Up." Debra fixed her gaze on Lisa Weinstock, the plump and brilliant editor whose department handled celebrity couples. "What's coming up, Lisa?"

Lisa brushed her magenta-streaked bangs away from her eyes. "Totally fresh scoop, including trouble in paradise for Jen and you-know-who. We've also got cell-phone pix of Ashlee flirting with Nick at Bungalow 8—nothing like hitting on your sister's ex to make a splash."

"Excellent," Debra said as heads bobbed in agreement all around the table. Of course, if Debra had agreed that a pictorial on donkey sex was "totally fresh," heads would've bobbed.

"Latoya?" Debra asked. "Center story?"

This was the department for which I was an underling. *Scoop* did one weekly four-page "article" in the center of each issue.

"I'm working on a piece with Demi's daughter Rumer,"

Latoya reported. "An inside look at her mom, Bruce, Ashton, blah blah blah. Her photographs; she'll write captions."

"Excellent, Latoya." Debra's head turned slightly until I was squarely in her gun sights. "Megan? What's your best new story idea?"

A dozen sets of eyes swung in my direction. I willed my face to remain this side of vermilion, but apparently, biofeedback wasn't working.

"Well...I was thinking about a story on..." Think, Megan, *think.* "Some new studies are suggesting that a decline in breast cancer may be connected to a decline in menopausal women's use of hormone replacement therapy."

Someone snickered, but Debra's face was inscrutable. She rolled a forefinger, indicating that I should continue.

"And that had me wondering what the connection might be to other forms of, um, hormones." I felt my face flaming. "Like the pill," I finished.

Debra raised her eyebrows at Latoya. "Did Megan discuss this with you?"

"No." Latoya was more than emphatic.

This was not good.

"Would anyone like to comment?"

Jemma raised a finger. "People read *Scoop* to *escape* reality, not to read about it. Cancer? Hormones? *Menopause?* I mean, ew."

I don't know if it was the weekend or my jealousy that James had gotten to write about something with a modicum of intelligence or that I'll always be my parents' daughter, but I couldn't help myself. "Don't you think we have some responsibility to our readers?" I asked. "We have a broader reach than almost any newspaper. Maybe we should do...*something*...with that."

Jemma glanced skyward in an apparent appeal to heaven to deliver her from me. "We write about important things *all the time*. But nothing goes wrong that a very expensive stint in rehab, or some very expensive plastic surgery, or perhaps a very, *very* expensive vacation on a private island can't fix. And *that's* what our magazine is about."

"I think—" Latoya began.

"Excuse me. Does anyone smell *smoke?*" Jemma wrinkled her irritatingly pointy nose, which got a dozen other noses twitching like bunnies' at a petting zoo. Shit. My shoes. I ever so casually shifted my legs away from Jemma and wrinkled my nose along with everyone else. There were murmurs around the conference table, until Debra asked Jemma to check with building security.

"Let's wrap up for now, people," Debra called as Jemma Minnie-Moused her way out of the conference room. The editorial staff shuffled toward the door. I was about to slip out with them, when—

"Megan?"

I turned back. "Yes?"

Debra slid her glasses onto her nose. "See me in my office in five minutes."

This was really *not good*.

Choose the analogy that best expresses the relationship of the words in the following example:

DOWNSIZING : SELF-CONFIDENCE

(a) stovepipe pants : plus-size model
(b) Page Six exposé : notoriety
(c) Britney Spears : K-Fed
(d) Grammy win : ticket prices
(e) drunken rampage : opening box-office number

chapter four

I stood outside the door to Debra's spacious office, listening to the wind howl around the corner of our building. NY1 had warned that the first real cold front of November was moving in. This seemed an apt metaphor for my life.

The mail guy wheeled his cart past me, careful not to make eye contact. Even the mail guy knew I was a *Scoop* leper. I glanced through the glass wall of Debra's office. She was on the phone but waved me in.

I stepped into her office for the first time since I'd been hired and was struck again by how spare and clean it was. Glass desk, Toshiba laptop, plus more of those floor-to-ceiling windows. She motioned me into one of the three black director's chairs facing her desk. The only decoration in her office was a silver Tiffany-framed photo of a much younger Debra at the beach, grinning at a little boy. Debra never talked about her personal life.

"Uh-huh. Okay. Fine... Yes, I'll let you know, Laurel. Talk to you soon." Debra finally hung up. "Megan."

"Yes?" I managed, folding my hands in my lap.

"Your instincts are scaring me." She swiveled her Aeron chair to look out the tall glass windows.

"I know my pitch was a little off," I admitted. She was staring at me as if I were a dead cockroach on her desk, but I plunged on anyway. "Sure, people like to read about the rich and famous, but if you think about it, we have a unique opportunity to reach so many different types of women. *Scoop*'s demographic is—"

"Jemma was right, Megan," Debra interrupted. "I'd hoped to move you from captions to articles by now—that's why I put you in Latoya's department. But it's been two months, and you're just not getting it."

My face flamed anew. "I'm sure I can come up with some better ideas." I hesitated, just in case Debra wanted to jump in at this point and agree with me. No such luck.

"I have to let you go, Megan."

I looked at my lap. Let me go? As in *fired*? Unemployed? Unemployed *again*? I gulped hard. "I understand. I'll just go clear out my—"

"I'm not finished," Debra interrupted.

"I'm sorry?"

She folded her arms. "I like you, Megan. Actually, you remind me of me at your age."

Evidently, she would have fired herself, then. I blinked my suddenly watery eyes.

"You're smart. Your ideas are intelligent and ballsy. And you're a hell of a writer—none of that is lost on me. But *Scoop* isn't the right fit for you. You should be writing for a weightier magazine. *East Coast. Rolling Stone.* Even *Rockit.*"

Gee, you think?

"I do have some good news," she continued. "There's a job in Florida. Teaching. It's only for two months, but I think you'd be perfect for it."

Teaching? In Florida? For two months? This was her idea of *good news*?

I started to stand again. I felt my throat tightening and hoped to escape before the tears bubbled up again. "Thanks for thinking of me, really. But I'm not a teacher."

I turned to go, but Debra raised a finger. "Wait. Hear me out. One. It's mid-November—publishing is practically dead from Thanksgiving until the first of January. No one is hiring. No one is even interviewing."

Unfortunately, I knew she was right. Of all the times of the year to get canned, this was the worst.

"Two." She held up another finger. "You won't have any expenses. The gig comes with room and board. And three. It pays better than *Scoop*. Much better."

Okay, this wasn't making any sense at all. I didn't have teaching credentials. Even if I did, teachers normally didn't get paid much. And what kind of two-month-long teaching job included room and board? Some fill-in gig at a rich kids' boarding school? No, thank you.

Then again, certain realities awaited me when I left the *Scoop* offices: I couldn't live with James, and I didn't want to live with Lily. I couldn't look for a job, and I had no savings to fall back on. Heading back to New Hampshire to work at *Earth Lovers* somehow didn't appeal to me; nor did getting a job at Bloomie's wrapping Christmas gifts for people who could actually afford them.

"When does this job start, exactly?" I asked cautiously.

"Exactly now. There's a black car waiting for you downstairs."

"*Now?*"

"Yes. To take you to the airport, should you choose."

"To go to Florida," I filled in.

"Palm Beach, specifically. By private jet."

Private jet? To be a *teacher*?

"All the details will be explained to you when you arrive." Debra shuffled a stack of contact sheets from a recent photo shoot. "And you've got nothing to lose. If you hate it, you can get right back on the plane and be home in time for the ten o'clock news."

"But I..." I wasn't even sure what the *but* was exactly, but... but *something*. It was all too bizarre.

"Sometimes you have to take a leap of faith, Megan," Debra said gently.

A leap of faith. I wasn't really a leap-of-faith kind of girl. Watch carefully from the side and suss it out—yes. Big leap—no. But what were my options, really? And even if she had just fired me, for some reason, I didn't want to let Debra down. Weirdly, I still liked her. "Okay. I'll do it."

She smiled. "Excellent. You're on your way, then."

I rose, feeling numb. "I'd say thank you, but I'm not sure what I'd be thanking you *for*."

"Have you read the new *Vanity Fair*?"

I shook my head. I liked *Vanity Fair*—it was on my Top Ten

List of Magazines I'd Like to Write For. But I'd been too busy having my life fall apart to pay attention to the latest issue.

"You might want to check it out during your flight."

She took a copy off her desk and gave it to me. I didn't bother asking why. Evidently, *why* was another piece of this bizarre puzzle. As I shook her hand and then left her office for the last time, I felt like Alice heading toward that damned rabbit hole.

If a private jet travels from New York City at 521 miles per hour, how much time will elapse before wheels-down in Palm Beach, a distance of 1,231 miles?

    (a) 1 hour
    (b) 2 hours
    (c) 4 hours
    (d) 6 hours
    (e) Does it matter? There's an inexhaustible supply of free champagne!

chapter five

*T*his can't be happening," I murmured to James. "It isn't real."

We sat together in the back of the black car that had picked me up outside my office. No, wait, my former office. The Slovakian driver had just gone over the George Washington Bridge to New Jersey. There was no traffic in the middle of day, since the rest of the world was, you know, *at work*.

James draped an arm around me. "Well, unless we're in the same delusion, it's real. Odd—very odd—but real."

Odd didn't begin to cover it. I was just grateful that he was able to go with me to the airport. Even before I'd left my *former* office, I'd called him and babbled about what had happened— how I was on my way to Florida after a pit stop at his apartment to pick up my Century 21 bargain-rack specials and my toothbrush.

"Thank you for coming," I told him again. He'd feigned a toothache and an emergency dental appointment to join me for the ride. "Don't forget to drool a little when you get back to work. Novocaine." I nodded seriously.

"Will do." He squeezed my hand as we approached a sign that said TETERBORO AIRPORT. Teterboro Airport? I'd figured we were headed for Newark, but judging by the low buildings and prop planes parked nearby, I wasn't heading to Florida in a 757. "Excuse me, sir?" I called to the front. "Are we in the right place?"

"Not to worry." The driver had a thick accent. His eyes met mine in the rearview mirror. "I know where you are going. Your boss, Debra Wurtzel"—he pronounced it *Vets-el*—"gave to Boris ex-plea-cit instructions. Sit back and enjoy ride."

Enjoy ride. That was a joke. How could you "enjoy ride" when you didn't "know destination"?

Boris turned onto a service road, showed some identification at a security checkpoint, and then—to my shock—drove right out onto a tarmac. We rolled to a stop next to a jet with a dozen windows and the letters LL elegantly entwined on the tail.

"Your plane," Boris announced.

"What's LL?" James asked.

"No clue." I made no move to get out of the car.

James squeezed my hand again. "It'll be okay. Maybe you'll have time to do some writing? And I'll see you in ten days for Thanksgiving."

What finally got me out of the car was remembering what Debra had said—if I didn't like what I found in Florida, I could get right back on this plane and fly home. Oh-kay, then.

I thanked Boris. Then, hand in hand, James and I crossed the tarmac to the Gulfstream. A flight attendant stood at the bottom of the steps. She wore an impeccable black suit with a nipped waist, the kind actresses wore in the forties.

"Ms. Smith?" she asked pleasantly.

My stomach was turning vomit cartwheels. "Yes."

"I'm Adrienne. I'll be your flight attendant today." She had the faintest trace of a southern accent. "You're traveling alone, correct?"

"Unless I can kidnap my boyfriend." I looked hopefully at James.

"Do you have any bags?" Adrienne asked.

"Just this." I held up my tattered navy blue JanSport. "But I can carry—"

"No worries." Adrienne took my backpack. "I'll see you aboard. We'll take off as soon as you're ready. May I prepare a beverage for you?"

My mouth opened. No sound came out.

"You can decide when you're aboard." She smiled and headed up the steps and into the plane.

Now it was just James and me, in a setting that felt way too much like *Casablanca*, except in, you know, New Jersey.

"I'll call you when I get there. Wherever *there* turns out to be. And just in case I don't come back tonight..." I pressed up against his chest and gave him what I hoped was a memorable kiss and my best Bogart impression. "We'll always have Teterboro."

Forty minutes, three hundred miles, and thirty thousand feet of altitude later, the Gulfstream was somewhere high above Virginia. There'd been a decent amount of turbulence, so I'd been confined to my plush white leather seat, where I sipped a bottle of FIJI water. Finally, though, the air had turned smooth.

Adrienne came to me. "Feel free to walk around. Captain says it's fine. Can I prepare your lunch?"

"Oh, I'm fine, really," I told her. "But thank you."

"Something simple, then," she told me with a wink.

As she moved back toward the galley, I unlatched my seat belt and gave myself a tour of the cabin, having been too freaked out before takeoff to do much more than huddle in the first seat directly behind the cockpit. Not that I was a stranger to airplanes. I'd even been bumped to first class once. But a good look at the inside of the Gulfstream was enough for me to conclude that people who own private jets do not fly like you and me.

Just behind me, there was a semicircle of white leather seats facing a sixty-two-inch plasma high-definition television and a state-of-the-art sound system. Each seat had its own pink marble TV table, with recesses for cups and plates. Beyond was a small room with a pink toile-covered queen-size bed. And then there was the bathroom.

I don't know about you, but I've always found airplane bathrooms a little nightmarish. Early in a flight, they reek from whatever disinfectant kills every germ known to humankind. Later on, they reek for other reasons. Not this one. The walls were white marble, veined with forest green. There was a glass shower stall with multiple gold showerheads. A green velvet swivel chair faced a white marble vanity that held baskets of hair- and skin-care products. A tower of fluffy white towels rested on a shelf. I ran my finger along the familiar embroidered initials: LL.

When I made my way back to my seat, the captain was standing in the open cockpit door.

"Miss Smith, hello. Welcome aboard. Don't be concerned—I've got her on autopilot."

"Good to meet you," I said, though the autopilot thing did not fill me with confidence. When I'm thousands of miles up, up, up, I like to see a human at the controls, controls, controls.

Though I didn't have the nerve to say that, I did muster enough courage for a question. "Would you mind telling me whose plane this is?"

"Laurel Limoges, of course."

Oh. Of course. Well, that solved everything. And by *everything*, I mean *nothing*. Who the fuck was Laurel Limoges?

"Anyway," the captain went on, "I wanted to apologize for the bumps. Should be smooth sailing from here down to Palm Beach." He checked his watch. "We ought to be on the ground by four o'clock. Anything we can do for you, just let Adrienne know."

He went back to the cockpit—whew—and I turned back to my seat to find Adrienne setting a place for me in the TV viewing area. There were a linen place mat and napkin, both with that damn LL logo, heavy silverware, a crystal goblet, and a water glass.

"Ready for lunch, Miss Smith?" My *something simple* included a salad of pears, endive, and Gorgonzola, a warm baguette, red wine, and bubbly mineral water.

I hadn't eaten since my jelly doughnuts with Lily, and this looked amazing. "Thank you. Really." I sat.

"Please let me know if there is anything else I can get for you."

"Actually... my backpack?"

"Right away," Adrienne said, verging on *Stepford Wives* agreeability.

I broke off a chunk of the baguette, slathered it with butter, and stuck it in my mouth. Taste-bud bliss.

"Here you go, Miss Smith." Adrienne set my backpack on the seat to my left. "Anything else?"

I sipped the bubbly water. "No, thanks. This is terrific."

"After you eat, if you'd like me to launder your shirt, we have facilities in the galley. There's a..." She motioned to the doughnut stain, which I'd completely forgotten about. "It will only take forty-five minutes. There's a robe hanging on the back of the bathroom door, if you want to change."

Okay. I was impressed.

I ate half the salad, then dug *Vanity Fair* out of my backpack. There was a piece by Dominick Dunne about a murder in Nashville and the husband's conviction ten years later. A feature on the former members of Talking Heads. Both interesting but seemingly irrelevant to me, Florida, or why I was going to Florida.

Then I turned another page and stared straight at a full-page photo of two blindingly gorgeous teen girls fully dressed and half submerged in a swimming pool. The simple caption said that they were Sage and Rose Baker of Palm Beach, Florida.

THE FABULOUS BAKER TWINS
by Jesse Kornbluth

Paris who?

If you're still snickering over her sexcapades or getting your gossip on over tabloid shots of the on-again-off-again best friend who wears anorexia like a couture accessory, then you're already five minutes ago. Welcome to the new millennium in white-hot-celebutante hype: Sage and Rose Baker, the Fabulous Baker Twins of Palm Beach, Florida.

Sage and Rose Baker are objectively better-looking than the tabloid titillators who came before them, and if the eighty-four-million-dollar fortune that will soon be theirs can buy it, they will be much, *much* more successful. They are also only seventeen years old.

They are nearly identical redheads—Sage is older by six minutes. Rose tans, and Sage keeps her flesh so pale she is nearly opalescent. Each is breathtaking, with cut-glass cheekbones, a slightly clefted chin, enormous emerald-green eyes, and full, pouty lips. They are a pair of throw-backs to the beauty of Jean Shrimpton, although when I mention this, they look at me blankly. Evidently, their ideas of beauty icons don't go further back than Christina Aguilera.

The Fabulous Baker Twins are the granddaughters of Laurel Limoges, founder and CEO of Angel Cosmetics.

Laurel Limoges. That's who the captain—
This was *her* plane?
Pay dirt. This was what Debra wanted me to read. I rewarded my brain synapses with a long swallow of some of the best burgundy I'd ever tasted and kept reading.

They lost their parents in a private-plane crash nine years ago, when they were in the fourth grade. Looks plus youth plus money plus pedigree plus tragedy plus unbridled lust and not just for fame equals what? Pop-culture platinum has been earned on much less.

Ever since their parents' death, the twins have lived with their grandmother on her vast Palm Beach, Florida, estate, called Les Anges. They share their own private eight-thousand-foot pink stucco mansion. Palm Beach, just south of Jupiter and north of Boynton Beach, is a sixteen-mile stretch of subtropical barrier island separated from the mainland by Lake Worth. Its ten thousand residents have more combined wealth than the inhabitants of Beverly Hills, Bel Air, Santa Barbara, and the United Arab Emirates collectively. Its estates are the most magnificent in the world.

J. Paul Getty once made this pithy remark: "If you can actually count your money, then you are not really a rich man." By this standard, when the twins' trust funds come due on their eighteenth birthday, less than two months after this issue of *Vanity Fair* is published, they will be truly rich.

Like the rest of young Palm Beach royalty, they attend Palm Beach Country Day. Both are candid about their dislike for, and boredom with, all things academic. When pressed, Rose murmurs that she "kind of likes music"; Sage bats her sooty lashes and says, "School is repungent [*sic*]." I don't correct her.

With care for the language of Shakespeare eliminated, what do the twins like? Rose shrugs and looks to her sister for the answer—she seems to do this a lot. Sage tosses the strawberry lioness curls from her perfectly made-up face. "Shopping, parasailing, driving fast, surfing, and sex, not necessarily in that order and sometimes all at once." She leans forward to look at what I'm jotting down in my little notebook. "I love sex. Be sure to write that down."

The hair artist sets Sage's hair in a tumble of flaming curls. Rose's locks are slicked back off her face. The makeup artist comes at them with loose powder on a makeup brush, and Sage shoos her away, complaining about the heat and the waiting around. "Why the fuck aren't we starting the shoot?" A worker ant explains that there's a problem with the light and hands her a frosted flute of Cristal and honeydew juice, her current favorite drink.

But Sage won't be placated; clearly, she's had enough. She stands, slides both slender hands into the bodice of her priceless gown, and rips it down to her navel. Time seems to stop. Even her sister gasps.

Sage smiles, obviously pleased to have all eyes on her. She takes five steps to the saltwater pool and jumps in. The curls and makeup are destroyed in an instant. As she floats on her back, her pierced nipples become visible beneath the soaked, ripped gown. She crooks a beckoning finger toward her twin.

Rose hesitates, but only for a moment. Then she jumps in, too.

"Shoot *this!*" Sage laughs and gives the photographer the finger.

For the Fabulous Baker Twins, being fabulous means never having to say you're sorry.

Maybe they weren't sorry, but suddenly, I was. Oh God. What on earth was I in for?

The wealthy and fabulous, having suffered as children, deserve all of the privilege and prestige that society affords them. They should be able to do what they want, when they want to, with no consequences. After all, they're worth it.

Discuss how well-reasoned you find this argument. Write your answer in the book labeled "Analytical Writing: Argument."

c h a p t e r   s i x

*M*egan Smith, I presume."

Those words found me gazing at the glorious view of the Atlantic through the picture window in Laurel Limoges's home office at Les Anges, an estate that *Vanity Fair* had not oversold. Thick raindrops hit the surface of the infinity-edged pool outside. It was hard to tell where the pool ended and the ocean began.

I whirled around and found myself face-to-face with a woman of a certain age. "Laurel Limoges."

"It's a pleasure to meet you." That was your basic nicety. I had no idea if it was going to be a pleasure to meet her, or whether in fifteen minutes I'd be asking her driver to bring me back to the Palm Beach airport.

As we shook hands, I was struck by her beauty. Anyone would be. Her alabaster skin was taut and flawless, stretched over high cheekbones. She wore a gray suit with a fitted jacket and a straight skirt that fell just below her knees. Her pearl-gray open-toe pumps matched the buttons on the suit. She wore a silver bracelet on her left wrist but no rings on her fingers.

"Please." She nodded toward a carved mahogany-framed couch and took a seat opposite me on a paisley chair. "Your flight was satisfactory? You did not get too—how do you say—drenched?" She had a slight French accent.

"Your driver had a *parapluie très bon et très grand.*" Translation: a very big and good umbrella. Thank you, four years of French at Yale.

The sky had opened up as soon as the Gulfstream landed in Palm Beach. During the limousine ride from the airport I could barely see out the windows. I'd flicked on the limo's mini TV and watched a Miami weatherman warning people in Palm Beach County to beware of hail as said hailstones pinged off the limo's roof.

The hail had abated by the time we pulled in to a circular gravel driveway in front of an enormous mansion the color of cotton candy. The car door swung open, and a very bald, cadaverous man in a black suit held an umbrella over me as I stepped out into thick, fetid air. "Miss Smith? This way, please."

He guided me toward an enormous mahogany front door and then into a foyer larger than my entire East Village apartment. It had a white tile floor, intricately carved woodwork, and a round marble pedestal in the center. On that pedestal rested a three-foot-high white onyx vase and dozens of enormous orange and purple bird-of-paradise.

"Welcome to Les Anges, Miss Smith. I am Mr. Anderson, Madame's butler," he intoned, touching the Secret Service–style earpiece in his left ear. "Your rucksack, please, Miss Smith?"

The butler—I immediately dubbed him the Skull—took my backpack and pushed a recessed metal button. A well-disguised elevator door swung open.

"Take this to the second floor," the Skull instructed. "Madame Limoges's office. She'll be with you shortly."

"Okay, thanks." I stepped into the elevator.

"And Miss Smith? Madame doesn't like her things to be touched."

The elevator closed automatically. The last thing I saw was the Skull two-fingering my backpack like week-old roadkill.

And now here I was, face-to-face with the woman to whom all this wealth and power belonged. I didn't have to be a Yale grad to figure out that she'd flown me eleven hundred miles to offer some kind of position involving her granddaughters, the Fabulous Baker Twins. But the what, where, why, and most of all, *how much,* were still a mystery.

"The flight was great," I told her now. "I mean, it was fine. Your plane is very nice."

Your plane is very nice? I sounded like an idiot.

"Thank you. Perhaps you'd like some tea or some other refreshment?" Laurel motioned to a silver tea set in the corner. I'd assumed it was for decoration only.

"No, I'm fine. I would like to hear about the position, though. If you don't mind."

"Ah. Normally, it is the employer who asks the questions in an interview, no?"

"Yes, normally," I agreed, feeling a little bold from the carafe of red wine on the plane. "But nothing today has been normal."

She laughed, and I liked her for it. "Actually, there is very little I want to ask, Miss Smith."

"Please, call me Megan." I leaned back a little on the settee, trying to look comfortable.

"Megan, then. Debra Wurtzel is a dear friend. We have known each other a long time. We spoke at some length about you. She recommended you very highly. You read the article about my granddaughters in *Vanity Fair*, yes?"

"Yes. On the plane. They're beautiful." I glanced behind her at the dozens of framed photographs lining the shelves. There were pictures of Laurel with heads of state and Hollywood elite, but not one of her with her granddaughters.

She offered a Gallic shrug and smoothed a nonexistent wrinkle in her skirt. "The good fortune of a gene pool. How much do you know about me, Megan?"

"Honestly? Only what I read this afternoon," I answered, and resisted the urge to put my fingernails in my mouth.

"Everyone, it seems, has written about me. Tom, Harry, Dick. No one gets it right."

I bit my lip to keep from laughing at the Harry-Dick thing.

"I started with nothing, Megan. I like to work hard, and I like this quality in others. Everything I have, I have earned." She entwined her fingers. "I have succeeded at many things. Anything worth doing is worth doing with excellence, don't you agree?"

I nodded. I did agree. But even if I didn't, what was I going to say?

"There is one thing—one important thing—at which I have failed. Raising my granddaughters."

For the briefest moment, I thought I saw a flash of genuine sorrow in her eyes. Then it was gone.

"Perhaps, over the years, I would not allow myself to see the truth," she continued. "But now the entire world is aware that my granddaughters do not use their brains for anything more complex than choosing a shade of nail polish. I blame myself for this."

As she looked toward the ocean, I thought I saw another flash of pain in her clear gray eyes. "I'd like to change that. I shall provide the motivation, which we shall get to in a moment. Unfortunately, I cannot be the one to help them put their minds to better use. For one thing, I travel far too much on business. You'll see me here at Les Anges only rarely. That is why the person to help them, dear, will be you."

So she wanted me to teach her granddaughters. But why? The twins were about to come into an eight-figure trust. Maybe they weren't bright, but they were filthy rich. I'd met enough legacies at Yale to know that filthy rich could get you a long way in this world even without a functional IQ.

Laurel waited for my eyes to meet hers. "You are wondering why this matters so much to me, no?"

"Yes," I admitted.

"Megan, the twins' late parents went to Duke University, in North Carolina," Laurel explained. "As did my late husband. I have always expected that the girls would go there also. To Duke."

I knew Duke. It wasn't Yale, but it was a really good school and hard to get into. But the twins were legacies, legacies whose grandmother could surely donate a building or ten to the school. The rules for mere mortals—grade point average, SAT score, killer application essay—simply didn't apply to legacies like that.

That's what I told Laurel, albeit a bit more diplomatically.

"In ordinary cases, you may be right," Laurel agreed. "But I received a phone call from Aaron Reynolds yesterday. He is the president of Duke. I've known him for years—my late husband and I donated the performing arts center."

See?

Laurel went on, "Yet he informed me that after *Vanity Fair*, he could not admit the girls. There would be—I believe he called it 'an alumni uproar.'" She held her palms up at the impossibility of it all. "Sage and Rose shall have to *earn* a place in next fall's freshman class, like anyone else. Or at the very least, demonstrate the ability to do so. I believe he will be willing to overlook some of their indiscretions if they can meet some specific standards."

From what I had read, the chances of these two earning legitimate spots at Duke was about as likely as the Gap using me instead of my sister in next season's ads.

"How are their grades at school?" I managed to ask with a straight face.

"Appalling." Laurel knitted her finely arched brows together. "Here is the thing, Megan. I know something about my granddaughters that they do not know. They are *not* stupid. Nor are you, evidently."

I had nothing to say to that.

"Yale is an excellent university, no? But frightfully expensive. Debra tells me that you incurred a significant expense to attend there. How much are your outstanding college loans?"

"Seventy-five thousand dollars," I reported, despite it being clear that she already knew. I remember discussing that very number, in fact, during my initial interview with my former boss.

"Seventy-five thousand dollars." She sighed. "So expensive in this country to attend a fine school. Not like in France."

Expensive for someone like me, I wanted to tell her. *Not someone like you.*

But she'd already pressed a button on a discreet box on the coffee table. "Please send the girls up."

"Right away, Madame," the voice through the intercom replied immediately. How was that possible? Then I remembered the Skull's earpiece.

"I should like to detail the rest of this arrangement with the twins in the room," Laurel explained.

Before I could protest that I'd agreed to no arrangement as yet, the elevator door opened again, and the two teenagers I'd seen in *Vanity Fair* stepped into the room. Both wore jeans and very high heels. One wore a white silk camisole. Her complexion was enviably translucent. Her flaming red hair hung in loose curls nearly to her waist—Sage, I figured. The other one, Rose, had a perfect golden tan with freckles dotting her nose and arms. Her streaky red hair fell stick-straight down her back.

I think I've conveyed how effortlessly beautiful my sister is, right? Well, these girls made her look merely average. If the theory of the bell curve applied to looks, somewhere on the planet, two severely butt-ugly girls were paying the price so that the twins could look this amazing. Let me say that I had a very superficial reaction to all this gorgeousness: I disliked them immediately.

Laurel stood, so I did, too. The girls towered over both of us. Sage—the pale one—shook her curls out of her eyes in what seemed to be a practiced gesture. "You summoned?" she asked Laurel, sounding incredibly bored.

"I did. There is someone I want you to meet. This is Megan Smith. Megan, my granddaughters, Sage and Rose."

Sage's eyes flicked to me for a bare millisecond. *"And?"*

"She will be your academic tutor for the next two months."

The twins exchanged a look, and then Sage put one hand on a prominent hip bone. "No, thanks." She turned to go, taking her sister's hand.

"Thanks anyway," Rose called over her shoulder.

I could third that. *No, thank you.*

Laurel sensed my hesitation. "Megan—you must hear me out. Girls, sit. I'm going to make each of you an offer you cannot refuse."

Any sacrifice—even the sacrifice of one's values and personal beliefs—is justified when the result of said sacrifice is financial independence.

Describe your perspective on this statement, using relevant examples to support your view.

c h a p t e r   s e v e n

Once the twins were seated on the other mahogany sofa, Laurel described the predicament with Duke.

Sage shook the hair out of her eyes. Again. "Okay. So what's-her-name is here to help us get in. That's it?"

"Megan. Her name is Megan," Laurel repeated. "If she accepts, she will be guiding you in two main areas—your regular studies at Palm Beach Country Day and the SAT examination that you will take on the fifteenth of January."

Sage rolled her eyes. "You've got to be kidding."

Once more, I caught a flash of sadness in Laurel's eyes, but the girls' faces remained impassive. Either they didn't notice, or they didn't care.

"I am not kidding. In fact, I would think that after that magazine profile, you would want to prove to the world—perhaps even to yourselves—that you are not *imbeciles*."

I noticed Rose's right foot jiggle nervously inside a pink

suede high-heeled sandal. Her sister threw her arms across the back of the couch. Not a care in the world.

"What do we care?" Sage asked, although she clearly wasn't looking for an answer. "We're already rich, and we're almost famous. Come on, Rose." She got to her feet. "We're out of here."

Laurel shrugged again. "Depart if you want. But understand this, Sage: You are not rich."

Sage sighed wearily. "Yet. We aren't rich *yet*. But we will be next month, on our eighteenth birthday. Eighty-four million dollars rich. That's what the trust says."

"No, that's what the trust *used* to say," Laurel corrected. "It was revised this morning."

Sage's pale face drained of what color it had. I watched her reflection in the silver tea set across the room. "What are you talking about?" she managed.

Laurel cleared her throat. "If you and your sister both earn places in the entering class at Duke—I have been told an SAT score and course average you must maintain by the president of the school himself—you will become recipients of the trust the moment the admissions office informs me of your acceptance. If one of you fails, you both do. You will be on your own."

"You wouldn't do that," Sage challenged.

"I already did," Lauren answered, and I thought I saw a little satisfied gleam in her eyes. She touched one of her enormous diamond earrings.

"But that's...that's so mean!" Rose looked like a little kid whose sand castle had been kicked over by a bully.

"It's for your own good, Rose." Laurel's voice was kinder

now. "And I am giving you the tools you need to succeed. I suggest you—and your sister—take advantage of them."

I waited for Sage to fire back. She didn't. The look on her face, however, spoke volumes, all of which were filled with expletives.

Laurel turned to me. "Megan, you have been very patient. Let me explain the terms of your employment. You will be with us until the Scholastic Aptitude Test in January. Eight weeks. Your pay is fifteen hundred dollars a week. It will be deposited into an account I've opened for you. You will have your own suite in the twins' mansion, all your meals, and use of any vehicle you'd like. We have a dozen or so in the garage."

I did some quick mental calculations. Fifteen hundred times eight weeks was twelve grand. Zero expenses. I'd go back to New York in January at prime magazine hiring season with a nice financial cushion. And all I had to do was live here in cushy splendor, endure the twins for two months, and try to teach them to spell their own names?

"I cannot fucking believe this," Sage muttered, reminding me of the reality of enduring these girls, even if only for two months. Not so easy.

"Megan, when we were talking earlier, you informed me that you have accumulated a significant amount of debt," Laurel said to me.

"Yes, that's true," I acknowledged.

Laurel nodded. "I am a fan of performance-based compensation, as you've likely concluded already."

"Yes, and your offer is very generous—"

"Kiss-ass," Sage cut in. "And what are you wearing, anyway?" she asked me, apropos of nothing at all. Rose giggled.

I turned back to Laurel, smiling tightly. "But I'm not sure your granddaughters are very receptive to the idea, so I'm afraid—"

"If my granddaughters are admitted to Duke," Laurel interrupted, "you shall earn a bonus that will allow you to eliminate that debt. In its entirety."

Holy.

Fucking.

Shit.

"Now. As you were saying?" Laurel set her hands on her lap once again.

"I...I..." I stammered. Then I looked at the twins, who looked as shocked by this proposition as I was.

"You're *bribing* someone to tutor us?" Rose asked.

"Paying, actually," Laurel corrected her. "So, Megan?"

My initial inclination was to do a happy dance around her office—I'd scored nearly perfectly on the SAT and graduated magna cum laude—but a brief moment later, reality set in. The issue here was not *my* academic abilities, but the twins'. Studying isn't a skill that can be developed overnight. Could I take two spoiled brats, who'd thus far majored in ennui and partying, and transform them into scholars? It was like asking a Neanderthal whose idea of seduction involved a club and a cave to discover the merits of dinner, a movie, and aromatherapy massage. But still. It was a hell of a carrot for me, to go along with the stick Laurel had just smacked against her granddaughters' Cosabella-thonged behinds. No wonder Angel Cosmetics was so successful.

"I trust that meets with your approval?" Laurel's eyes met mine.

I made a quick decision, heavily influenced by dollar signs both certain and chimerical. "Okay. I mean, um, yes. I'll do it."

Laurel smiled. She even looked relieved. "Excellent. I will be leaving in the morning on a business trip to Paris, but I shall check in on a regular basis." She rose gracefully. "Megan, a bookstore in Miami sent me everything you'll need—Kaplan, Barron's, and Peterson's SAT prep materials, SparkNotes, Cliff's Notes. If there's anything else, just tell Mr. Anderson. Why don't the three of you get to know one another and then get to work? Please excuse me."

She crossed her office and summoned the elevator. A moment later, I was alone with the Baker twins. Sage regarded me coolly.

"Listen, Molly, Mandy, or whatever your name is—"

"Megan."

"Whatever." Sage flipped her hair. Again, again. "You understand we're not studying, right?"

"I'm pretty sure I just accepted a job." I attempted a laugh.

"Okay, there's a little problem, Frizzy. You don't mind if we call you Frizzy, do you? It describes your hair so well."

"I prefer Megan," I answered her, feeling very thirsty and more than a little panicky.

"Uh-huh. So listen, Frizzy." Sage did the hair-tossing thing again. "I *puke* cuter than the outfit you're wearing."

Rose snorted a giggle. Sage turned to her sister. "Rosie, you know who Frizzy looks like?"

"Who's that, Sagie?"

I felt like I was being set up for some particularly cruel knock-knock joke.

Sage turned back to me. "Actually, it's not really a who but a what: baboon ass. Bright red and fat all over."

I was right. Except it wasn't a knock-knock joke, and it didn't entirely make sense. Still, I felt my cheeks turning a deeper shade of baboon-ass red. *Fifteen hundred a week*, I told myself. *Fifteen hundred a week.*

"Just out of curiosity, Sage?" I asked. "Does it give you pleasure to insult someone you just met?"

Sage put a slender finger to her lips as if pretending to ponder this, then she stood up. "Actually . . . yes. When it's someone who looks like you." She beckoned to her sister. "We don't need our grandmother, and we definitely don't need you, Frizzy. So I suggest you head back to whatever godforsaken place you came from."

She strode to the elevator with Rose in her red-haired wake. I sat there, my eyebrows frozen in shock, until the elevator door had closed.

I slid down on the couch and stared up at the domed ceiling overhead. Then I let out one dramatic sigh and pulled myself upright.

Outside, the sky was clearing. The late-afternoon sun glittered on the water. I watched it, reviewing my exchange with the twins in my head. They were horrible. Awful. Nasty and wretched.

But their grandmother might be right. Maybe, just *maybe*, they were not stupid.

Choose the most correct definition for the following word:
HEIRESS

(a) female destined to inherit millions without working a day in her life
(b) 50 percent physical perfection, 50 percent emotional cruelty
(c) vacuous, without possession of reason or, apparently, a soul
(d) entitled, prissy bitch
(e) all of the above

chapter eight

W here are you again? Palm Springs?" Charma asked me. "Like, in California?"

"Palm Beach. Like, in Florida."

"Never been there."

"Me, neither, but evidently, this is where the beautiful people congregate and tell each other how beautiful they are." I leaned back on the plush magenta-and-white-polka-dotted divan in the den of my suite at the twins' mansion. It was a few light-years nicer than the found-it-on-the-street futon that used to pass for a couch in my apartment.

A half hour before, charm-free Mr. Anderson had led me silently through the muggy evening along a long white gravel walkway from the main mansion to the twins' mini-mansion.

Tall French-style hedgerows guarded the sides of the path, which meant I couldn't see the rest of the estate. When we arrived at the front of the twins' manse, though, there was no missing it. Done in a pink one shade lighter than Laurel's house, it was a dead ringer for Tara from *Gone with the Wind,* right down to the columns, and minus the color scheme.

"Addison Mizner," the Skull intoned.

"Excuse me?"

"The architect," he clarified, which clarified nothing for me. He opened the door and led the way through a foyer only slightly less spectacular than Laurel's to an enormous winding staircase. Upstairs were two corridors leading in opposite directions. "The twins," he uttered, casting his eyes to the left. "You," casting his eyes to the right.

Down the corridor we went, until he stopped at a large white door. "Your quarters. Good night."

He headed back the same way we'd come, and I opened the door to what would be home for the night—maybe longer if I could stomach ever coming face-to-face with the twins again. The wallpaper was muted pink and white, and a velvet divan had been placed directly under a picture window overlooking the Atlantic. It was too dark to see the water, but a few sparkling lights twinkled in the distance. There was a white antique desk where I could set up my iBook, along with a high-backed pink leather chair and several hassocks. On the far wall was what I guessed to be a sixty-inch flat-screen TV. An archway opened into a massive bedroom with a canopied king-size bed and a walk-in closet that—like Les Anges's foyer—was roughly the size of my entire East Village apartment.

I went back into the den and called James, but I hit his voice mail. My second call was to Charma, who took the news of my rapid deployment to South Florida with her usual deadpan aplomb. I tried to describe Sage and Rose, suggesting she picture the biggest bitch from when she'd been a senior in high school, multiply her times infinity, and then split her in two. *That* was the Baker twins.

I told her I loathed them. I also told her how much I would make in a week.

"Hire a Cuban dominatrix from Miami to lash them to a bed if you have to, Megan," Charma droned as I opened the mini-fridge in the closet. It was empty, but inside was a note: *Summon Marco for provisions.* Who the hell was Marco? "Stay there and bring Mama home something nice," she told me sternly.

"Seriously, Charma. I don't know how I can possibly—"

I stopped midsentence. Was someone knocking on my suite door? I listened. Yes. There it was again.

"Someone's here," I told Charma. "Call you later."

"Wait, wait. Laurel Limoges has a wine cellar, right?"

My finger hovered over the "end" button. "I haven't had the grand tour yet, but probably."

"If you do blow out of there, grab me a couple bottles. She'll never miss 'em."

I hung up and padded down the corridor to the door. There stood Sage and Rose.

"Could we . . . speak with you a minute?" Sage asked tentatively.

Where was the sneer? Where was the attitude? Why hadn't she called me Frizzy?

"Sure," I told them cautiously. "Come in."

They trailed behind me back to the pink-polka-dotted sitting area. "So, what's up?" I asked as they settled onto two of the hassocks.

They shared a hesitant look. "We came to apologize. Earlier...we weren't so nice." Sage twisted the bottom of her camisole nervously between her fingers. "It was just such a shock, you know. What our grandmother did."

Rose nodded. "Eighty-four million dollars is a lot of money. You don't get that taken away from you every day."

"And that stuff about college?" Sage went on, her green eyes watery and earnest. "That was news to us. She *never* said anything about Duke before. How were we supposed to know?"

"Don't sweat it," I told them, surprising myself. It would be shocking to hear you couldn't go on being the spoiled princess you'd always been. It might even have ruptured their one shared brain cell. "Let's start over. I'm Megan," I said lamely, holding out my hand.

"Sage." She giggled, extending her hand, too.

"Rose. How do you do?" She stood up, then curtsied. Okay, that was kind of cute.

All I knew about the Baker twins was what I'd read in *Vanity Fair* and seen in Laurel's office. Maybe there was more to them than that.

"As long as we're starting over..." I took a seat on the carpet and motioned for them to join me, which they did. "How about if we get to know each other a little? What do you guys do for fun?" I nearly rolled my eyes at myself to save them the trouble.

Sage put her knees up, circling her long legs with her arms. "To tell you the truth, we're kind of wild."

Rose's head bobbed. "*Very* wild."

"I can be wild," I said confidently, recalling my oh-so-recent East Village beavering.

Sage rose to her knees and put her head close to mine. "Tell us the wildest thing you ever did."

Hmmm. Save the unintentional beavering, my wildometer was a total flatline.

Sage grinned. "Sex in public?"

Whether I had or I hadn't—okay, I hadn't—it didn't seem like bonding over my sex life with my two students-to-be was a really professional way to go. But I wanted to prove that I wasn't afraid to meet them halfway.

"Let's save that for another night," I dodged.

"Fair enough," Sage agreed, though I could see her shoulders sag with disappointment. I feared I was losing my audience, but Sage's next words belied that impression.

"You know, you're not really what we thought," Sage told me. She tilted her head as if looking at me anew. "You seem almost...cool."

Rose nodded emphatically. "Yeah."

"So..." Sage perked up again. "Maybe this could work after all. Let's try studying tomorrow."

"Sure," I said. "Yeah, let's." Laurel had been right. These girls might be dumb, but they weren't stupid enough to turn their back on the family fortune. "How about nine o'clock?"

"Ten," Sage said.

"Ten it is."

Sage grinned the biggest, whitest grin in the history of big, white grins. "You're on—if you'll do something for us first."

"Yeah," Rose agreed.

Fine. They wanted to prove to me that they had some power

by making it an exchange. I understood. It was Sociology 101, only they couldn't spell the "sociology" part. I was willing.

"We're going to give you a chance to prove that you're wild," Sage declared.

"Okay, fine. As long as it isn't illegal. Or sexual," I added hastily.

Sage nibbled contemplatively on a manicured forefinger. Then she waggled her eyebrows at her sister. "How about... skinny-dipping? In our saltwater pool? There's a freshwater pool over at Grandma's house, but I *know* you aren't wild enough do it there."

Skinny-dipping? *Skinny-dipping* was the best they could come up with? Honestly, I was mildly disappointed in the Fabulous Baker Twins. I'd gone to hippie New Hampshire sleepaway camp. Skinny-dipping was nothing—or rather, it had been nothing when I was twelve and still had wonderfully prepubescent hips and perky almost-breasts. Sage's fat-ass jab still stung a little.

"And where would you guys be?" I asked.

"We aren't going to stand around watching, if that's what you think." Sage sounded insulted that I'd even consider such a thing. "We'll get the champagne for when you get out. To celebrate our new start together and our eventual entry into the shallowed halls of Duke University."

Shallowed? Oy. I definitely had my work cut out for me.

Identify which part of the following sentence is incorrect:

Swimming nude in the (a) <u>presents</u> of one's students (b) <u>is a remarkable</u> way to make (c) a big <u>splash</u> (d) in a <u>new job.</u> (e) No error

chapter nine

In the half hour between my "okay, I'll do it" and the actuality of the act, there was more than enough time for second thoughts.

It didn't take a Yale grad to balance the equation. Maturity was not the twins' strong suit. Plus, it was only *after* I'd dodged their query about my wildest sexual escapade that Sage had decided on my saltwater plunge in the buff. I added the elements together and came up with the obvious answer: photographs. Sage and Rose would be waiting, camera in hand, when I climbed out of the pool. They'd probably post the pix at www.ratemytits .com and cast a thousand "1" votes against me.

It couldn't be too difficult to outsmart two not-so-smart teen girls.

I found the deck on the east side of the twins' manse. Bright gaslight torches illuminated the perimeter. The deck was dotted with cerulean chaise longues and a cabana with a fully stocked bar. A stone seawall separated the deck from the beach and, beyond that, the ocean. As I'd anticipated, the twins were waiting for me. I didn't see any cameras, but that didn't mean they weren't stashed behind the bar.

"Right on time," Sage called cheerfully. Too cheerfully. Fine, I would play along.

"Hey. I'm on time tonight. You be on time tomorrow." I dragged a chaise to the edge of the pool and turned my back to them as I began unbuttoning my white shirt. The salty ocean air felt thick and warm on my bare skin. It was hard to believe I'd been in nearly freezing New York City just that morning.

"Are you shy?" Sage asked.

"Sometimes," I called over my shoulder as nonchalantly as possible. I draped my shirt over the chair, careful to leave one of the sleeves within grabbing distance of the water. I figured if I saw candid photography in the offing, I could pull the shirt into the pool and put it on. It would get soaked, but it was long enough to hide what needed to be hidden.

Rose nudged her sister. "It's kind of sweet, really."

"Yeah, sweet."

I stepped out of my skirt and draped it across the chair, too. The girls recoiled in horror.

"Have you no pride?" Sage was aghast.

I figured she was insulting my body again, and the words *Screw you, you brain-dead twit* came to mind. However, that wouldn't have been entirely conducive to building a productive teacher-student relationship. Before I could decide whether immediate satisfaction outweighed temperate maturity, Sage clarified herself. "Your *underwear*. How could you?"

Remember that I'd been under severe duress, both financial

and psychological, only yesterday at Century 21. I had found the yellow semi-granny panties in a two-pairs-for-six-bucks bin, which allowed me to buy—you guessed it—two pairs. As for the bra, I had to cope with the lingerie buyer's Hello Kitty fetish, because that was all I found in the other bargain bin.

"It's *ironic*," I explained, not in the mood for a heart-to-heart about either the fire in my apartment or the pitiful state of my balance sheet. They looked at me blankly, and I realized they had no clue what *ironic* meant. All righty, then. I started to unclasp Hello Kitty, then stopped. "You two planning to take notes?"

"We said we wouldn't watch," Rose reminded her sister, then offered me a pair of swim goggles. "You might want these. It's salt water."

That was kind of thoughtful. "Thanks."

"Okay. So, twenty laps?" Sage suggested.

"Sounds good." To prove how chill I was with everything, I shrugged out of Hello Kitty and twirled one strap from a forefinger.

"Woo-hoo!" Sage cheered. "That's the spirit. Enjoy. We'll be back with champagne and chocolate. Or maybe just champagne. And remember, no wet underwear!"

"Wet means you cheated," Rose explained.

"No cheating," I promised.

As they headed back toward the manse, I stepped out of my three-buck panties and jumped in. The water was heated, the salt gave me extra buoyancy, and my shirt was within easy reach. I could feel the tension oozing out of my muscles as I floated on my back, listening to make sure the twins weren't returning. They weren't. Was it possible that I was wrong? Not likely, but still—this was *nice*.

I used to swim in a lake near our house in New Hampshire. I'd dive down and run my hands along the mucky bottom, wondering what it was like for the frogs that my sister had explained slept down there all winter. I did a surface dive now, swimming down, down, down until I touched the rough bottom of the pool. From there, I swam underwater, pulling with my arms, kicking with my legs, wholly enjoying the exercise. Maybe I'd start swimming every day, might as well take advantage of having a pool to—

Pop. Suddenly, bright lights blinded me. I touched my goggles, my eyes adjusting to the light.

Oh, God. There were people. Lots of them. Behind a Plexiglas window in some sort of underground party room. Sage, Rose, and half-dozen others, pointing and laughing. Standing in the front row was a boy in faded jeans and a baby-blue linen shirt, just *staring*. And that was when I saw my own reflection: bubble-eyed, magnified by the water's refraction, naked little-ol'-not-so-little me.

Allow me a moment here. When I was twelve and starting to get a figure, I had the same nightmare as a lot of girls: Running late for school, I'd dash into my seventh-grade homeroom only to realize I'd forgotten my clothes. I couldn't move my feet; all I could do was stand there while everyone chortled and pointed.

Who knew that ten years later, I'd live out a version of that terror?

I shot to the surface and powered toward the shallow end, intent on only one thing—getting to my clothes before the twins and their friends got to me. Because sure as I was that Sage and Rose Baker didn't know the meaning of irony, I was fully confident that they knew the meaning of cruelty.

I wasn't fast enough.

"It's the little mermaid!" Sage mocked. She held a champagne bottle in her right hand.

A chubby guy chugging a Stella inadvertently flashed a couple inches of belly between his red Polo and the top of his khakis. "Killer breaststroke." He smiled.

Ew.

If the twins wanted to humiliate me, they'd succeeded. I wanted to get out of there—*there* being the pool, Palm Beach, and Florida in general—as fast as humanly possible, with as much dignity intact as possible. I hoisted my naked self up the rungs of the ladder. The cool night air on my wet skin turned on my anatomical headlights, so to speak.

"Oooh-la-la!" Sage squealed. "Frizzy's face isn't all that blushes!"

"And the hair on her head isn't all that frizzes!" Rose added.

I glanced downward and saw a red rash of embarrassment spreading upward. Bitches.

I wanted nothing more than to grab my clothes and run—all the way back to New York, if necessary. But I wasn't about to give these assholes the satisfaction. Charma had told me once about an acting exercise in which you try to embody a person you know in order to act out a character. Charma had embodied her ex to play the part of a completely flaming but very closeted gay guy (don't ask). I knew who I needed to be. *You don't look like you. You look like Lily.* I slapped on a casual smile and stepped up to the guy who was taking his beer belly for a walk.

"I don't think we've met. I'm the twins' tutor, Megan." I offered my hand. "You're . . . ?"

"Pembroke Hutchison." His gaze traveled back to my breasts, but he managed a sweaty-palmed handshake.

"Here." The baby-blue-shirt, front-row-seat guy held out a towel. He was looking away from me, probably stifling his own giggles.

"Thank you," I said, wrapping it above my chest sarong-style. "I'm Megan."

"Will," he told me, looking up. "Phillips."

"Nice to meet you." *Asshole*, I added silently. Incredibly hot asshole—his almost navy eyes were framed with thick strawberry-blond lashes—but asshole nonetheless.

I introduced myself to the rest of the crowd. The tiny blonde was Precious Baldridge. The athletic girl with the straight raven hair tied back in a ponytail was Dionne-not-Dianne Cresswell. The brunette with obvious implants was Suzanne de Grouchy. In addition to Pembroke and Will, there was a short guy with a soul patch—Ari Goldstein.

"Well, nice to meet all of you," I declared. "I hope you enjoyed the entertainment portion of our evening."

"You've got balls, I'll give you that." Pembroke finished his beer and fired the empty can at a pink metal bin but missed. The can rolled into the pool. He didn't bother to retrieve it.

I arched a brow. "If that's what you saw, I'd lay off the Stella."

Will let out a loud *ha* from behind a chaise. "Good one," he murmured.

Um, thanks.

"Yeah, *hilarious*," Sage spat, her eyes narrowing.

"Look, Sage," I said. "I get it. It was a practical joke. I'm still good if you are."

Sage did her patented head-shake thing. "You're not even close to good, Frizzy."

"Oh, this shit is rich," Pembroke crowed, putting up his fists in an exaggerated boxer's stance. "Catfight!"

"Shut up," Rose told him.

"I love it when you talk dirty," he mock-groaned. He held out his arms, edging backward toward the pool. "Come to Papa."

Everyone laughed again. Abruptly, Rose gave him a two-handed push. He fell awkwardly into the pool with a massive splash.

"Thar she blows!" Ari bellowed as Pembroke came up sputtering.

I'd had more than enough and gathered up my clothes. "Enjoy your party, guys. Sage, Rose, I'll see you in the morning."

I pivoted to depart, but Sage's voice stopped me. "Hold it, Frizzy."

The smooth walkway pebbles felt cold on my feet. "Face it, Sage. You wanted to humiliate me. You failed. Good night."

The twins' friends oohed like a sitcom sound track.

"You *still* don't get it," Sage sneered. "We've got a really big agent, Zenith Himmelfarb. Maybe you've heard of her?"

"And I would care because?"

"Because we're going to be stars," Rose explained.

Sage smiled smugly. "Everyone in the business has seen *Vanity Fair*, and Zenith is fielding offers for us. Film, TV, modeling—"

"For really a lot of money," Rose put in.

Sage folded her arms. "We're not going to college, we don't need Laurel's money, and we *definitely* don't need you. So why don't you and your ugly clothes and your fat thighs waddle their way back to New York, fuck you very much?"

The only sound was the squishing of Pembroke's clothes as he sloshed to the bar for another beer. Everyone else waited to see what I would say.

Let 'em wait. I had nothing to say to any of them. First they'd tried to be rude. When that failed, they'd come to my room to manipulate me into doing something humiliating. They'd succeeded. There hadn't been a moment when they'd actually considered studying with me. I made sure my towel was wrapped tightly enough, put one foot in front of the other on the white pebble path, and wondered whether Laurel's plane was still at the airport.

Fuck this.

Fuck the money.

And definitely fuck the Baker twins.

Choose the definition that most accurately describes the following word:
LIE

(a) an intentionally false statement
(b) a petite bending of the truth
(c) a totally justifiable act, in times of desperation
(d) a sin, in some circles
(e) standard operating procedure at any number of tabloid
publications

chapter ten

*H*ate is not a strong enough word," I ranted to James,
cell phone pressed hard against my ear. I'd discovered
a small balcony off my den that overlooked the pool deck and
the ocean, and I had gone out there to call him. The deck was
now empty—only discarded champagne bottles and crushed
beer cans served as evidence of my humiliation. "*Detestation.
Abhorrence. Loathing.* Yeah. *Loathing* comes close."

Even after a fifteen-minute scorching-hot shower to wash
off both the salt water of the pool and the fallout of the Twins
from Hell, I was still raging. I had already called the Skull to say
I needed to speak with Laurel immediately, but he told me she
was currently en route in her jet to France, and I could speak
with her in the morning. Fine, then. I'd quit at sunup.

I'd called James immediately thereafter and told him to expect me back in New York tomorrow. "So, anyway," I continued into the phone, "can you leave a key with your doorman? You'll probably be at work when I get in."

"Yeah...sure..."

Like the hesitation in his voice wasn't obvious. This was an emergency, for God's sake. "James? I could really use the help right now." I hated myself for sounding both demanding and needy, but what choice did I have?

"Hey, I got it covered," he assured me. That was more like it. "For a few days," he added.

A few days. And then what? Move in with Lily? Head up to New Hampshire? But I'd figure that out once I was back on Planet Earth with actual humans instead of Palm Beach celebutard robots.

A breeze stirred the muggy night air, carrying the delicious aroma of orange blossoms and the ocean. Out at sea, boats bobbed, their lights flickering. I forced myself to take deep yoga breaths. I didn't know the first thing about yoga, but fuck it. *In with the good, out with the bad. In with the good...*

"It's so beautiful here," I murmured, finally calm enough to settle in to one of the two wicker chairs. "And the kids with the keys to the kingdom—so gorgeous on the outside, so ugly on the inside..."

"Sounds like *The OC* on steroids," James joked.

"Except this is real." I stood up and leaned against the balcony wall. Les Anges's property spread out on either side of me. I could see the rooftops of equally extravagant estates lining the beach in the distance. "You should see this place, James. It's completely removed from anything that resembles reality.

These girls and their friends...I mean, that *Vanity Fair* profile was *nothing*. If anyone had any idea what it was really like—" I stopped myself in midsentence. "Wait. Holy shit."

"Wanna run that by me again?" James asked.

In the graphic-novel version of my future autobiography, this is the frame where shafts of light shoot out from around my head. What did I love to write about? Not what people saw but what was underneath. And here I was with girls so perfect on the surface and so nasty inside. The same could probably be said about Palm Beach itself. And it was all right in front of me.

"James? I changed my mind," I told him. "I'm not coming home."

"Wait, what? What's going on?"

I explained my epiphany as I paced around the balcony, my mind flying with the possibilities of a Palm Beach–Baker twins exposé. "It's the ultimate outsider-insider story. Who wouldn't publish it?"

It wasn't like the twins could throw me off the estate—only Laurel could do that, and she was currently en route to France, as the Skull had so haughtily put it. She'd be there for another two weeks, which basically meant I was getting paid to be on an undercover assignment for fourteen glorious sun-filled days. Of course, I'd have to leave as soon as she returned and it became immediately obvious that the twins were still brain-dead assholes, but until then...It was freaking genius.

"It's great," James enthused. "Seriously."

Okay, so it wouldn't be eight weeks at fifteen hundred a week. And it definitely wouldn't be a seventy-five-thousand-dollar bonus for getting the twins in to Duke. But if I wrote a first-class, kick-ass insider piece on all things young and Palm Beach and secretly smarmy and corrupt—*that* could launch my writing career.

I was sitting on a journalistic gold mine. Let the excavation begin.

Choose the definition that most accurately matches the following word:
GAY

(a) a person who is sexually attracted to people of his or her own sex
(b) the best friend to have in a fashion crisis
(c) current de rigueur "accessory" for talk-show hostesses and B-list actresses
(d) safe arm candy at red-carpet events
(e) all of the above

chapter eleven

The next morning—despite my lack of both coffee and food (since I still had no clue how to "summon Marco")—I awoke early and dressed in the second of my profoundly hideous Century 21 outfits on the off chance that the twins would come knocking on my door with pencils and calculators in hand.

Ten o'clock came and went with no sign of the girls, so I set off looking for them. I went down the hallway past the top of the spiral staircase, then followed the white corridor to the twins' wing. It wasn't hard to figure out whose door was whose. Each girl had her name spelled out in electric-pink neon tubing.

Rose first, since she was marginally less detestable. When there was no answer to my knocks, I went in, taking mental notes. Her suite was gigantic, with rooms twice the size of mine. There was a bedroom with a balcony, a kitchen, a den, a dressing room, and a bathroom whose vanity held every cosmetic and beauty product known to humankind, and not manufactured by Angel Cosmetics. Everything was furnished in stark modern white. There were fresh white roses in a white vase on the nightstand, and white gardenias in the bathroom. I was struck by two strange—okay, kind of creepy—things in her den. There was a dollhouse that was an exact-scale model of her suite, right down to the tiny fake floral arrangements. Inside that dollhouse, two identical red-haired girls played jacks together on the den floor.

When I tried Sage's suite, I found it similarly empty, identical in layout, but completely different in decor. Her king-size bed was swathed in leopard fabric. The safari theme carried through to her den, which had a working waterfall and a six-foot stuffed parrot on a perch. Her bathroom and dressing area were as well equipped as Rose's. I peeked into her clothes closet. Jesus. There was enough couture here to dress the state of New Hampshire.

What could it possibly be like for this to be the norm? The reality? How did you look at the rest of the world when you'd known nothing but this kind of excess?

My next stop was their pool deck. Still no girls. I decided to go up to the main house. The white gravel of the path crunched under my black loafers—at least the aroma of eau de smoke seemed to be gone. It was a perfect morning: The sky was azure, and the air was fresh, without the mugginess of the day and night before.

I was surprised to find the mansion's door open but then remembered that it would be impossible for an intruder to get past the security gate. In the foyer, I called for Sage and Rose. Nothing. Something smelled fantastic, though—garlic and cheese—and my stomach rumbled.

My nose twitched like that of a dog picking up a familiar scent, and I followed the aroma down a hallway and into a French country kitchen. A floating island in the center of the room held an eight-burner stove. Copper pots and pans hung from ceiling hooks. There was a sturdy stone table with about twenty straight-back chairs surrounding it, as well as a six-person round table nestled in one corner. The backdrop was the ocean, glistening through a twenty-foot wall of glass.

"Ah, just in time for breakfast!" A handsome silver-haired man, wearing a white chef's jacket over a white linen shirt and off-white trousers with a perfect knife pleat, was whisking eggs in a copper bowl.

"I was looking for the twins," I explained. "I'm Megan Smith, their new tutor."

"Delighted!" He flashed me a smile, then poured the eggs into a frying pan on the stove. Another pan held sizzling cloves of garlic. "I'm Marco Devine, Madame Limoges's chef."

Marco. Summon Marco. *This* was Marco.

He flipped the garlic on top of the eggs. "I thought you might be hungry. I was going to have one of the maids deliver this to your room, but now you can enjoy it here. I hope you like garlic. I'm afraid I'm entirely incapable of cooking without it."

"I love it. And I'm starving," I confessed, leaning against the center island. "Do you have coffee, by any chance?"

He laughed and motioned to the small round table. "Black carafe is French roast, brown carafe is Ethiopian, red carafe is Venezuelan, and white is decaf that no one in their right mind should drink." He pulled an earthenware mug from a cupboard and handed it to me. "Help yourself."

After I poured the French roast, Marco leaned over and popped a fresh cinnamon stick into my cup. "French roast should never be consumed without a cinnamon stick," he explained. "They were made for each other."

"Thank you," I said, meaning it more than he could know. It was the best coffee I'd ever tasted. "Have the girls been here for breakfast?"

He chuckled again and moved the pan around on the stove. "They're allergic to breakfast, darling. Actually, they're allergic to morning entirely."

"Well, they're not in bed—I checked."

"You mean they're not in their *own* beds." Marco flipped the eggs. "You'll see them around noon. Maybe."

Interesting. This guy seemed to know a lot about the twins. What a good place to start my research.

"Have you worked here a long time?" I asked innocently.

"Since the twins were in the terrible twelves." His eyes glinted with good humor. "I believe that would be the terrible twos times six."

"You must know them well, then."

"I doubt they know themselves well yet, darling," Marco opined as he slid the omelet onto a white china plate, then tore various fresh herbs from small pots on a ledge and sprinkled them over the omelet. Next he fanned bright green avocado slices around the plate and added a dollop of sour cream. "The twins lead what Socrates would call 'an unexamined life.' Sit." He pointed to the smaller table and then put the omelet down in front of me.

I took my first bite. Incredible. "Wow."

"I shall take that as a compliment." Marco poured me a glass of orange juice, then brought a tiered silver tray that held croissants, brioche, and small silver pots of jellies and jams. I reached for a brioche, still warm from the oven, pulled off a flaky hunk, and put it in my mouth. He went on, "Not to brag, but my omelets are so good, they've been known to entice married men to offer me favors they normally reserve for their wives."

"Oh my God, I'd go to bed with you, too, if I could eat this every day."

"I'm afraid I play for the other team, darling. Also, my VSO—very significant other—frowns on such things. Pity."

I chuckled and chewed, savoring every bite as I considered Marco's unexamined-life comment. "Marco? I was wondering..." I dabbed at my lips with the napkin. "I met the twins last night..."

"Let me guess." Marco took a sip of coffee. "Didn't get off on the right foot?"

"You could say that," I admitted. "We're just sort of ...different. I think they're going to be reluctant pupils."

Marco smiled. "The words 'Sage,' 'Rose,' and 'pupils' have rarely been used in the same sentence before, unless someone is referring to their eyes, late at night, and very dilated."

"Maybe if I knew more about them. Like, what do they do for fun?"

"In the case of Sage, that would be *who* does she do for fun?"

"You mean she likes to party," I clarified.

"No, I mean she likes boys. And she likes to party."

I swallowed another bite of omelet. Marco was turning out

to be more than a cook—he was fast becoming my number one source. "You've probably seen some outrageous things around here."

"Indeed, indeed," Marco replied, but he didn't take the bait. "If you're done, how about a tour? Perhaps we'll run into the twins along the way."

He started our walk in the main mansion. I'd been nominally prepared for the three different living rooms filled with priceless eighteenth-century French antiques, the dozen or so bedrooms done in different themes, and an actual dance studio with a ballet barre that Marco said Laurel used daily whenever she was home. It was the extras that blew me away: a movie theater for fifty with pink velvet seating, a salon, a four-lane bowling alley, a gym with every piece of high-tech equipment invented, plus a sauna, steam room, whirlpool, and hot tub. Marco took me down stone steps to a twenty-thousand-bottle wine cellar and humidor and noted that Laurel did all her wine tasting and selection herself.

"Even I've learned not to advise her," he confessed. "And I'm a certified sommelier."

Next came a stroll around the estate. He shared his knowledge with obvious pride. I tried to remember everything he told me, knowing that detail would be critical for my article. "The exterior walls of the mansion are made of coquina. It's a very rare pink stone scraped from the ocean floor. Rumor is that Mizner required ten years and five million dollars to gather enough to start building."

"How much is this place worth?" I prompted.

A smile tugged at Marco's lips. "There's a saying down here: If you have to ask how much, you can't afford it."

Well, *duh*.

From there, we toured the greenhouse, Laurel's pool, the two tennis courts (one grass, one red Roland Garros clay), the putting green, and a gazebo that perched on a pink arched bridge over a tilapia pond.

"So this is what a cosmetics empire can buy, huh," I marveled as we stopped in the gazebo to rest.

"Laurel was born poor, you know. She lived in a squalid coldwater flat in Paris. I'm sure you've read about it."

"Actually, I haven't."

"She mixed her first shampoo in the hallway toilet and peddled it from salon to salon. She built Angel from nothing." Marco motioned to the estate in front of us. "I quite admire that."

"Do you think the twins have that same drive?" I asked. As if I didn't know the answer: *Surely you jest.*

"They're wounded, you know." He studied me a moment. "You're very curious about them."

"It's just that I want to get to know them." I felt a flicker of guilt. It didn't last long. All I had to do was to picture Sage's jeering face from the night before.

"That isn't going to happen, my dear," he said, not unkindly. "They are all about appearances. To them, you look like a 'before' photo in one of their magazines."

I felt my face begin to flame, and I looked down. "I lost all my clothes...there was this fire in my apartment," I mumbled.

He put a hand to his chest. "That wasn't said to hurt your feelings, I assure you. Palm Beach can be a very superficial place, I'm afraid. To get along, one must fit in. To gain the twins' confidence for your endeavor, they must believe you're part of their world. Or at least look that way. You need to think of yourself as a living accessory."

Being likened to a handbag did not make me feel bright and perky. "That's ridiculous!" I laughed.

"Of course it is," Marco agreed. "But you must understand: The rest of America is driven by money. Sage and Rose? Money is no object. So they are driven by appearances."

"I am who I am," I lamented, realizing the biblical allusion and not giving a damn. "And I look how I look."

"Perhaps not. My VSO, Keith, is famous for turning Palm Beach's wealthy sows' ears into silk purses. Something for which they are quite willing to pay delightfully hefty sums that shall keep me in face-lifts until I'm gumming my food in a home. He's Mr. Keith to those in the know."

"What does he—Keith—do, exactly?" I asked Marco as he ran his hand along the gazebo's white banister.

"Hair, makeup, wardrobe, everything, and anything." Marco ticked off. "He's booked a year in advance outside of the season, and two years in advance for the season."

"The season is?"

"Dear God, child. Do you know *nothing*?"

I must have looked like the stranger in the strange land I was, because Marco took pity.

"The Season—capital T, capital S—runs from late November through the early spring. It's when all the social balls are given, mostly for charity. The first event of The Season is to-night—the Red and White ball, darling. Everyone who's anyone in Palm Beach does The Season, darling. And one cannot do The Season without looking The Season–worthy."

I did a quick self-assessment. Un-The-Season-worthy clothes. Un-The-Season-worthy hair. Makeup? That was the biggest un-The-Season-worthy of them all, because it didn't exist. Great.

Palm Beach was heading into The Season, and no one was ever less prepared for it than I. Nor did I have the "delightfully hefty sum" I'd need to secure Mr. Keith's services, even if he were available. I was destined to remain a "before" to the twins—I'd remain outside their circle and just out of reach of my story. So much for the inside scoop.

"Fifteen years ago, I was cooking in a diner in Point Pleasant, New Jersey, and wearing knockoff golf shirts from Wal-Mart." Marco touched my arm gently. "How I got here is a story that I shall save for my scathing autobiography. Suffice to say that Keith helped me. Saved me, really." He tapped a forefinger against his chin. "And now ... he needs to save you."

"But *how?* I really don't have the money, and—"

Marco smiled. "There's nothing Keith loves more than a good Cinderella story. And tonight will be your ball! Just think of me as your fairy gaymother!"

Choose the pair of words that most closely resembles the following
analogy:

NATURAL BEAUTY : SOCIETY BALL

(a) intelligent : Paris Hilton
(b) unattractive : Brad Pitt
(c) earthy : Jennifer Lopez
(d) subtle : Anna Nicole Smith
(e) talented : Nicole Richie

chapter twelve

think I'm going to barf."

"Hang in there," Keith urged, giving my knee a
fraternal tap. "You look hot. The straight men will want you,
the gay men will want beauty tips, and the women will want to
scratch your eyes out. If that isn't the stuff of fairy tales, I don't
know what is."

We were stuck on South Ocean Boulevard, part of the long
line of cars and limos approaching the pink walls and narrow
stone archway of Donald Trump's Mar-a-Lago resort. What the
hell had ever made me think I could go to the first society ball
of The Season and pass as one of them? I tried the deep breathing exercises that I vaguely recalled from the one and only hatha
yoga class Charma had dragged me to. As soon as the instructor

announced something called the upward-facing dog, I was out of there.

"Relax, Megan," Keith instructed me. "Marco and I will have your back."

It was more my front I was worried about. I was fully expecting some Palm Beach grand dame to take one look at me, point an accusing finger, and shout, "Impostor!" But I reminded myself that if Keith didn't know how to make a girl pass, no one did. Keith Genteel—that was his real name, though here on the island, he was known as either Mr. Keith or *the* Mr. Keith, depending on how crucial he had been to one's fashion rehabilitation—had grown up wealthy in a Charlotte suburb. But his mother had signed an onerous prenup that made money tight postnup, though she did get to keep the family manse. When other boys were playing sports or chasing girls, Keith was deconstructing and then reconstructing her gowns for each new social occasion so that it looked as if she had purchased something new and very expensive.

After four years at FIT in New York, he'd moved to L.A., where he'd become the most sought-after costume, hair, and makeup person in Hollywood—a bona fide triple threat who was the go-to guy for every major movie studio and director in town. When a well-known French actress had offered him an obscene amount of money and invited him to Palm Beach to prep her for the annual Red Cross ball, after which she'd merited a full page of photos in the *Palm Beach Daily News—The Shiny Sheet*, to those in the know—the legend of Mr. Keith had been born. In a town where appearance was everything, having style was a skill more valuable than the ability to perform open-heart surgery. I'd gotten most of this information from Marco, who'd been in a voluble mood when he'd driven me to his partner's beachfront cottage at the south end of the island. The three of us had a quick cup of French-press coffee on a back deck that opened onto the beach, and then Marco left to return to Les Anges. Keith, who was dressed casually in khaki shorts, a white golf shirt, and leather flip-flops, looked me over carefully. He correctly guessed my shoe, dress, and, much to my chagrin, bra size, then uttered five fear-inspiring words: *The hair has to go.*

"Bald is really not a good look for me," I'd quipped nervously, but he was already leading me to a salon chair set up in what probably was once his den. He sat me down and spun me away from the mirror.

"It's more fun if it's a shock," he explained.

Two hours later, he turned me back around. He was right. This was definitely fun. He'd cut three inches and layered bangs around my face, added butterscotch highlights, and blown it out.

"You look freshly fucked," he decided, clearly happy with his work. "In the best possible way."

If *freshly fucked* meant I looked as if God had blessed me with the world's best hair, then I had to agree.

After a break for lunch—French bread, several types of cheese, sliced hothouse tomatoes, and duck confit—Keith started on my makeup. He ticked off the brands as if he'd invented them. Crème de la Mer moisturizer was followed by a variety of paints, powders, and creams from Angel (of course), Laura Mercier, Chantecaille, Paula Dorf, and NARS. I made mental notes.

The process took more than an hour. Again, Keith wouldn't let me see until he was finished. I, a nonmakeup girl, expected the worst. Jack Sparrow in drag. So wrong. I looked...like me, only better. Cute. Make that *really* cute. My skin glowed, my eyes looked enormous, my eyelashes were Bambi-esque.

Sometime between my above-the-neck transformations, Keith must have made a few discreet phone calls, because people with garment bags began arriving during the final phase of my makeup transformation. Keith directed them all to the guest bedroom. When he led me inside, I saw what the visitors had left behind: a pale pink strapless cleavage-enhancing bra with matching silk panties. Five pairs of shoes nestled in their marked boxes. Jimmy Choos, Manolo, Gucci, and Stuart Weitzman. And a single fire-engine-red dress that Keith held up for me. "Zac Posen. No one else cuts like him."

I frowned. "That will never fit."

His only reply was a Cheshire-cat grin that revealed his dazzling white veneers. "Trust me."

He was right. Which was why I was now in the passenger seat of his Rolls, wearing the exquisite lingerie, the black Gucci pumps, and a dress so beautiful, I felt it should be hanging in a museum rather than on me. It was strapless, with chiffon layers gathered at the waist. A cowl back exposed a red silk boned bodice so fitted, I'd needed power assistance to be zipped in. The fabric fell in graceful folds to just below my knees. Long gowns, Keith decreed, were much too stuffy this year. And besides, according to *the* Keith, I had great legs. Who was I to argue?

"Remember, Megan," Keith began, "sip a single glass of wine or bubbly. That demonstrates breeding. But do not, under any circumstances, eat."

I nodded. No need to ask why. If my diaphragm expanded by a centimeter, the gown's rigid corset would not expand with it. Tomorrow's *Shiny Sheet* headline would read: "Baker Tutor Boned to Death."

"Okay, darling, we're here. You have my cell?" Keith asked. "And Marco's? For an emergency?"

I nodded, fearful to make any movement below my collarbone.

"Lip-gloss check," Keith ordered as a valet opened my door. "Smile." I did. "You're good to go, princess."

A white-gloved hand reached for mine. I swung my legs out, careful to keep them together, and managed a graceful departure from the Rolls. "Welcome to Mar-a-Lago." The valet flashed a movie-star smile.

Keith came around the Rolls—he wore a black tuxedo and a ruby stud in his shirt, since the Red and White ball had asked that everyone wear one or both colors—and offered me his arm. "Shall we, my dear?"

"We shall," I agreed. We stepped forward onto a path strewn with red and white rose petals.

Right before we reached the imposing doors, my eyes darted to Keith. He squeezed my hand. "You will fucking own the place."

❧ ❧

Many years earlier, Lily and I had rented *Pretty Woman*, which she loved and I despised. You, too, can be a hooker and end up living happily ever after. Lily said I was taking it too literally—it wasn't supposed to be real life, and everyone knew it. Well, *of course* it wasn't real life. In real life, Cinderella did not get transformed and then—*poof*—get to go to the ball.

Color me shocked when it happened to me.

There I stood, at the top of the grand stairway that led down to a massive ballroom of gilt and ivory, lit by what seemed like hundreds of ornate crystal chandeliers. It was wall-to-wall with some of the most beautiful and wealthiest people on the planet. They ranged in age from young to doddering. At the far end of the ballroom, on a raised stage, Valerie Romanoff's Starlight Orchestra was playing "Bad, Bad Leroy Brown"—I kid you not—and a few dozen couples were dancing. There were four bars and four different buffets, plus white-tuxedoed waiters passing around food and drink.

"Straight through the crowd to the middle, then turn to the bar to your left," Keith instructed. As we started down the steps, I felt eyes swing in our direction.

Don't trip, don't trip, don't trip, I told myself.

We hit the hardwood floor, where Keith escorted me through the throng of Palm Beach royalty. All around us, people whispered as we passed.

"Who is she?"

"She's gorgeous."

"That gown."

"That hair."

"I saw her in Torremolinos last spring!" And then Pembroke stepped in front of me, wearing a tux so well cut that it camouflaged his seven-month-pregnant middle. "Megan?" His eyes dropped to my cantilevered cleavage as if he were hoping the dress would somehow melt from the force of his heat vision. "*Damn.*"

"Thanks," I said. "Pembroke Hutchison, Keith Genteel. Keith, Pembroke."

Pembroke laughed. "I know Keith. He does my mother. Not literally, of course. So how do you know Keith, Megan?"

"She's a friend of a friend." Keith grinned devilishly, then kissed my cheek. "I'm going to find Marco. You're fine?"

"More than," I assured him. It was ridiculous, I know, but Pembroke's *damn* had provided a wave of confidence.

As Keith moved off, Pembroke insisted on getting me an apple martini. He took my arm as we moved toward the bar. We didn't get more than ten feet before I heard my name again.

"*Megan?*"

It was Sage, in a long crimson gown whose neckline was cut down to her diamond-stud-pierced navel.

"Oh, hi, Sage." No shocker that her sister was right behind her, in a stunning halter-neck floor-length white gown. With her was diminutive Precious Baldridge, from my swimming-pool humiliation, wearing a spray-on tan and a lipstick-red silk dress cut low in the back. Sage gawked at me. So did Precious.

"What are you *doing* here?" Sage could barely get the words out.

"The same thing you're doing: helping to raise money for NARSAD," I replied.

I'd done my homework. Most of the events during The Season were ostensibly given for charity, though in actuality, they were excuses for the ridiculously rich, shallow, and self-involved to try to outdress and out-bling one another. This particular ball was being given for the National Alliance for Research on Schizophrenia and Depression.

Sage pushed some curls that had tumbled from her updo behind her ears. "I meant, how did you get *in?*"

"Uh—"

"What difference does it make?" Precious exclaimed. "She's

here, she obviously belongs here. Ohmigod—I love your dress. Why didn't my stylist show me that one?"

Pembroke grinned at me. "I almost didn't recognize her with her clothes on." He guffawed at his own cleverness.

"I could strip and remind you, but I'm sure you have a vivid imagination." I dearly hoped this came across as playful teasing, since I felt like feeding him my fist.

He laughed. "How about that apple martini?"

"Something else," I replied, and then I looked at Rose. "What are you all drinking?"

"Flirtinis."

No clue what those were.

"Fine, then," I told Pembroke. "A flirtini."

"Flirtini it is."

He trotted off, and his place was taken by another of the twins' friends from the night before, the one with the eye-popping implants. What was her name again? It had something to do with *Sesame Street.* Big Bird? Cookie Monster? Oscar the Grouch? That was it. Grouch. Suzanne de Grouchy. She stared at me with unabashed admiration. "Zac Posen, right?"

She didn't even attempt an apology for the night before. I played along like I was too cool to want one.

"Of course," I lied. I had zero recollection of who'd made my dress.

Sage narrowed her eyes at me, and I willed myself to stay calm. "What happened to the frizzy hair and the crap clothes?"

This one I was ready for, thanks to my former not-so-brilliant career.

"Please, Sage. All I ever wear when I'm traveling is an Evian spritz, lip gloss, and my most comfortable clothes." I did my best imitation of her patented hair toss. A month ago at *Scoop*, I'd written the photo captions for an interview with three top models. Kate Moss had explained that she never wore makeup while traveling. "It's not like *I* need to impress anyone."

This moment shall be forever seared into my brain. Sage blinked. The superior sneer fell from her face, and she sniffed. "Well, you could have told us."

I smiled sweetly. "As I said, it's not like I need to impress anyone."

And yet I was impressing someone. Sage and Rose. Exactly whom I had to impress. They might not like me, but there wasn't an ounce of disdain in their eyes. By any measure, it was progress.

"Here you go!" Pembroke was back, handing me a pink drink in a martini glass. "One flirtini."

"You're a sweetheart." *Sweetheart?* Who was I? I was tempted to gulp the thing down, the better to fuel my farce, but I remembered Keith cautioning me to sip, so I did, feigning great interest in the couples dancing to something by the BeeGees that no one should dance to, ever.

"Dance?" came a voice from behind me.

I turned to find myself staring into the impossibly blue eyes of the guy who'd handed me the towel the night before. Will Phillips. Now, instead of a full-body blush, I was wearing a red dress. It seemed fitting.

"How can you dance to this shit, Will?" Sage asked. The orchestra had just started "Strangers in the Night." I hesitated as couples old enough to have lost their virginity to Sinatra—no, Edith Piaf—took to the dance floor.

"Think of it as really, really retro," Will told Sage, then looked back at me. "So?" He held out a hand.

"Sure." It was momentarily hard to look away from his eyes until I reminded myself exactly who this guy was friends with and precisely what those eyes had already gazed upon. *I'm working*, I told myself. I had two weeks until Laurel would return and see that the girls were no closer to getting in to Duke, and then I'd be out on my ass—two weeks to learn everything I could about the rich, wretched, and repugnant of Palm Beach. I slipped my hand into his. Every minute counted.

"Sorry about last night," Will said as he slipped his arms around me. "That surprised me, too."

To believe or not to believe, that was the question. I'd muse on it later.

"No biggie," I said smoothly. "It was just a silly prank. So how do you know the twins?"

"I live next door, at Barbados." We began to move to the alleged music.

The next-door neighbor who'd known them forever. Perfect.

"Barbados is an island in the Caribbean," I said teasingly.

"Also the name of our property. People in Palm Beach can't resist naming their houses. I think it's in the water."

"So you kind of grew up with Sage and Rose?" I asked.

"Not exactly. I'm twenty-three. I graduated from Northwestern last June."

He was my age. Which begged the question: Why was he hanging out with a group of high school kids? Which led me to an obvious conclusion: He was sleeping with one of them. Where I come from, we call that criminal. And no matter where you come from, it's just ... *icky*.

"How about you?" He pulled away just far enough so that he could look at me.

"Yale," I replied diffidently.

He whistled softly. "And you're a tutor? By choice? What'd you study?"

"Literature." The truth seemed safe enough. "You?"

"Art history. My dad's a dealer. I'm trying to decide whether to go into the business. His flagship gallery is on Worth Avenue, actually. I'm sure you know it—the Phillips Gallery."

I resisted the urge to roll my eyes at this guy's totally self-important spiel. Did all these people assume their little world was the center of the universe? "This is actually my first time in Palm Beach," I told him, trying to keep my research in mind. "I haven't seen the island at all yet."

I hoped he'd take the bait I'd just floated. What better tour guide could I possibly have than Barbados Boy?

"My dad's showing some Corots at the gallery. Maybe you'd like to see them. I'd be happy to show you around tomorrow."

Oh, yeah. Hook, line, and sinker.

"Love to."

I smiled over his shoulder, imagining all the inside dish I could get from him the next day. And when an old codger in a red dinner jacket bumped me closer to Will, well . . . I didn't even mind.

This was starting to be *fun*.

c h a p t e r   t h i r t e e n

*D*espite the minor progress I'd made with the twins
at the party—at least I was Megan again instead of
Frizzy—I'd decided not to chase after them the morning after.
I figured I'd go to the main mansion to get breakfast and my
predictions for my afternoon with likely-statutory-rapist-slash-
Baker-twins-neighbor Will Phillips.

It turned out that I didn't have to. The twins' pounding on
my door woke me at the almost reasonable hour of ten o'clock.
They were dressed for fun in the sun. Sage had on a three-Post-
it-notes-size gold bikini, while Rose wore a black tank suit cut up
to the waist on the sides, making it look as if her legs were about
eight feet long.

Sage spoke first. She folded her arms, eyes narrowed. "We
know who you are."

Busted. So much for Marco and Keith's attempt to pass me off
as one of them. It was fun while it lasted. All sixteen hours of it.

"Okay, fine," I began. "So I'm not really—"

"We Googled you," Rose interrupted me. Sage nodded. "You're Megan Smith from Main Line Philadelphia—Gladwyne, Pennsylvania, to be exact. Your family sponsored a ball last spring to benefit the University of Pennsylvania Hospital's transplant center. Your mother wore Chanel, and you wore Versace. We read all about it."

Sponsoring a benefit last spring was so far from the reality of my life that it was laughable, but the puzzle pieces rearranged themselves in my head. Smith wasn't exactly an uncommon name, and neither was Megan. That there was another girl out there with my name who came from a super-rich family shouldn't have been a surprise. I'd Googled myself once or twice. Okay, ten or twelve times. Except for a few hits on Yale-related websites, my real self was an Internet nonentity. But there were about 93,700 other Megan Smiths mentioned. And apparently, one of them was rich.

"At least we know how you got invited to the ball," Rose muttered.

"And where the dress came from," Sage added. "You should have just told us, Megan."

They flounced off. I took a chance and shouted after them, "Are you guys ready to study with me?"

It's amazing how quickly a pair of twins can shout the word *no* over their shoulders.

<hr />

I ended up ordering breakfast from the main house—two fresh-baked croissants, a plate of sliced fresh tropical fruit, and a carafe of Ethiopian coffee—and spent the morning out on my private deck, doing a little online research myself about Gladwyne, Pennsylvania, home of the other Megan Smith. Gladwyne was another one of those places that made Concord, New Hampshire, the town where I'd grown up, seem like a third-world country.

It was in the midst of my Gladwyne research that a scary thought hit me. When I went to meet Will later, he'd expect to see the girl he'd danced with the night before. Only, that girl didn't exist. I was terrible with my hair, and I had no clothes. Short of having *the* Mr. Keith materialize in my den, I was screwed.

In a panic, I showered, washed my hair, and put on a combination of hideous Century 21 outfits numbers one and two. Then I dashed over to the main mansion—deliberately skirting the pool deck, where the twins might be—to find my fairy gaymother.

With few preliminaries, I explained my crisis. Not the whole story, of course—Marco couldn't know that I was actually going undercover as a journalist—but I did work in how the twins had mistaken me for another, much richer Megan Smith. He thought this was hysterical and seemed to understand the importance of not doing anything to dissuade them from the notion. For purely, um, academic reasons.

"Not to worry, dear heart," Marco cooed, setting cinnamon buns on a cooling rack. "It's a stroke of good fortune. I believe I can come to your rescue. Have a bun."

I wolfed one down, both relieved that he thought he could help and newly guilt-ridden. Marco had been nothing but nice to me from the first moment we'd met, and I was being less than honest about my intentions in Palm Beach. *This is what journalists do,* I reminded myself.

As Marco led me to his pink bungalow at the north end of the property, my remorse abated. It turned out that I wasn't the only one who had a secret. When Marco wasn't Chef Marco, he was Zsa Zsa Lahore, the most glamorous drag queen this side of the intercoastal. And he just happened to be my size.

We walked though his red and black living room with a lizard-print couch—he was currently in a western phase—and into his bedroom. Unlike his general demeanor, it was aggressively masculine, all silver and chrome, with a painting over his bed of two cowboys eying each other with lust. How *Brokeback*.

"My closets are your closets," he announced, opening double doors to a walk-in nearly as large as his bedroom.

How generous could one fairy gaymother possibly be? The walk-in was filled with rack upon rack upon rack of gorgeous designer clothes. He began pulling out possibilities. "For the gallery with Will, I'm thinking Bottega Veneta high-waisted black crepe trousers and the Fendi ivory chiffon blouse. Now let us find you more."

I tried to protest, but by the time he was done, he'd filled one large suitcase and a king-size garment bag, saying that I'd need these clothes for the future.

"My advice for what you're wearing, darling?" he offered. "Burn it."

Next came hair and makeup. Marco didn't share Keith's genius for hair, but he did teach me to use a flatiron. Next was makeup, which he had more than perfected, and then I changed into the outfit he'd suggested. It fit. I looked down at my black loafers and bit my lip in concern. Even I knew they were a *nonono*.

"Oh, dear." Marco nibbled on a perfectly manicured fingernail. I wore a women's eight. He wore a women's ten. Then he snapped his fingers. "Stretch Chanel ballet slippers, darling. Just the thing."

I tried them—still too big, but they stayed on because of the elastic. He promised to call Keith and have him bring over some other options. I protested one more time, but Marco was hearing none of it.

"Dahling," he drolled in a near-perfect Zsa Zsa Gabor accent as he coated my lashes with mascara, "you look stunning. Which car will you take?"

I hadn't given it a moment's thought, which was what I told Marco. In exactly fifty minutes, I was supposed to be downtown on Worth Avenue, where Will would give me the grand tour of his father's gallery and then take me to the Breakers for tea.

"Take the Ferrari," Marco advised. "The red Ferrari. It's the most fun to drive. You can handle a stick?" He smirked at the sexual innuendo.

"I sure can." I laughed. My father's pickup truck had a manual transmission.

Marco smiled. "My advice, my dear? When given the opportunity to handle a stick, handle it."

The Phillips Gallery was located at the north end of Worth Avenue, and it had but a single painting in its picture window: a stone bridge in the French countryside. An even more discreet sign announced PHILLIPS GALLERY: PALM BEACH. JEAN-BAPTISTE-CAMILLE COROT, WORKS. NOVEMBER 13 TO DECEMBER 23.

I left my car at the valet stand directly in front of the gallery and then stepped inside. So this was it. The gallery that Will's father wanted him to run. The front room was stark white with a polished wood floor. The air-conditioning offered relief from the sun and humidity.

I was greeted by a young woman in a very fitted black suit, with a de rigueur Palm Beach tan and blunt-cut shoulder-length blond hair. "Welcome to the Phillips Gallery. I'm Giselle Keenan," she said to me. Then she turned her head and regarded me again. "I hope you don't mind my asking, but... who did your color? The streaks are *wonderful.*"

"Um, Keith," I told her, his last name escaping me for a moment.

"*The* Keith?" Giselle uttered the name with hushed reverence. "I've tried and tried to book him. How did you do it?"

"I'm staying at Les Anges—"

"With the Baker twins? We were all on the Hearts and Hopes ball committee last season. Tell them Giselle said hi, okay? I loved their *Vanity Fair* thing."

"Sure," I told her, filing away some mental notes. "And I'm actually here to see Will Phillips? He's expecting me. I'm Megan."

"Right away." She pushed a few buttons on her phone system. As she did, a well-dressed guy with shaggy hair and the ruddy complexion of someone who spent lots of time on boats, or golf courses, or both, entered the gallery. He smiled at me in the way that I had seen so many guys smile at my sister. My first instinct was to turn to see if he was smiling at some really hot girl standing behind me. Apparently, the Cinderella effect had lasted after the ball.

Just as my golfing sailor took a couple of steps in my direction, Will materialized. "Megan? Welcome to the gallery."

He wore a blue sport coat, an open-collar light blue shirt,

khaki pants, and maroon loafers with no socks. I would soon learn that variations on this outfit were Palm Beach's unofficial male uniform. My sailor offered me a little nod of recognition and a good-natured look of regret. Then he turned and walked out.

"Have you had a chance to look around yet?" Will asked.

"Not much. But this room is gorgeous."

"I grew up with it. I don't even see it anymore," Will confessed.

I wanted Will to be comfortable enough around me to be himself—what better poster boy for an article about Palm Beach could there be?—but it was hard to squelch my desire to kick him in the shins for being so spoiled.

"Want to take the two-cent tour and then a walk on the avenue?"

"Sounds good," I answered him.

Will mostly talked, and I mostly listened, as he showed me through the two expansive white rooms of the gallery. He had an encyclopedic knowledge of Corot's work and life, and he took me through the artist's three distinct periods, then turned to me. "Let's go."

We walked out into the dazzling early-afternoon sunshine and turned right on the sidewalk, passing one designer shop after another. Ferragamo. Gucci. Hermès. Tiffany. There was nary a Gap nor a Starbucks in sight. The pedestrian traffic was light, and the day was warm. The only real action was in front of a restaurant named Ta-boo, where a team of valets was efficiently parking a substantial lineup of Bentleys, Mercedeses, and Rolls-Royces.

I noticed a speed-limit sign that was posted with a minimum

as well as a maximum. Why would you possibly have a *minimum* speed requirement?

"What's up with those signs?" I asked.

"They don't have those in Philadelphia?" He looked puzzled. "It's to keep the tourists from slowing down to gawk. People around here like their privacy."

"Who said I'm from Philadelphia?"

"Sage."

Well, okay. This could work to my advantage. For research purposes, it couldn't hurt for Will to also think I was the other Megan.

"So I've never been to Philly," Will said. "Tell me about where you grew up."

Thanks to my Internet research that very morning, this wasn't hard. I told him where I liked to eat (Tre Scalini), where I liked to shop (the Smak Parlour), and where I liked to go on vacation (Gstaad, for the skiing, and Brussels, for the shopping). I was having so much fun inventing myself that I barely noticed we had done the full circle of Worth Avenue and were standing in front of the gallery again.

Will looked at his watch. "I have to get back to work."

Wait, what about the Breakers? "Thanks for the tour." I touched his arm. "Maybe we could get together another time."

This was my shameless way of saying: *Ask me out for cocktails, pretty boy*. Who knew what I could get out of him after two or three drinks?

"Yeah, maybe. Take care, Megan." I couldn't help but think he looked a little confused as he stepped backward into the gallery.

Choose the best antonym (pair of words possessing an opposite meaning) for the following set of words:

DIVIDE and CONQUER

(a) invite and party
(b) separate and destroy
(c) highlight and blowout
(d) unify and submit
(e) mani and pedi

chapter fourteen

I was walking on the now-familiar white pebble path between the main mansion and the twins' manse, going over the bizarre end to Will's and my walk, when I heard shouts coming from the pool deck. The twins—I couldn't yet tell their voices apart—and someone else.

How intriguing.

The expletives were flying as I stepped off the path and hid behind a palm tree just west of the pool deck. From there, I could see across the deck to the cabanas, where the battle royal was taking place. The girls were still in their swimsuits, and the other woman was dressed in a beige pantsuit.

"I can't fucking believe you, Zenith!" Sage screeched. "You call yourself a fucking manager? You *suck*!"

Manager? As in the manager who was supposed to be getting the twins all that priceless film, TV, and modeling work?

Zenith took a deep breath, clearly attempting to maintain her composure. "Look, this kind of thing happens all the time—deals fall through when it comes time for people to write checks."

"You said you were going to get us our own TV series. Our own movie. Our own chain of clubs," Rose whined. "You said we were going to make the world forget about Paris and Nicole!"

"Look, there *is* an offer on the table. If you weren't such spoiled brats, you'd be grabbing at it," Zenith fumed.

"Golden Glow spray-on tan? And I'm the fucking 'before' picture? Sage Baker is *never* a 'before' picture!"

Sage Baker as a "before" picture? Priceless.

"Are you finished?" Zenith asked quietly.

"Get the hell off our property," Sage responded.

"Nothing would make me happier. Don't ever call me again." Zenith started back across the pool deck, thankfully taking a path that wouldn't cause her to run into me.

"No, you don't ever call *us* again!" Sage took off one of her jewel-encrusted sandals and hurled it at her retreating manager. It plunged into the pool. "And you look like shit in beige!" Sage turned back to her sister. "Fuck her. We'll find another manager. Come on, Rose, let's go get plastered."

"No." Rose looked like she was on the verge of tears.

"*No?*" Sage echoed, sounding incredulous. I was incredulous, too. I hadn't known that Rose was capable of saying that word to her sister.

"Everything's... ruined." Rose dashed across the deck and down the stone steps to the beach, leaving Sage alone. For a brief moment, it seemed like Sage was going to go after her. But then she strode back toward their house, kicking her other sandal into the pool on the way.

Divide and conquer, I told myself. The twins' house was already divided. All I had to do was conquer.

I took the back way to the beach and tried to look casual, like I merely happened to be going for an afternoon stroll. Almost immediately, I saw Rose taking baby steps along the surf line, dancing away from each oncoming wave and then daring the ocean to soak her feet.

"Out for a walk?" I asked as I approached. Her lower lip was trembling. "Hey, are you okay?"

She shook her head. The tide was on the way in, and a wave came dangerously close to soaking our feet. I jumped back, figuring Marco's ballet slippers were not waterproof.

"Where's my sister?" Rose asked, looking concerned.

I shrugged. "Don't know."

Rose started up the beach and sat down against the stone seawall. I followed her there, realizing that if Sage looked out at the beach, she couldn't see us together. That was the point.

"We're totally fucked," Rose finally muttered. "Sage and me."

Well, then. "Fucked how?"

She kept her eyes on the water. "You remember what Sage told you the night you arrived—about our manager out in Los Angeles? All the offers and how we were going to make our own money?"

I nodded and waited for her explanation. And waited some more. Finally, she let it all spill out in a monologue that challenged every law of punctuation and syntax: "Sage said doing *Vanity Fair* would make us famous, and we wouldn't be able to go anywhere after a while without television cameras following us, and I mean, that sounded like fun because that's how famous people are, like, all the time and everything . . . So Sage hired this manager in Los Angeles, and there were going to be all these offers, like for a movie, and our own reality TV show, and, like, makeup companies but not like cheap ones, you know?"

I nodded again. It seemed like the thing to do.

"Well," Rose went on, "as it turns out, none of those deals worked out, but I don't know why and, like, there was only this spray-tan thingie? Oh, and maybe this other thing that wasn't for sure, but it was for a chain of stores in the South that carries, like, Jessica Simpson jeans, which she doesn't even wear."

"Wow."

My sympathy seemed to encourage Rose. She went on, "Anyway, we wouldn't have made enough to live for, like, a year. But we already said fuck you to Grandma's money we never should have made you swim naked because now you hate us and you'll never want to be our tutor but even if you did what good would that even be?" She blinked twice. "Does that make sense?"

In an alternate grammatical universe, maybe. But I got the gist, because the gist seemed like the opening I'd been hoping for. Sage had sold Rose on the notion that they wouldn't need their grandmother's money because they were going to make so much of their own. Ergo, they could blow me off. All wrong. Rose was confiding in me because she was scared shitless of being fundless.

There's nothing like being needed.

"So . . . can you help us?" she asked.

I could tutor her, which would buy me more time in paradise—a good thing. No. A great thing. But could I get her in to Duke? Even if I worked with her night and day for seven and a half weeks, I wasn't sure she had the IQ of a tennis ball. Plus, *both* twins had to be accepted, and being the Palm Beach version of Heidi Fleiss was likely Sage's preference over being tutored by me.

At least I was getting somewhere with *one* of the twins. Maybe her sister wouldn't be so far behind.

That night, like any good investigative journalist, I worked on my notes. Between Marco, Keith, Will, and the twins, I had more than enough dirt to bury the Palm Beach privileged.

From Suzanne de Grouchy, after one two many flirtinis at the Red and White ball: A society princess who stabbed her husband with a Wüsthof-Trident classic kitchen knife, after catching him with one of Suzanne's friends, had received two months of house arrest. The friend was shipped off to the South of France.

From Keith, during another makeup application: Last year a shelter called the Peace Place canceled their usual fund-raising ball for The Season and instead sent out invitations announcing that "guests" could stay home in comfort and send a donation in their place. Peace Place normally received more than a million dollars in donations at their event. The year they canceled, they raised five thousand. "Charity balls during The Season," Keith decreed, "are Palm Beach's contribution to society."

From Rose herself, with a napkin folded in her lap: Sometimes chewing your food and then spitting it out is just as satisfying as, like, eating . . . you know?

Seriously. I couldn't make this stuff up if I tried.

I'd thought I'd be here for only two weeks. But Rose had given me the possibility of a two-month sojourn. To make that work, I had to get Sage on board, too. So the next morning I flatironed my hair, put on one of the more casual outfits Marco had lent me—low-rise Joe's jeans that had shrunk in the wash, plus a white Petit Bateau T-shirt—and settled myself at the fork of the corridor between our two suites.

Around eleven, Sage strode out, wearing dark skinny jeans, a white tank with angel wings on the front, and impossibly high strappy sandals. Save for the shoes, we were similarly dressed.

I took it as a sign. "Sage!"

She looked irritated before I even opened my mouth. "What do you want?"

"Well..." I sagged back against the wall and tried to look as forlorn as possible.

"What?" she snapped. "You catch crabs from someone at Bath and Tennis or something?"

I stopped sagging. Evidently, Lily had the acting talent in our family, but it was too late to stop now. "Listen, Sage, I'll level with you." *True. In a journalist-who'll-do-anything-to-get-the-story kind of way.* "I know you don't care about studying, but honestly?" *Fingers crossed.* "I really, really need this job."

She looked at me with something approaching professional interest. "Because you're in debt?"

"Exactly." *Totally true.*

"Big debt?"

I nodded.

Sage nodded gravely. "I kind of figured. Two years ago Precious had front-row seats during Fashion Week in New York, and the clothes were to die for that year. And she ended up, like, three hundred thousand dollars in debt, and her mom *freaked* because her credit card only had a hundred-thousand-dollar limit."

This was amazing. And priceless.

"What did Precious's parents do?"

Sage leaned forward. "They cut off her allowance," she whispered, as if imparting a national-security secret. "Precious was so upset, she nearly *gave birth*. When we Googled you, I sort of figured it must be something like that."

Ah, the irony. Never in a million years would it have occurred to me that Sage would jump to the conclusion that I had run up a couture debt and not an educational one.

"So you can see why I really need this job," I said without correcting her misimpression. "To try to whack it down."

"Make Mommy and Daddy Smith happy, you mean," she interpreted. "Did they push back the release of your trust? God, it's just so *mean*!"

"Right," I agreed. I'd known a girl at Yale who used to moan all the time that she wouldn't get her trust until she was thirty, which was, she used to say, like, *ancient*. "So if we could do a few study things so that I have something to show your grandmother . . . I mean, I can pretty much stay out of your hair. And at some point, if you decide the Hollywood thing isn't working for you, well . . . at least we'll have studied a little."

I could practically see the blank thought bubbles coming from her head. She heaved a very irritated sigh. "Fine."

Fine? Hot damn.

"Thanks *so* much," I gushed. "I really appreciate this."

"Whatever. When do we start?'"

"This afternoon?" I asked tentatively.

"Okay," she agreed with an eye roll that emphasized what a huge favor she was doing for me.

She had *no* idea.

Choose the analogy that best complements the following phrase:
YACHT : SOCIETY PRINCESS

(a) cardboard box : wino
(b) Chihuahua : rock starlet
(c) cocaine : supermodel
(d) Fendi Baguette : Sarah Jessica Parker
(e) drug arrests : Robert Downey, Jr.

chapter fifteen

A fundamental truth came clear to me four days later, my seventh day in Palm Beach: There was a reason for all those stories of famous scholars surviving on bread and radishes, sleeping in a garret, using the same water to boil their eggs and wash their armpits—a life of luxury is not an atmosphere conducive to learning. When given the choice between mastering quadratic equations and watching a not-yet-released DVD in a home theater nicer than any multiplex, who wouldn't opt for the distraction of hot popcorn and Orlando Bloom?

Despite the twins' ostensible new commitment to studying, they spent a lot more time playing than working. If I'd been an actual tutor, I might have cared. But I wasn't, so I didn't. Instead, I did my best to bond with them under the pretext of teaching.

Rose was reasonably pleasant to me, because she was nicer by nature. Sage tolerated me, because with my new Marco wardrobe and look, I was, as he had predicted, an acceptable accessory. Teaching-cum-bonding-cum-research was exactly what I was doing this late afternoon out on Laurel's hundred-and-fifty-foot yacht, the *Heavenly*.

As we motored out of the Palm Beach Yacht Club, the new deckhand, Thom, gave me a quick tour. He was skinny, with messy sun-streaked hair and a winning smile. The boat spread out over three levels: one down below that held staterooms; a main level with a huge open rear deck, living room, dining room, and kitchen; plus a helipad upstairs so that guests could be ferried to and from shore without having to contend with the waves.

Post-tour, I found my way to the rear deck, where the girls were already stretched out in their swimsuits. Sage's tangerine bikini had shirring across the ass that made her backside look like a peach. Rose wore a white one-piece halter with a back so low, it displayed a peek of rear cleavage. I, on the other hand, was wearing Marc Jacobs white stretch cotton pants and a black T-shirt with a giant cross on the back. Marco had worn it during his Cher stage.

"Where's your suit, Megan?" Rose asked. "Aren't we going to take a hot tub before we get started?"

Marco could provide me with a lot of things, but a bathing suit wasn't one of them. I pleaded cramps and enjoyed the ride while the twins lolled. A sauna followed their hot tub, and then they summoned Thom to bring food—caviar, water crackers, chocolate-covered raspberries, and a bottle of Taittinger, their favorite champagne. Since water crackers were actual carbs, they mostly stuck their fingers in the caviar and popped them in their mouths.

After that, they were ready to tackle some math. As they got out pencils, paper, and calculators, I tried to tailor the problems to their interests. "Karen was able to find a classic Chanel dress on sale for two thousand, six hundred and fifty dollars."

"Who's Karen?" Rose asked, flipping onto her stomach.

"It doesn't matter. It's just a name for the word problem. Just take down the main info." I pulled my T-shirt sleeves off my shoulders so I could at least get a little sun.

Sage sighed with irritation. She'd been trying—without success—to find another manager to represent them. In the meantime, she had started participating in our study sessions. *Participating* can be defined very loosely. "Can you start again?"

"Karen was able to find—"

"Hold on," Sage ordered. She grabbed some SPF 50 and slathered it on her opalescent chest, arms, and legs while Rose waited. "Start again."

"Karen was able to find a Chanel dress on sale for twenty-six hundred and fifty dollars."

"I thought you said two thousand, six hundred and fifty dollars?" Rose asked.

I smiled and filed that one away. "Same difference. When that dress was designed and sewn in the forties, it cost eighty percent less. What did it cost back when it was made?"

Rose propped herself up on her elbows and began scribbling on a piece of scrap paper. Sage stared at me blankly.

"Did you need me to repeat the question?" I asked.

"Are we talking actual cost or cost as adjusted by inflation?" she asked coolly.

Huh. Score one for Sage.

"Actual cost," I said.

"Does Karen have a trust fund or an allowance?" Sage asked.

"Karen doesn't exist," I said carefully, thinking that maybe we ought to move on to geometry. "It's just a made-up problem to—"

"Hold it," Sage decreed, raising a finger and cupping a hand to her left ear. Then she pointed to the western sky. "Yep, that's them."

I could barely make out an approaching helicopter. "That's who?"

"Suzanne turned eighteen yesterday," Sage explained. "We're celebrating tonight. If you're not into it, you can go hang in my grandmother's *library*."

I was fine with the surprise. A party was a lot more likely to result in Palm Beach dish than Karen and her fucking Chanel dress.

The noise was deafening as the chopper approached and then hovered a hundred feet above the rear deck. I watched helplessly as the workbooks and papers we'd been using were blown out to sea by the backwash from the blades.

The chopper touched down, the doors opened, and three of the twins' friends hopped out. I recognized Ari and Suzanne, and there was a tall athletic guy I'd never seen before. Next came an orgy of hugging, kissing, and shouting of "Happy birthday!"

As the helicopter went airborne again, I considered how the twins could so blithely risk their fortune by being so unfocused—unless they had the misguided notion that what they were doing with me *was* being focused. In just over six weeks, they were going to find out how wrong that assessment was.

Sage immediately flounced off with the tall guy to good-natured catcalls from the others. I got an actual hug from Suzanne, who then called for a beer and headed for the hot tub, shedding clothes as she went.

"How goes the work?" Ari asked, offering me a fist bump. He was wearing cutoff Brooks Brothers khakis and an old CBGB T-shirt. He looked like he could have been in my East Village neighborhood instead of on a multimillion-dollar yacht in the middle of the bay.

"They're...making progress. How about you, Ari? What are your plans for next year?"

"MIT. I've got better than a four-point GPA and 2400 SATs, so I'm pretty confident."

I nearly choked on my own spit. One of the twins' friends was...*smart?*

"I wish you could take the SAT for me, Ari," Rose said with a helpless sigh.

"What your grandmother did was so—" Ari began, but I didn't hear the rest, because yet another helicopter was approaching. No. *Three* helicopters, making the yacht the center of their airborne isosceles triangle. Then I spotted a few powerboats motoring our way, and Thom lowering a ladder that would allow their passengers to climb aboard.

Thirty minutes later, I was in the midst of a full-fledged birthday bash. All the twins' friends I'd met so far were there, as well as forty or fifty other kids. The only person missing was Will Phillips, whom I hadn't seen since he'd blown me off on Worth Avenue. Not that I cared.

Really.

As the sun went down to the west, most of the kids were

in seriously altered states. The new Gwen Stefani album wailed over the boat's sound system. Girls were dancing with guys, girls were dancing with girls, girls were kissing guys, and a couple were kissing each other, too, much to the enjoyment of the guys. Everyone had drink or drug in hand. It made a Yale frat party seem like a Quaker meeting, so when Pembroke told me not to look so stressed—we were the requisite twelve miles off the coast that put us in international waters, i.e., beyond the threat of the Coast Guard—I actually did breathe a sigh of relief.

As the music switched to an old Smashing Pumpkins song, Pembroke pulled me close—well, as close as I could get with his stomach in the way. His eyes were glassy.

"You're so *hot*," he whispered in my ear, and I felt a bit of spittle hit my earlobe. Oh, *ick*. "The whole teacher thing is fucking, like, *wow*."

Fucking, like, wow was right.

chapter sixteen

*W*hen I'd agreed to spend Thanksgiving with James at his parents' beach house, I'd known the holiday would not be the over-the-river-and-through-the-woods experience I was used to at home in New Hampshire. I would miss the early snow and the crackling fire in the fireplace and my father doing an acoustic run through Bob Dylan's greatest hits as my grandma made her world—okay, family—famous cranberry sauce (secret ingredient: orange peel).

I'd spoken to my parents the day before. Lily was going up to New Hampshire by limousine so she wouldn't miss her Wednesday-night and Friday-night shows. I felt a pang of homesickness made worse by the knowledge of what lay ahead. Turkey Day in Florida with the quasi-in-laws who hated me.

On Thanksgiving morning, I put the Macy's parade on the plasma TV and flatironed my hair, a skill that I'd nearly mastered. I was still a walking disaster with makeup, so I ran to Marco's cottage and let him do me. For clothes, I chose an Oscar de la Renta sleeveless cashmere sweater from Marco's Ann-Margret phase and a camel-colored Burberry skirt. As I got into one of the spare BMWs for the hour-long drive down to Gulf Stream, I thought I looked pretty good for a girl who was going into battle.

James's parents' place was right on the beach in a town that would be considered extremely wealthy compared to anywhere but Palm Beach. As I pulled in to the driveway, James stepped out the door. The next thing I knew, I was in his arms.

"Hey," he murmured into my hair. "I missed you." Then he held me at arm's length. "Holy shit, what ... *happened* to you?"

Ouch. And here I thought I'd been looking kind of—you know—cute.

"Oh, I just changed a few—"

"You look *beautiful*."

I grinned. "Really?"

"Spin," he commanded, managing to make the instruction sound as ungay as possible. "The hair, the clothes ... Wait till my parents see you."

I chafed a little. Had I not been good enough before? But since I knew he meant it in a nice way—that he was proud of me—I gave him a soft kiss and kept my mouth shut. He slung an arm around my shoulders and led me inside.

If you've ever seen Stanley Kubrick's *A Clockwork Orange*, you have a pretty good sense of the Ladeen beach house. Starkly modern, all surfaces bled of color, furniture in straight lines. A glass and chrome table in the living room held the only signs of life: the morning *New York Times* neatly laid out in overlapping sections and an abandoned cup of coffee.

There were also a half-dozen chrome-framed family photos on the table—the usual portraits and vacation scenes, and one of James from Yale graduation. There was a portrait of the Ladeens laughing on a ski slope: James and his parents bundled in sweaters and parkas, their ruddy-cheeked faces smiling at the camera. All good. But James had his arm around something else as well. *Someone* else. Heather.

True confession: It happened after James and I had been together about a month. The morning after a great night, he'd left me in his bed at his apartment to go buy us some breakfast. I was crazy about him but unsure if he was equally crazy about me. Coming right out and asking him seemed way too needy, so I did the only thing a halfway normal girl can do when left alone in a new boyfriend's apartment: I snooped.

I don't know what I was looking for, exactly. Another girl's undies? Lipstick in his medicine cabinet? My perusing took me to his desk, and in the bottom drawer of that desk, I found a cigar box. Inside were old love letters signed from Heather, and in one envelope was a photo. A naked photo taken in that very apartment . . . in the bed I'd just been sleeping in. It was then that I gave her the nickname by which I'd thought of her ever since: Heather the Perfect. Heather's body was . . . *perfect*. When I'd finally met her at one of James's family's parties last year, she'd been wearing a Diane von Furstenberg wrap dress that clung to her every enviable curve. Suffice to say, my theory had been more than confirmed.

And now I was gazing at her photograph again, this time with my boyfriend. At least they had clothes on in this one.

"Oh, that." James gave me a little hug when he saw what I was looking at. "My parents must have forgotten about it."

"Have a handy flamethrower?" I quipped.

"Come on." He took my arm and led me to an exterior patio that opened directly onto the beach.

"Megan!" Dr. Ladeen greeted me warmly, setting down the grilling tongs he'd been flipping turkey breasts with. "Wow, don't you look fantastic. Veronica, doesn't Megan look fantastic?"

Mrs. Ladeen looked up from the cucumbers she was slicing. She wore skinny jeans, which she was thin enough to pull off, a coral-colored peasant blouse, and a pile of silver and turquoise necklaces. Her dark hair was done in a new short choppy cut not unlike Debra Wurtzel's.

"Hello, Megan, dear," she said, air-kissing me somewhere near my left cheek. "You look lovely."

Now, on the face of it, this was a very nice thing to say, so I shall have to try to convey her tone. It was cool, supercilious, and patronizing all at the same time. I would have bet anything that the Ladeens and my parents voted the same way and gave money to the same political and social causes. It was something bigger than politics that made me not measure up to some mythic standard—Platonic standard, actually—of what and who James's girlfriend should be. A Platonic standard doubtlessly embodied by Heather the Perfect and Heather's Perfect Family.

I thanked Mrs. Ladeen and handed over the bottle of 2001 Calera Jensen Vineyard Mt. Harlan pinot noir that Marco had insisted I take from the wine cellar. Apparently, Laurel kept dozens of cases around as small thank-you gifts.

"We're doing barbecued breasts this year," Dr. Ladeen explained. "So much healthier. Tofu and bulgur stuffing, the whole nine yards."

"Sounds great," I told him, though of course it did not.

"We'll be inside, Mom, catching up," James told his folks. "See you later."

We went back inside and down the hallway to a den that had as little color and personality as the rest of the house. At least it was filled with books, most of them review copies that had been sent to James's mother at her magazine, and others that had been gifts from writer friends.

James tugged me onto the gray suede couch. My body quickly reminded me of how long it had been since it had gotten any attention. His hand crept under my—well, Marco's—skirt.

I grabbed his wrist. "Your parents."

"What about 'em?" He nibbled at my neck.

"You know what." I lightly pushed him away and smoothed down the skirt.

"Fine." He groaned. "So, tell me what's going on. What're the twins like?"

I slid to the other side of the couch. "Let me draw you a picture: their brains." I made a circle with my middle finger and my thumb. Then I puffed some air through it, which got me a laugh.

"You getting good stuff for your article?"

"By the time I'm done, James, I won't have an article—I'll have a book." I told him a few stories from the last ten days.

"A couple of editors my mom works with are coming to dinner. You've got to tell them about it." He kissed me again, sliding his hand over my chest. "How about if I come to Palm Beach tomorrow?" he murmured in my ear. "You and I can stay at a little hotel on the beach—I'll show you how much I missed you..."

"I'd love to have you come visit," I told him, meaning it with every aching-to-be-touched muscle in my body. "But Laurel will be home in five days, and I have no way of knowing if I'll have a job after that."

The truth was, I hadn't even persuaded the twins to take a practice SAT test. Since getting the girls to sign on as various-degrees-of-willing study buddies, I'd been a heck of a lot more concerned with observing them for my article than with teaching them. Laurel would likely come home, see how little (read: no) progress had been made, and I'd be on my way back to New York—but *with* article notes in hand.

"Meaning you need to spend every moment doing research," James filled in.

"Exactly."

James laughed. "That e-mail you sent me about how you're pretending to be this blue blood from Philadelphia—funniest thing I ever read."

"And as far as they know, Megan Smith from Main Line Philadelphia doesn't have a boyfriend. You'd be amazed at the dirt I've been able to flirt my way into."

If I had thought James would be upset at this news, I had another think coming. He actually looked at me with admiration. "With your new look, no, I wouldn't."

I leaned over and kissed him. "It's only for five days."

"Hey, journalists have done a lot worse to get the story. Count me impressed."

By the time we returned to the patio, all the guests had arrived. There was Alfonse Ulbrecht, who had just written a scathing assessment of the Bush family that was currently on the *Times* nonfiction best-seller list. There was Simon Chamberlain, very British, who held an endowed chair in poetry at the University of Chicago and whom James's mother called, quote, the second coming of T. S. Eliot. There were two edi-tors from New York named Barbara Fine and Janis Lapin. Both were in their fifties and cackled at everything the other one said.

Dinner was served by a nameless Cuban woman. I couldn't help but wonder if she was missing her own Thanksgiving to serve ours.

Janis, cackling editor number one, turned to me as tea was being served. "So . . . it's Megan, right?"

"Right."

"What do you do?"

Interesting question. Hard to explain. I went with simple. "I'm a college prep tutor."

"Really? And you went to Yale with James?" her partner asked in a way that said, *How sad that you couldn't get a real job.*

"Hey, she's no ordinary tutor. She's working for the Baker twins," James offered. "Did you read the piece in *Vanity Fair?*"

Barbara looked over her teacup at me. "They give bimbos everywhere a bad name!" Janis laughed as if this were the funni-est thing she'd ever heard.

"And how can you stand Palm Beach?" Mrs. Ladeen looked closely at me. "It's full of Republicans!"

"We haven't really talked about politics," I said, despite the uproarious laughter all around the table.

"I did a reading there last week," Alfonse reported. "The women looked like they'd been dipped in formaldehyde. I'm actually writing about it in my piece for *East Coast.*"

It turned out that he was writing two thousand words for the magazine on the horrors of book tours, with the focus on a fat, middle-aged woman who fancied herself his groupie and followed him from reading to reading, including to the Botox Barbie event in Palm Beach, as he put it.

An hour later, when I had escaped from the Ladeens', I was glad. I missed James, and I definitely missed sex, but as I stepped out of their cold and rigid home, I breathed a sigh of relief into the humid Florida air.

Standing in the crushed-seashell driveway was the Cuban woman who'd served us dinner, packing a brown paper sack into the trunk of her rusting Corolla.

"Hi," I greeted her, awkwardly eyeing the gunmetal-silver BMW I'd driven up in. "Did you...I was just wondering...Did you miss your own Thanksgiving for this?" I motioned back at the Ladeens' house. "I'm Megan, by the way."

"Marisol," she replied, taking my extended hand. "Yes, but they'll save me some stuffing." She winked.

Another cackling fit of laugher came from inside. We both looked back at the house and then at each other.

"They think they are very funny, no?" she asked.

"Sí," I told her, laughing lightly. *"Sí."*

"Happy Thanksgiving, Megan," she said, taking her keys from her pocket.

"Happy Thanksgiving." I pulled the keys to the BMW from my loaned Goyard bag and opened the driver's door. "And Marisol?"

She closed the trunk of her car with a loud clunk and looked at me expectantly.

"Just...thank you."

Choose the definition that most closely matches the following word:
SALACIOUS

(a) nauseating
(b) juicy and gossipy, à la Page Six
(c) cold and withdrawn
(d) nervous
(e) a really big trunk sale

chapter seventeen

By the end of the twins' Thanksgiving break, we had settled into something of a study routine. This was all thanks to a combination of cajoling, guilt-jerking, and putting the best possible spin on the work that they were actually doing. We'd meet poolside around noon and order lunch from Marco. Prawns, lobster, filet mignon, fruit and vegetables so fresh they tasted as if they had just been plucked from tree or bush, mashed potatoes with capers, yam fries, Italian arborio pearl rice ribboned with shiitake mushrooms and pecans—I could go on. But the twins barely touched their food. They would pick at a lobster salad, followed by half a prawn and maybe one mouthful of mashed potatoes.

Unfortunately, I not only had touched everything but also

had *swallowed* everything. When I wasn't wheedling and charming information out of all of Palm Beach, I was alternately working on my story notes and stuffing my face. I didn't know if I had enough for a decent story, but I did know I would be heading back to New York ten pounds heavier. That morning I'd had to lie on my bed to zip my Joe's jeans, and even then I'd felt my femoral arteries being squeezed into submission.

After the twins and I ate we'd put in an hour or so of so-called studying. Then they would go to Bath & Tennis or one of their friends' mansions, and I would go upstairs to work on my notes or read.

Today, five days after Thanksgiving, we'd—*I'd*—lunched poolside on crab cakes and seafood quiche, followed by fresh pears and figs with candied pecans. I'd gone to the cabana for another bottle of iced pomegranate juice and come back to find Sage and Rose in a hell of an argument. Over—color me shocked—an actual SAT vocabulary word.

"*Salacious* means *scandalous*!" Rose maintained, pushing herself upright on her chaise.

"You're retarded, Rose. It means something you lick," Sage shot back.

"No, it doesn't. Should I get the dictionary?"

"I don't need the goddamn dictionary to know it means something you lick. You think you're suddenly smart because you're friends with her?" Sage pointed at me.

"No. I think I'm smart because *I* pay attention when we work," Rose maintained. "*You* don't."

"Fuck off," Sage told her sister, flipping her hair over her shoulder.

"No, *you* fuck off," Rose challenged her.

"You are such a suck-up, Rose!" Sage threw a pencil at her sister.

Finally, I jumped in. "Guys, stop it," I told them more forcefully than I'd intended. There was something about seeing two sisters fight that reminded me of . . . well, me. "This is kind of like me and my sister, Lily——" I started, and then I stopped. I'd always felt like I was the everyday loser in the competition that was life with my sister. Instead, I said, "She, um, always wanted to do everything I did—talk like me, dress like me. I couldn't ever just be, um, on my own, you know?" I'd recently adopted their *you know?* as an important part of my vocabulary.

Sage glared at her sister. "Then you know how *I* feel."

"Anyway." I sighed and sat back down at the table. "Lily eventually started to see herself as a separate person from me, thank *gawd*."

To my surprise, Sage flinched at this comment. The reaction had been subtle—a double blink of the eyes—yet I was sure I had seen it.

"All right, we're okay?" I asked.

"Sure," Rose was the first to agree.

"Whatever," Sage said, but she got up to retrieve the pencil she'd thrown at her sister.

"Hello, girls."

I looked up and across the still aquamarine pool. Laurel Limoges stood in an impeccable fawn pencil skirt and a taupe cashmere sweater. *Shit shit shit.* She wasn't supposed to be back until tomorrow, when I'd planned on looking like "before" photo Megan again. I quickly ran my hand through my hair in every possible direction but the right one.

"Welcome home!" Rose called sarcastically.

"It's the Wicked Witch," Sage muttered under her breath.

No. It was the end.

"Hi, Laurel. Mrs. Limoges. I mean Madame Limoges," I corrected myself, standing. "You're home."

Oh, that was brilliant. Yep. I sure would want the brain trust who'd come up with that observation to tutor my granddaughters.

"Girls, could you leave Miss Smith alone with me for a few minutes?" Laurel asked.

"Take advantage of the time," I urged the twins. "Review."

Sage gave me an *are you kidding* look, but she and Rose trudged off to their manse. When they were gone, Laurel sat in Rose's chair. I knew that bullshitting her would be futile. But I tried anyway.

"The twins have made so much progress," I began. "They really—"

She held up one palm: *Shut it.*

I did.

"The twins were arguing. By the pool."

"Usually, our study sessions go more smoothly—" I started, but she once again cut me off with her raised palm.

"You were wonderful with them."

Say *what?*

"I was quite impressed. They listened to you."

There were many scenarios I had envisioned for how I'd be sent packing, but this was not one of them. "Um, thank you."

"And you said they are progressing?"

"Mm-hmm." I nodded. They had improved. Sort of. Maybe. "I think they've begun to take this seriously. Especially Rose."

"She feels she isn't as bright or as good as her sister, you know. So this is really a very good sign." Laurel smiled. The palm trees overhead rustled in the breeze. "Clearly Debra Wurtzel was right to recommend you for this position. Is there anything you need?"

"N-no," I stammered. Some vintage R.E.M. blasted from the twins' side of the property. Baby steps, baby steps.

"I shall add another thousand dollars to your account for pocket money," Laurel said. "I hope you find it helpful. And, Megan?"

"Yes?"

"The new look suits you. Tell Marco he did well."

I practically fell to my knees and kissed the pool deck as Laurel headed back to the main mansion. Praise, continued employment in paradise, a designer wardrobe, and *much* more spending money than I'd made in a week at *Scoop*—all to write an exposé that was going to launch my career. Hell, yeah.

Choose the most closely related analogy:
TWEED JACKET : CHANEL

(a) tacky crap : Kmart
(b) wedding dresses : Vera Wang
(c) boots : Prada
(d) bondage wear : Gaultier
(e) sweater-vests : Ralph Lauren

chapter eighteen

wo weeks later, I'd reached the halfway point of my now-extended tenure in Palm Beach—December 15—and things were going swimmingly. After a weeklong sojourn at Les Anges, Laurel had returned to France until the Christmas holidays, so I didn't have her looking over my shoulder and bugging me about the twins' study schedule. To my surprise, they were spending a bit more time with their books and with me. They were up to an hour or two after school and ditto on weekends. Sage—who was a lot nicer to me when her sister wasn't around—told me that she was hedging her bets. Hollywood shut down between Thanksgiving and New Year's, so there was no way they'd find a new manager or sign any deals. In that case, if the studying continued to be relatively painless, she'd participate.

The weird thing was, paltry as their efforts might be by Yale standards, they were actually paying off. Rose proudly brought home a test from Palm Beach Country Day that had asked her to compare and contrast various sets of characters in Bradbury's *Fahrenheit 451*. Not only had she read the book, as opposed to doing what she and Sage normally did—watching the movie—she'd written a halfway coherent essay. Her teacher had written "Good job!" along with a circled B– atop the paper, and you would have thought Rose had been the recipient of the Presidential Medal of Freedom. As for Sage, she'd pulled an actual C on a math test, and without Ari texting her the answers.

It confirmed a theory of mine about school. To do brilliantly, one had to be brilliant. To do well, all one needed was willingness to make the effort. Brilliance was absolutely not a prerequisite. Unfortunately, nothing I'd seen from the twins led me to think they were either hardworking or brilliant. But it was a start.

What was pretty brilliant, however, was what happened when someone knowledgeable like Marco took you shopping for lingerie on Worth Avenue. I was looking forward to James's return to South Florida so I could, *ahem*, show him how I'd learned to take advantage of my assets and a growing collection of La Perla and push-up bras. *East Coast* shut down for the Christmas holidays, and he was flying down on Christmas Eve.

It was Sunday morning, and I'd just gotten off the phone with my parents, who'd told me it had been blizzarding all weekend and they were on their eleventh Independent Film Channel movie. It inspired me to find an art-film house in West Palm Beach, which was currently showing a double bill of Truffaut films—*The Last Metro* and *Small Change*—and I was dying to go. I knew better than to disturb the twins this early, so I read on the balcony and watched a couple of porpoises swimming in the breakers. At noon, I butterflied my book and made my way to the twins' wing. If I could move up their study session, I'd be off to the theater.

"Sage," I called quietly. There was no answer, which meant she was out cold, out, or putting on her game face at her vanity.

I tiptoed inside to discover that she wasn't asleep and she wasn't at her vanity, either. But then something caught my eye. Sage's computer was booted up, and on the twenty-one-inch flat-screen monitor were four photographs: one of Sage wearing the same outfit that I'd seen her in the night before—a gold chain-link miniskirt with stiletto-heeled gold slouch boots and an off-the-shoulder black cashmere sweater. There were front, back, and profile shots, and a fifth thumbnail photograph that I clicked on to enlarge. It showed a front-view picture of her with Rose. Rose wore low-slung brown trousers and an aqua vest with nothing under it; she'd worn that outfit the previous night.

There were various other buttons on-screen. I clicked on one, and more images popped up. The first two were extreme close-ups of Sage's and Rose's faces, also from the night before. There was also a detailed food-and-weight diary of the day for each girl, complete with a bar graph at the bottom that showed daily weight fluctuations and could be manipulated to show change over a week, a month, or a year. Every morsel they ingested was recorded, right down to "one mouthful of mashed potatoes."

Next I found a two-paragraph narrative report on the evening's proceedings that covered who was with whom and who was wearing what. Turned out the twins had gone to a private party at the Leopard Lounge. Various friends' names, like Suzanne and Precious, were highlighted. I clicked on Suzanne's name and was taken to a page that listed her outfits from the last eighteen months, contrasted with what Sage and Rose had been wearing. One more button, called "history," brought up a calendar with small thumbnails of Sage and Rose on each date. I clicked on the date, and it blew up to full size.

I shook my head in disbelief. I was reasonably adept with my iBook, but inputting and maintaining the data of a relational database went far beyond my capabilities. The time it must take to maintain was staggering. And Sage had already made her entries for last night's activities, which meant she'd done it either before she'd gone to bed or first thing when—

"What the fuck do you think you're doing?"

I whirled. There were Sage and Rose, standing in the doorway.

"Get away from my computer," Sage ordered.

"I'm so sorry," I sputtered. "I came in to see if we could move up our studying, and I saw the screen with your pictures...it's just *amazing*. Why didn't you tell me about it?"

Sage stared at me as if I'd lost my mind. "Are you kidding? Why would we tell you we had something like this? You'd tell someone, and before we knew it, *everyone* would make one!"

"Wait, *make*?"

"With Oracle," Rose replied, as if making a freaking database were no more challenging than matching your foundation to your skin (natural light was the key, I'd learned from Marco). "It took a couple of weeks for us to put it together."

Sage put her hands on her hips. "Which is why we don't like anyone touching it. Or even looking at it."

If someone had told me five minutes earlier that the Baker

twins would be capable of creating and configuring a database like this, I would have bet my Yale degree that the person was lying. Or tripping. Or both. "How'd you think of it?"

Rose shrugged. "Clueless."

"Come on, you had to get the idea from somewhere," I prompted.

"Clueless?" Sage yelped. "The movie?"

I had seen *Clueless* with my sister. There was a scene in which Alicia Silverstone used a computer database to help co-ordinate her fashion looks. But the *Clueless* database was to the Rose and Sage database what the Wright brothers' first biplane was to the space shuttle. I couldn't help my next question. "But how does it—"

"Work?" Sage filled in with an eye roll.

Rose looked tentatively at her sister. "I think it's okay."

"Fine. Megan, go stand in my three-way mirror. Rose, open a new page for Megan."

I went to the dressing room. Sage followed me. I hadn't no-ticed before, but there was actually a scale on the floor between the mirrors.

"Step on the scale. See the cord to your left?" Sage pointed. There was a thin white electrical cord dangling between the side-view and front-view mirror with a button at the bottom. As I looked up at the top of the mirrors, I saw three tiny cameras angled down at me. "Push the button, wait five seconds, then turn slowly left and slowly right."

I did. I could hear the cameras whirring.

"Coming through okay?" Sage called to her sister in the other room.

"Yeah."

"Okay, step off the scale, and let's go see," Sage instructed me. "And if you tell anyone—I mean *anyone*—that we've got this, I'll kill you slowly and painfully."

I held up a hand. "My lips are sealed, I promise."

So this was how Sage and Rose made sure they didn't wear the same outfit twice. It was totally ingenious. I was even more impressed when Rose showed me my own computer page, with the three different angles, a close-up of my face, all cross-referenced to the information picked up by the floor scale—both weight and BMI (*eek!*)—and somehow transmitted electronically to the computer.

"We've got a hookup from the mirrors in my room, too," Rose confided. "WiFi. That was my idea."

Back at Yale, I'd read Kuhn's *The Structure of Scientific Revolutions,* in which the author posits a theory on the nature of change. As I stood there, looking at myself from three points of view on their flat-screen monitor, Rose typing away at a computer program she and her sister had created, I experienced one of those paradigm-shifting moments. Everything I'd believed in was crumbling. In its place, as Kuhn had posited, a new and radically different paradigm was arising: Rose and Sage Baker of Palm Beach, Florida, were . . . *smart.*

chapter nineteen

Over the next few days, I don't think the twins knew what had hit them. I couldn't turn into a drill sergeant, exactly, but I did up study time from two to four hours a day and insist they not paint their nails while taking their practice tests. I told them it was because we were heading into the final month of prep—which seemed like a perfectly legit explanation—when the reality was the bright green dollar signs flashing in my eyes. The possibility, admittedly small, that I might actually be able to triple-dip—get these girls in to Duke, get myself seventy-five thousand dollars richer, and also get my story—had indeed proved a great motivator.

As a reward for two bona fide Bs that the girls brought home on a biology test, we took off the fourth night of the nouveau regime. Sage went clubbing in West Palm with Suzanne and Dionne. When Rose told me that she'd probably be tagging along, I decided to take a drive down the coast to the town of Hollywood, just a little bit north of Miami Beach. I thought it would add texture to my exposé to compare Palm Beach with another area of South Florida that was geographically close and, at the same time, light-years away. Rose had told me Hollywood was the anti–Palm Beach—as in: "Darling, he dresses so Hollywood, I'm surprised they let him on the island!"—although I had noted a particular lilt in her voice as she'd described it.

It was nearly ten o'clock when I arrived in Hollywood, but there were still plenty of people around as I walked the boardwalk past the bandshell and all the way to the Ramada. They ran the gamut from déclassé to distasteful—an old man on Rollerblades with a white ponytail and a deep tan, a drunk couple arguing about their children, and a group of Russian tourists all wearing the same FBI: FEMALE BODY INSPECTOR T-shirt in different colors.

I hadn't been sure what to wear for this trip, lest I seem too Palm Beach; I had settled on Prada jeans with flat sandals and a low-cut T-shirt Marco had purchased for "Britney: Before and After" night at his favorite South Beach club. (He also had a T-shirt with I AM THE GOLDEN TICKET printed on the chest, which was large enough to accommodate a pregnancy prosthetic. I turned that one down.)

I stopped for a drink at a beachfront place called O'Malley's, an open-air joint with a rollicking karaoke section, cheap plastic tables and chairs, and a semicircular bar facing a bank of TVs tuned to ESPN. There were a few lone guys at the bar, mostly middle-aged, ignoring the karaoke and watching SportsCenter. I asked the chubby, balding bartender for a flirtini. He brought me a martini and a suggestive wink. "On the house," he said.

"What's your name?" I asked.

"George. Yours?"

"Vanessa," I replied. It was my go-to fake name, though I didn't even like it. "Thanks for the drink. Can I ask you something?"

"Anything, babe."

"What's the hottest place for fun around here?"

He gestured at himself. "You're lookin' at it."

"Ha." I couldn't help but laugh. I'd thought that with Christmas coming in under a week, the Hollywood social scene would be in full gear. Wrong. I drank half the martini in a couple of gulps and set the glass down on the wooden bar.

"I hear Palm Beach is pretty kickin' this time of year," came a voice from across the bar.

"Thanks, but—" I looked up and saw Thom, the handsome deckhand from the *Heavenly*.

"Hey, Thom." I smiled as a very sunburned man peeled off his electric-blue FBI T-shirt and shook his man breasts at his friends. "You live around here?"

"Not far—I'm playing a show at a place down the boardwalk. But what are *you* doing here?" Thom looked around. "This doesn't seem like a Megan Smith kind of place."

Think fast, think fast. "I'm, um . . . I was just—"

"Megan?"

I turned around. *Rose?*

You'd have thought I was a security guard who'd just caught Rose pulling a Winona Ryder at Neiman Marcus. Her tanned face drained of color, which left it a sickly shade of gray.

"What—what are you doing here?" She was wearing a pink-and-green-leaf-print halter and white skinny jeans.

"I just bumped into Thom." I smiled in a way that I hoped would be reassuring-slash-convey that I was definitely not doing anything sketchy.

"Hi, sweets." Thom got off his bar stool and wrapped his arms around Rose. I looked on in shock. "Thanks for coming."

I waited for some kind of explanation, but all I got was a pleading look from Rose.

"I'll go find us a table," Thom told her with a kiss on the cheek. "Nice to see you, Megan. Maybe you'll come to the show, too?"

"Um...sure." I hoped I didn't look as confused as I felt. *Rose and Thom?* I never would have guessed.

As Thom settled into a corner booth, Rose pulled me to the other side of the bar and sat me on a stool. Then, staring straight into my eyes, she said to me: "You can't tell Sage."

Oh-kaaaay. "Sage knowing would be a problem," I surmised.

Rose sighed. "You have no idea."

I looked over at Thom, who was fiddling with his guitar case and looking so handsome. "Can I ask...why?"

"*Why?*" Rose echoed, as if I had to be incredibly dense not to get it. "Let me draw a picture for you: last year there was this guy named Richard who I really liked, but every time Sage saw him, she'd go, 'Oh, hi, *Dick*,' and hold up her pinkie finger. She told all our friends his nickname was the Big Inch. After a while I just couldn't take any more."

"That's a bitchy thing to do," I commented, noticing how Rose's eyes were actually tearing up over the little-dick story.

"Then there was Scott, who I met at Bath and Tennis," Rose continued. "Sage claimed he had BO and held her nose around him. Then everyone else did, too." She sniffled.

When I was in high school, and even at Yale, how many angst-filled hours had I spent worrying that I would never, ever be in Lily's league? One nod of approval from her, a smile, a "cute outfit, Megan" had meant the world to me.

So, God help me if I didn't reach out and hug Rose. Seeing her cry, I thought she looked as sweet as any seventeen-year-old—well, any seventeen-year-old with a navel piercing, sitting at a bar—could. "You're not Sage's shadow, Rose. You don't need her approval."

Rose shook her head. "You know how you told us you were the cooler sister? I'm sure you were the smarter sister, too. It's...different when you're like me."

I looked away at that one. My chest tightened. "Rose, just think about how well you're doing with the studying. If you just try a *little* bit harder—"

"I don't think I *can* study any harder. This is the hardest I've ever worked in my life."

For one instant, I wished that I had the magic power to materialize the Yale library right here on the beach across from O'Malley's so that Rose could absorb the reality of hundreds of college students pulling all-nighters during exam week.

"For tonight I'll let it go," I told her, glancing back at Thom. "You guys look like a good couple."

"Speaking of good couples..." Rose smiled. There was a new, knowing look in her eyes. "I was talking to Will the other night."

"Will Phillips?" I asked. As if I didn't know. Yuh.

She nodded. "He wanted to know how you were doing."

Hard to believe. I still felt hurt by his frozen-tundra treatment at the end of our "I'll show you Palm Beach" walk on Worth Avenue.

"If he wants to know how I'm doing, he can call me."

"Or we could call him." Rose took out her Razr and put it to her ear. "Will?" she asked. "I'm with Megan down in Hollywood.

I ran into her here . . . yeah, I know . . . Anyway, she says you could call her." She listened for a moment and then smiled. "Fine. I'll put her on."

Before I could protest further, the Razr was in my hand and against my ear.

"Hey," Will said.

"Hi." And then silence. I had no idea what else to say.

"Rose was telling me what a great tutor you are," Will continued. "She couldn't stop talking about you."

"Really?" I glanced over at her and smiled. "That's really nice."

"Yup," Will went on. "I got a lot of *Megan this* and *Megan that*."

I kept my voice low so Rose couldn't hear. "She's smarter than she gives herself credit for."

"All her Megan talk got me thinking," Will said as I readjusted the phone against my ear. "I'm sorry about cutting out the other day, but maybe I can make it up to you."

I smiled. Evidently, Rose's seal of approval had redeemed me. "What do you have in mind?" I asked him.

"If you're interested, I'm taking a drive in a couple days. I was thinking maybe I could show you a side of Florida that most people on the island don't know at all."

"I'd love to," I answered quickly and felt myself blush. Then I blushed some more, though he obviously couldn't see me through the phone.

"Good," Will said, and I could hear him smiling. "I'm glad you're interested."

Interested? God help me, I was.

The key theme of the myth of Sisyphus is:

(a) Don't fuck up in this life, or you'll pay dearly in the next.
(b) Manual labor sucks!
(c) Do unto others as you want others to do unto you.
(d) Live each day as if it's your last.
(e) The grass is always greener....blah blah.

chapter twenty

Two days later—two days before Christmas—I did three solid hours of work in the morning with the twins. We were prepping for the writing portion of the exam, and I was trying to get them to grasp the importance of using actual examples to illustrate a point. I extracted a promise that they'd each write two five-paragraph essays over the course of the afternoon; I'd review the papers when I came home. I gathered my papers into a pile and stood up.

"What?" Sage asked. "You're leaving?"

"Taking the afternoon off," I reported, and offered Rose a quick wink as I strolled back to the pink manse to change.

Next came the most important test question of the day: What would parallel-universe rich-girl me wear for a drive to the folksy side of the Sunshine State? When he called that morning, Will had mentioned a drive to the Everglades, so I was thinking casual and comfortable. Interestingly enough, designer clothes are, by and large, not very comfortable. They're also, by and large, not very large, and God knows I wasn't getting any thinner. I chose a pair of deconstructed Stella McCartney white stretch—thank you, God—cotton capris and a white tank top under an over-size navy linen shirt. I managed the low-maintenance version of my makeup and flatironed my frizz but tied it back in a simple ponytail.

When Will picked me up at the main mansion in his Beemer, I was pleased to see him dressed casually, too. Gone were the Palm Beach preppy blazer and the loafers without socks. He had on jeans and a navy T-shirt—no muss, no fuss, no designer labels.

As he got us off the island and pulled onto the state road that he said would cut across the peninsula, he asked for a progress report on the twins.

"They're doing well," I told him, which was mostly true. "Especially Rose."

"Sage isn't as tough as she acts," he replied, and I wondered if there had ever been anything between them. "So what have you been doing with yourself when you're not tutoring?"

Playing my role perfectly, I filled him in on the parties and the dinners and the club hopping.

"What about O'Malley's down in Hollywood?" He glanced into the rearview mirror. "What were you doing there?" So. This was how it was going to happen. My cover would be blown on the middle of an interstate. I felt my palms sweating and wiped them on my white pants. They left dirty marks behind. "I was just..." I tried to imagine what on earth Heather the Perfect would have been doing at a place like O'Malley's. "Truthfully," I lied, "I got lost on my way home from shopping in Bal Harbour and was just getting directions."

"Yeah, I figured that wasn't really your kind of place." I wasn't positive, but I thought something in Will's voice sounded almost disappointed.

"Not exactly," I agreed, wondering what the problem was. Then I rattled off some names of places I'd been to with the twins or heard them talk about. Those were more my kinds of places, I told him. They were nothing of the sort, of course, but the more I pretended to be rich-girl Megan, the easier it was to get comfortable on my nondate with Will. If I wasn't the real me, the real me had nothing to be nervous about.

It wasn't until he yawned that I realized he wasn't really paying attention.

"I take it the only social life you're interested in is your own," I said, trying to sound light. I was a little surprised to hear the edge in my voice.

"Sorry. I was thinking." He took a right off the exit ramp and then a quick left onto a hardly two-lane road. "Check this out: Right now we're heading into the Lake Okeechobee region. There's a big lake filled with largemouth bass and not much else."

We passed a wooden sign that said CLEWISTON: AMERICA'S SWEETEST TOWN, then slowed for a stoplight in front of Norm's bait store. Norm was advertising a special on all spinner baits and crank baits, plus guide service that guaranteed CATCH A HAWG OR YOUR MONEY BACK!

Clewiston looked like the land that time forgot. No Ta-boo for lunch, just a place called the Okeechobee Diner. Actually, it said DI ER, since the N had fallen off and no one had bothered to replace it. I saw a little boy running on the sidewalk with bubbles floating out of a bubble wand, his thoroughly ordinary-looking parents walking behind him, hand in hand. The boy looked happy, just having fun. You never saw happy kids just having fun in Palm Beach. You either didn't see them at all, or you saw them dressed up and trotted around like show dogs.

I let my face catch the warm Florida sun through the window. "I like it here," I murmured, forgetting all about being some other Megan for a moment. I could feel my shoulders unhinging from my earlobes. Turns out pretending to be someone you're not can take some energy.

"Me, too."

When the light changed, Will gave the Beemer just enough gas to get rolling and pointed out a state trooper's squad car neatly hidden behind a parked bread truck. "They look for people with Palm Beach County plates. I guess they think we can afford the ticket."

"Well, you can." I lowered the passenger window.

Will glanced at the open window. "You sure about that? There's mosquitoes here the size of a small child."

"Yeah, I'm sure." It had been a long time since I'd breathed country air. Warm and humid as it was, it reminded me of hot July evenings in New Hampshire when Lily and I used to chase fireflies until Mom called us to bed. "Now, *this* is relaxing. No Palm Beach. No twins." I turned to Will. "Maybe you can help me with something."

"What's that?"

"Sage. I don't understand her. You'd think eighty-four million dollars would be a great motivator, but teaching her is a Sisyphean challenge."

Will glanced at me, bemused. "Wasn't Sisyphus the Roman guy with the rock?"

"Greek, actually. The gods punished him by making him push a boulder up a hill only to have it roll back down to the bottom again, over and over and over. Some scholars think the Greeks created the myth to make sense of the sun rising every day in the east only to set every night in the west."

"You Yalies," he teased. Safely past the police car, he sped up to thirty miles an hour.

"Northwestern is a good school. You must have spent some time studying." I didn't mind taking the opening he'd given me. We could talk about Sage another time. Or not.

He shrugged. "I was a legacy frat brat."

I studied the perfection of his profile. "Are you still?"

"Hey, I *like* to party," he insisted. "But I'll give you that it's not necessarily a life calling." He gave me an enigmatic half-smile. "Did I tell you what we're doing on this outing?"

"No, Mr. Phillips, I don't reckon you did." Will slowed behind a rusty red pickup truck towing a bass boat. "Care to *elaborate?*" I prompted.

That smile flashed again. "Her name is Hanan Ahmed. She's an artist."

"And you're interested in her for your dad's gallery..." I knew I was leading, but interviewing Will was proving a frustrating task.

"Not at all. She came to America from Yemen on a student visa to go to the Art Institute of Chicago. I saw her work at a student show there. When you see what she paints, you'll understand why she applied for political refugee status. Her home country is a pretty conservative place. It was a big deal even for her to come to America to study."

Wow, an entire paragraph, and an intriguing one at that.

"So if you're not interested in her art for your dad's gallery..." Come on, Will. Fill in the blank.

"At Northwestern, when I wasn't partying"—he offered me a sidelong glance—"I majored in art history." It didn't answer my question, but there was no way he'd been an art history major at Northwestern without hitting the books, and now, apparently, he went to art shows, too. Interesting.

"So, Hanan, she lives in this sleepy place by choice?" I asked.

The bass truck turned off toward the big lake, and we finally cleared the sign beckoning us to return to Clewiston. Will sped up.

"She hates noise—it gets in the way of her work. She was in a bookstore in Chicago and came across a book of photographs of Okeechobee and the towns around it. She fell in love. That was, like, three years ago. Then her visa got approved, and here she is."

"Are you two...involved?" *What?* I had to ask. Research. And BTW, I was impressed I'd held off that long.

"Megan, she's gay."

Oh.

Just beyond another bait-and-tackle shop, Will turned right on a gravel road canopied by lush foliage. After spooking a great blue heron resting in the overhanging branches, Will stopped the car in front of a ramshackle house badly in need of a fresh coat of paint. "We're here."

He honked the horn twice. Almost before the second beep had died away, a beautiful young woman came bounding around the side of the house. Her thick raven hair was tied back in a messy ponytail with what looked like a shoelace. She wore paint-spattered jeans, a white T-shirt smudged with crimson and ocher, and a huge smile.

"Hanan!" Will greeted her as we got out of the Beemer.

"Hello, both of you! You're just in time to help me," Hanan exclaimed in admirable English. She shook my hand heartily. "You must be Megan."

Evidently, Will had told her he was bringing a friend.

"Nice to meet you." I couldn't help smiling at her; she had an infectious energy.

"Welcome to my little corner of the universe." Hanan opened her arms wide. "Far, far away from that peculiar place called Palm Beach. Come."

She ushered us around to the side of the house; I was surprised to see an immense vegetable garden in full bloom, protected by a chicken-wire fence. I recognized cucumbers, three different kinds of peppers, zucchini vines, and six or seven enormous tomato plants ripe with fruit. Wow. Would my parents ever covet this kind of growing season. In New Hampshire, there was usually snow on the ground by mid-November.

But Main Line Megan wouldn't know anything about growing seasons. Main Line Megan would not understand Hanan, or this oasis of sanity, at all.

"You really like living here?" I asked, throwing in a head toss for Will's benefit. "Where do you *shop*?"

She shrugged. "I don't need much. I tried New York City, but the whole art scene, all the parties, all the gallery openings . . . so boring." She raised her face to the afternoon sun and closed her eyes. "All I want to do is paint. Here in Clewiston, I can work without anyone bothering me." She opened her eyes and looked at me. "If you don't love to fish, there's really no good reason to be here. The whole town thinks I'm a hopeless eccentric, but it doesn't bother me at all. I probably am. I'll tell you more . . . while we work." She handed a hoe to me and a cultivator to Will. "I always take advantage of visitors."

I got to work as they chatted, hoeing up weeds between two rows of succulent cucumbers hanging from their vines. The smell of the rich earth and the sun on my back reminded me so much of home, the many hours I'd spent in my parents' garden. There was a cycle to things, my mom always said. Planting, watering, weeding, cultivating—

"Megan Smith, don't you wield a mean hoe."

I looked up. Will was staring at me as if I had just grown horns.

"Your friend Megan has done this before," Hanan observed. "You see, she holds the hoe like a broom—no backache her way. Megan, you must put Will to work for the first time in his life. I'll be right back."

As she skipped into the house, I saw the question in Will's eyes. "I . . . took an organic farming biology elective at Yale," I invented lamely. "Easy A." I held the other hoe out to him. "Try it."

He was aghast. "Barbados has a twelve-man team of horticulture specialists. You wouldn't want me to infringe on their right to work, would you?"

I grinned. Disaster averted. "Your secret is safe with me."

He pretended to roll up nonexistent sleeves. "Okay, okay. I give in. What do I do? I put myself in your capable, dirt-encrusted hands."

I took one dirty palm and ran it down his cheek, leaving a brown track of smudges. "This will help you get into the mood,

Farmer Will." Then I showed him the finer points of cutting off the roots of weeds.

"Will kill weeds," he joked in a robotic voice as he hoed clumsily. "Will kill weeds. Will kill."

"Hey, Will? Megan!"

We turned. There was Hanan with a digital camera. She snapped a couple of photos of sweaty us.

"I'm sending this to off to Northwestern's alumni magazine," she joked. "Otherwise no one would believe Will Phillips with actual earth on his face. Come on in, you guys. Will, you'll be glad to know I got air-conditioning since the last time you were here."

We followed Hanan inside and were hit by a blast of cool air. "There is a God," Will exclaimed.

In stark contrast to its shabby exterior, the bungalow's interior was bright, airy, and immaculate. Whatever interior walls had once existed had been mostly knocked down and replaced by white columns. There were just two rooms. One was a combined living room/kitchen/sleeping space with a kitchen. The other was Hanan's studio.

"Come see my work." Hanan beckoned to us. "Don't be too harsh. I tried something new."

As we entered her studio, I expected to see paintings, some finished and others in progress, paint cans, and an easel. Instead, the studio was immaculate, too—white walls, white floor. Leaning against the windowless walls were several massive canvases, all of them completed. Each was a scene of romantic lesbian love. The first canvas showed two clothed women in a warm embrace. The next depicted the same scene, but the women were nude. All the others focused on one section of the larger picture, as if magnifying pieces of a puzzle—entwined hands, thighs, breasts meeting breasts.

"It's amazing," I breathed.

"It's more than that," Will said, then expounded. "What's brilliant is not just Hanan's mastery of color and light but the progression. Once you've seen the lovers clothed, and then nude, she forces you to imagine them that way when you look at the isolations. But if you view the isolations before you see the whole series, you're creating the subjects in your mind automatically, and your subject might not look the same as hers. Which kind of makes you, the observer, an artist, too. Do you see what I mean, Megan?"

The most I could manage was a nod. I was dazzled.

"Will is my biggest fan," Hanan admitted.

"I'm your second biggest," I told her. "Your work should be in museums."

"Thank you." Hanan bobbed her head gracefully. "You see why I am waiting for Will to open a gallery so he can represent me. So get on with it, Will."

My recently waxed eyebrows headed for my flatironed hairline. "Your own gallery?" I asked him.

He didn't respond.

"Will commissioned this entire series," Hanan explained.

I felt like hugging him. "I didn't know that."

A phone rang in the other room. Hanan excused herself to answer it.

"Don't look at me like that," Will protested, noticing my awe. "I'm a capitalist scoundrel from the word *go*. I commissioned her so I could put them in my gallery and sell them."

"For that to happen, you'd need a gallery." My eyes held

his. He took my hand. "Come on. There's a place I want to show you."

"Where?"

Instead of answering, he ran for the back door. We headed past the garden, through a grove of trees, across a broad meadow, and down a dirt embankment to a beautiful farm pond sparkling in the afternoon sun. Will already had his T-shirt over his head. The perfect golden six-pack was not lost on me.

"What are you doing?" I asked. Of course, I knew exactly what he was doing, short of streaking the bullfrogs, but it seemed like the thing to say.

He undid his belt buckle. "Come swimming with me."

The question before me was: Were the jeans and the boxers coming off? And if so, did he expect me to follow suit? As in, the birthday suit he'd already seen me wear? For the fiftieth time in the last three weeks, I lamented the quality and caloric quantity of Marco's efforts in the kitchen.

Just as I was dealing with this quandary, Hanan came whooping through the trees, shedding clothes as she went. Once she got down to a very utilitarian bra and panties, she leaped into the water.

No birthday suit. I breathed a little easier. But still. Off came the jeans and the linen shirt. Then, clad in just the skinny white tank top and panties I'd bought at the Target in West Palm, I jumped into the water. It was cool against the heat of the day. If skin could sing, mine was humming "Stairway to Heaven."

Will surfaced and pushed on my shoulders. I went down with a sputter and came up with my flat ironed hair ruined, the nonwaterproof mascara I'd so carefully applied that morning tracking down my face.

Palm Beach me should have screamed and scrambled out of the water. But God, I didn't want to do that. For this second, screw the research. I just wanted to be myself.

For the next half hour, we splashed like little kids. We played Marco Polo. We had a water fight. We did cannonballs off the embankment. We stopped only when my cell phone rang. It was the twins, telling me they'd finished their essays. When was I going to be home? I looked at Will.

"An hour and a half," he said. "If we leave now."

Hanan said she'd run back to the house to get us towels. Will and I sat on the muddy bank. I was filthy, I was wet, and I was the happiest I'd been since I arrived for this crazy experiment.

"There's something I don't get." He dug a pebble out of the dirt and threw it into the lake.

"Which is?"

He turned to me. "One minute you're this typical, boring rich chick. The next you're . . . not."

"Oh, really, Mr. I Majored in Partying?"

He laughed. "That wasn't a lie, trust me."

I pushed my wet hair off my forehead. "Now I get to ask you one. Why did you invite me here?"

"When I first met you—that crazy night when the twins were so awful to you—I thought I saw something . . . Then you came to see me at the gallery, and she was gone." He threw another pebble into the water. *Plunk.* "But then Rose went on and on about how much she'd learned from you, that you were the first person who ever made her feel like she had a brain. So I invited you today because I was curious to see which girl would show up."

"And?"

"Easy. Both. But not in a bad way." He stared down at me, then lifted his free hand to my cheek and rubbed his thumb gently across it. "Mud."

I shivered a little. Something shifted inside of me. The real me. "Thanks for bringing me here, Farmer Will," I said.

His eyes were on my lips. Was he about to kiss me?

"You're welcome. Can I bring you someplace else?"

"Sure. Where's that?"

"The Christmas Eve ball at the Norton Museum of Art. I know it isn't much notice, but I really would like—"

"I'd love to."

A cell-phone company charges 3 cents per minute for a long-distance call. What algebraic expression shows how much a 20-minute call from Florida to New York City would cost, if 5 of those minutes are nighttime freebies?

(a) $y = 3 + 20 \div 5$
(b) $5z = 20x$
(c) $x = 3(20 - 5)$
(d) $c = 20 + 5 + 3$
(e) $x = 3 \times 20 \times 5$

chapter twenty-one

That night I read quickly over the twins' essays from the afternoon, ignored the question in Rose's eyes about how my time with Will had gone, and then retreated to the privacy of my bathroom for the longest, hottest bath in the history of long, hot baths. As the water ran, I poured in Heavenly Holly bubble bath, part of Laurel's new spa collection. It smelled like the woods in autumn and turned the water into an Emerald City sea under a blanket of white bubbles.

I'd like to call a time-out here to say one thing: Fantasizing isn't cheating. Okay. So long as we're in agreement.

I lay there with my eyes closed, the hot water dribbling in, feeling all warm and...um...wet, playing the afternoon with Will over in my mind and wondering what it would have been like if Will had done what I thought he was about to do by the side of the pond. That is, kiss me. Just as I began heading for an underwater expedition, I heard my cell phone faintly.

It was him. I knew it was him.

I jumped from the tub and slid across the bathroom floor, leaving wet footprints on the bedroom hardwood, then I dove wet and naked over my bed. I managed to get my purse open and yank out my phone in time to answer on the fourth ring.

"Hello?" I asked breathlessly.

"Hey, babe. Wow, you sound... winded."

Him. The wrong him.

"Oh, hi! James!" I wrapped my soaked self in my bedspread, knowing that if I needed another, it would be delivered from the main mansion, no questions asked. "I was taking a bath. I had to run to the phone. I'm so glad it's you!"

Okay, so fantasizing is *kind of* cheating. What kind of person is thinking about the *wrong guy* when her *boyfriend*—the boyfriend she barely gets to see, much less get horizontal with—calls? The boyfriend whom she'd be seeing on Christmas morning? As in, under thirty-six hours.

"Great news. I just spent twelve hours editing that asshole's short story. Songwriters who think they can write fiction—it's painful. Then the wanker has the nerve to call and ask for approval on any changes."

"That's the great news?"

He laughed. "No, that's the buildup. My boss took pity on me. He's letting me split at noon tomorrow. I'll be in Gulf Stream in time for dinner. Great, huh?"

Guiltier and guiltier.

"That sounds fantastic."

"I can't wait to see you."

"Me, too."

"So, listen," James went on. "My mom called a little bit ago. Some friend gave her two tickets to this Christmas Eve ball at the Norton Museum. You know about it?"

Uh, yeah. Actually, I said yes to this other guy. "I think the twins are going," I hedged.

"Oh, sweet!" he crowed. "Because I was thinking that you and I should, too. I know the whole thing about you pretending to be single, which is totally cool. We'll act like we're strangers. It'll be hot."

Not good, not good, not good. Why had I said yes to Will? I obviously knew the answer, but what was I supposed to do now that my actual boyfriend was asking me?

"You could write about it in your article," James went on. "It's hilarious, like something Hunter Thompson would have done. Plus, I'll get to meet the twins without them knowing I'm your boyfriend. It's perfect."

I pulled the bedspread closer and tried to match James's enthusiasm. "That does sound like fun! But you know, I think I'm coming down with something. I just...should probably stay in bed and get better for Christmas."

"Oh, no. Well, then, forget the ball. I'll come to Les Anges, and we can play doctor."

"That's so sweet of you. But I think I'm going to stay in bed tomorrow and beat this thing—whatever it is."

"If you're sure." He sounded disappointed. Or maybe the shame I was feeling magnified my sensitivity.

"Yeah, you can hang out with your parents tomorrow night; they'll like that. What time do you want me to come over on Christmas Day?"

This was the guilt asking.

"Eleven. And I'll call you when I get in tomorrow." I heard someone say good night to him. Poor guy—he was still at the office at midnight, two days before Christmas. "Megan?"

"Yeah?" I asked as I stood up from the bed and walked to the window. The dark spilled out in front of me.

"I love you."

I swallowed. "I love you, too."

We said our goodbyes and hung up. What had I just done? I'd lied to my boyfriend so that I could go to a ball with someone else. It was terrible. I knew it was terrible.

And it had been so easy to do.

In a novel, a "turning point" represents a moment in which a character:

(a) has a change of heart.
(b) sees something in a new light.
(c) is surprised by an unexpected development.
(d) experiences emotional growth or change.
(e) all of the above

chapter twenty-two

According to the College Board, which created the test, the SAT assesses how well you analyze and solve problems. Colleges use it as a rough predictor of how well the test taker might do at any given school. I'd told the twins this many times. And then I'd added that in my humble opinion, what the SAT really measures is a person's ability to prepare for and take the SAT.

There was no way I could make up for their twelve years of academic neglect in eight short weeks. But I knew from seeing the intricacy of their beauty database that they had the raw intelligence to succeed. My bet was that if I could get them accustomed to how this system operated—to think the way the testers thought—they might be able to squeak by.

The twins had trouble with abstract concepts. But when I made the learning relevant to them, that also made it memorable. I resorted to first-grade tactics. My best weapons were flash cards.

For example, rather than displaying a trapezoid and asking for a description of the area and perimeter, my flash card outlined the dimensions of the ladies' room at the Everglades Club. Instead of working out theoretical proportions, I'd sketch a picture of a mirror, give its length, and ask how many girls, each using ten inches of mirror space, could repair their Stila lip gloss at the same time. For vocabulary building, I used pertinent examples. Purgatory was described not only as a place between heaven and hell, but also as being stuck in coach next to a screaming baby on a transatlantic flight from New York to Paris.

There was academic progress being made. Not enough, but enough to keep me from losing all hope. And enough to keep them going, too. The biggest problem was effort. No matter what I did, I couldn't impress on them how studying was a cumulative process, and how extra hours put in on day one paid huge dividends on day seven or day eight. It was hard to undo seventeen years of relative sloth. Basically, when you can call room service, cooking for yourself becomes a massive challenge, even if you stand in front of the stove for four hours a day.

Since we had decided to take off Christmas Day, the twins and I started work on Christmas Eve day at an absurdly early hour—nine A.M. This schedule would leave them—and me— free in the afternoon to prepare for the ball that night.

We ordered coffee and croissants to eat poolside and started our work on vocabulary. I held up a homemade card for Sage.

Suzanne used _____ to steal her rival's boyfriend.
   (A) chary
   (B) coeval
   (C) duality
   (D) chicanery

"D," Sage pronounced. "Definitely D."

I praised her, since she was the queen of misusing words. Next card.

White pants after Labor Day is no longer considered an _____ wrong.

    (A) aggravating

    (B) egregious

    (C) ergonomic

    (D) astute

"B," she said. "Egregious."

Damn. Two in row. It was followed by three wrong answers, but two in a row felt like a milestone. Rose took over and doubled her sister's feat. We moved on to sentence structure, and between the two of them, they successfully identified topic sentences, compound sentences, subjects, predicates, though the concept of conditional clauses still eluded them. Yes, this is stuff most of us learn in middle school, but the twins had missed it along the way.

To make it all relevant, and to hone their writing skills, I asked them each to write a five-paragraph essay comparing and contrasting their looks for tonight's Christmas Eve ball with what they wore to last month's Red and White ball, and then identify the topic sentences, subjects, predicates, etc. I heard the requisite bitching and moaning, but they did settle down with pens and paper. As for me, I retired to a chaise while they worked, enjoying the morning sun on my face, thinking of what I would tell James when he called that afternoon. Forty-eight-hour flu? Something like that.

I must have dozed off, because I was jarred awake by Sage nudging my ankle.

"Megan? You fucked up yesterday."

I opened my eyes. She was on the chaise next to me. "You finished your essay?"

"No, I stopped midway with an overwhelming urge to enjoy your scintillating company," she droned. "Of course I finished."

I looked over at Rose, who was still writing, and then closed my eyes again and smiled. "Good."

"Why didn't you just tell me that you're crushing on Will?"

That comment got me not just to open my eyes but also to sit up. "What are you talking about?"

"I saw him at the Breakers last night. He told me everything."

"What's everything?" I asked cautiously.

"How you spent the day together, how he boned you in a pond—"

"He did *not* bone me in a—anywhere!" I sputtered, feeling that familiar heat creep up my face.

"Kidding. Don't go all tomato on me. He did say you hung out and that he likes you. Happy?"

Actually, yes. But I didn't say that. I didn't say anything.

"You could have just told me yourself." She sniffed.

"I was trying to be professional."

She yawned. "Bullshit. Rose knew. Like I give a fuck. He also said you're going to the ball with him."

Rose came padding over to me with her essay, which had taken her approximately twice as long as it should have to write, and sat down next to her sister. "So you like him, Megan?" she asked eagerly.

Maybe it was because I never really got to do the cute-girl-

crazy-for-the-cute-boy thing in high school. Maybe it was because I had gone to my senior prom with Bruce Peterson, he of
the formidable IQ and dubious skin, with whom I had about as
much chemistry as a Rich Text file. Or maybe it was because
my sister, Lily, got all the pretty-girl moments and I could never
hope to compete. Whatever the reason, some dormant girly-girl
thing rose up and forced out my one-word answer.

"Yes."

Let me admit something here: It's very hard to convince
yourself that you're going to a ball with a guy for research purposes after you admit to your students that you're into him.

"So what are you wearing?" Sage pressed.

"The same thing I wore to the Red and White ball, I guess," I
replied, hoping I could still squeeze my Marco-fed ass into it.

I'm sure you're familiar with Edvard Munch's most famous
painting, *The Scream*. Give yourself double vision, substitute the
twins' faces for the terrified guy on the bridge, and you'll have
a reasonable approximation of Rose and Sage's reaction to my
statement.

Sage was, as usual, the first to manage words. "Is *that* how
they do it in Philadelphia?"

"Like, you're so rich, you don't care if people see you in the
same thing twice?" Rose clarified.

Of course. Main Line Philly Megan would already *know* not
to wear the same gown. She'd be as horrified as the twins at the
thought. Backpedaling furiously, I explained that I'd brought
only one formal with me to Palm Beach and had no time to shop.
I figured I could use that excuse tonight, too, if it came up.

Sage nodded. "We understand."

"We do?" Rose yelped.

"Yes," Sage insisted. "Let's order lunch. Although it will probably suck, with Marco on vacation."

"Where'd he go?" I asked. Marco was on vacation? This was news to me.

"To New Jersey with Keith," Rose explained while Sage called in the food order. "They go every year to see his family. He'll be back for the New Year's Eve ball, don't worry. Grandma puts him in the charge of the caterers." She got up and took off her jeans and T-shirt; she was wearing a green tartan-plaid bikini underneath. "I'm going to swim till the food gets here. Want to come?"

I shook my head, feeling the blood drain from my face. No Marco *and* no Keith for tonight? And I was supposed to be ball-ready in only a few hours? I couldn't even zip myself into my own damn dress without Marco's help. Cinderella was going to end up looking like Cinder-hella this time around.

"What's up with you?" Sage asked me as she stepped out of her jeans and left them in a pile at her feet. "You're reverse-blushing."

"At home... well, I always think of makeup as art. And—don't tell anyone—I'm a terrible artist. Stick figures give me trouble. So I never, ever do my own makeup." That wasn't a lie. Exactly.

"And you don't have Marco to help you tonight." Rose dove into the pool, her wet hair fanning out behind her as she resurfaced. "He told us Keith knows your stylist back in Philadelphia."

"He *did*?" Bless him for covering my ass in more ways than one.

"Sure." Sage stepped into the shallow end. "But you're still kind of fucked for tonight, huh?"

Rose giggled. Sage giggled. Nice of them to enjoy the schadenfreude even if they didn't know what it was.

"Come," Sage barked to her sister, if giving an order to a well-trained dog. She stepped out of the pool and slipped her flip-flops back on. "We'll call the main house and tell them to bring the food inside."

She headed toward her manse while I waited for Rose to climb out and towel off. Then we found Sage in her den, in front of her computer monitor. She clicked once, and a close-up of my face appeared on the monitor.

"How did you do that?" I marveled. My face had on makeup I'd never worn.

"That's one more feature we built in to our system," Rose said proudly.

"Watch and learn," Sage ordered. With a few quick mouse strokes, she thickened my eyebrows. "Although the Brooke Shields thing is so not a good look for you." She thinned them out again.

As the girls illustrated on Sage's computer and I watched, I got a double-barreled lecture on correct makeup and hair for a girl with my particular features. Then they switched to a full-length body shot and treated me to a speech on body proportion, how to hide "figure flaws below the waist," and making the most of what could kindly be called my modest cleavage.

"Okay. Come to my dressing room," Sage ordered. "Let's see what you learned."

A moment later, she pushed me into a seat at her vanity. Rose opened what looked like a tackle box finished in pink pearl. Its pink-velvet-lined compartments were full of new upscale cosmetics.

For the next hour, the twins worked on my face. Unlike Marco, they took pains to explain everything as they did it. Then they handed me step-by-step instructions so I could duplicate what they'd done if they weren't around, simplifying things so I could do it no matter how clumsy my hands were. *Then* they handed me the box.

Yes, it was mine. They'd bought it for me. Before I could begin to thank them, we'd moved on to my hair, which Sage deemed clean enough, because updos actually stay better if your hair is slightly dirty.

Who knew?

Sage flatironed it and slicked it up in a ponytail. "There are two key elements to making this look work," she decreed, "Hair U Wear and tendrils." With that, she brought out a gorgeous hairpiece, perfectly straight and exactly my color. She attached it over my own hair, and voilà, I had a ponytail halfway down my back. Then she artfully arranged tendrils around my face to soften the look and added a lavender grosgrain ribbon to the ponytail. Rose completed the process by spackling my lips with another layer of gloss. From the neck up, I looked fantastic.

Rose had to run back to her room for something, and Sage placed her hands on my shoulders. "You do understand that you can't wear the gown from the Red and White ball tonight, right?"

"I—"

I'd gotten no further than that one syllable when Rose reappeared with a lavender gown worthy of a princess draped over her arm. "Versace Atelier. Lavender is your color. Look at this."

She handed me a *Scoop* with Emmy Rossum in the "Purple

Is Royal!" fashion section, wearing the exact same dress. And I had to admit that I *did* look a little bit like her. If she put on ten pounds, that is. "It won't fit," I protested.

"Try it on," Rose insisted.

Off came my Juicy warm-ups and T-shirt. I was wearing only panties, a positive, they decreed, since the bodice would hold up my breasts. With their help, I dropped the gown over my head, then held my breath while Rose zipped it.

"You can exhale," Sage instructed.

I stood up straight and faced them.

"Oh, yeah. We're good." Sage offered her sister a fist bump.

I turned to the mirror. The bodice was strapless and fitted. They were right; a bra would have been superfluous. The skirt was pleated chiffon and georgette.

"How did you . . . when did you . . . ?" I stammered.

"When you drop six figures a year on clothes, your personal shopper is your best friend," Sage explained. "We gave her an order last night. It was here before breakfast."

"You look beautiful," Rose said, grinning hugely.

"I can't believe you did all of this for me."

Sage nodded. "Me, neither. We must have been on drugs."

But I could tell she was kidding. Was it possible that I had gotten through her facade and hadn't even known it?

"Before you start giving yourself all kinds of credit," Sage went on, as if reading my mind, "just think of the anguish we're saving ourselves. If you went to the ball in an *already-worn gown*, we would have been totally humiliated to be seen with you."

I smiled in response. They handed me my new train case full of cosmetics, the diagram of instructions, and then shooed me

out so they could get ready. I left, but not until after I thanked
them. Sincerely. How would this turn of events fit in to my article? As I floated to my suite under layers of butterfly-wing-thin
chiffon, I couldn't help but think that the shallow Baker twins I'd
planned to write about never would have done something like
this. So who was shallow now?

Socializing romantically with more than one person can be considered:

(a) ludicrous
(b) foolhardy
(c) equestrian
(d) decadent
(e) misanthropic

chapter twenty-three

When Will picked me up that evening, he told me I looked beautiful. The weird thing was that I believed him. It was as if I'd started to see myself as the person I had pretended to be. Not rich, maybe—some fantasies are too ridiculous to buy in to, even for someone who had gotten as good at lying as I had—but pretty. When I looked in the mirror, I no longer saw Lily's ordinary little sister.

The annual Christmas Eve ball to benefit the Norton Museum of Art didn't start until eight. We arrived in West Palm at seven, the better for Will to show me around the museum before the masses arrived. It was so early that the valets weren't yet on duty and he had to park his car himself, but he was excited to lead me through before the paintings and sculpture had to compete with the couture and cocktails.

The exhibition spaces were deserted of all but workers. Musicians were setting up and doing sound checks, and the waitstaff was loading buffet tables and stocking bars. No one paid any attention as Will walked me through the various exhibits.

The Norton had sections for nineteenth- and twentieth-century European, American, Chinese, and contemporary art, plus an extensive collection of photography. It was in the contemporary collection where Will really came alive. We both loved a painting called *Isaiah: Grass Will Grow Over Your Cities,* depicting the biblical prophecy come to life in a modern metropolis.

"Because everything is temporary," I mused aloud. I was thinking about how true it was in my own life; I'd lost a job, and lost an apartment, and—

"Merry Christmas, guys." Thom clapped a hand on Will's shoulder. He was dressed in a standard-issue white-jacket tuxedo with a waiter's white towel draped over his arm. "Hi, Megan."

"Hey, Thom." I gave him a quick kiss on the cheek. It was nearly eight and the room was beginning to fill up around us. "Merry Christmas."

"You working, dude?" Will asked.

"Money's good." Thom nodded toward the bar behind us. "Just wanted to say hi before the party really gets started. I'll catch you guys later."

After Thom was out of hearing distance, I turned to Will. "How do you know him? I would have thought you guys ran in different circles."

"From the *Heavenly*. I try not to care about things like that," he offered, and I wondered if he thought I did. How ironic that would be. "I'm the one who told Rose to go for him."

I spotted the twins and their friends making an entrance across the room. Sage was wearing a Bordeaux-colored chantilly lace gown lined in pale pink silk that made the dress look almost completely sheer. Rose wore a scoop-neck black sheath with feathers and gold beading trimming the skirt. Their reddish manes rippled down their backs. They were a living advertisement for a lifestyle about which most people only dreamed.

Thom stood next to the bar, watching Rose's every move. I waited for her to turn around and say "Merry Christmas," or at least offer him a we're-madly-secretly-in-love smile. Instead, she grabbed her sister's hand and pulled her toward the central hall next door.

"She doesn't seem as open about their relationship..." I let the comment hang there.

"Yeah, well, I understand why." Will winked at me quickly. "Come on, I think we should probably see if the crowds have descended."

He took my arm and led me through the museum back to the enormous white-on-white central hall, which was serving as the main reception area for the party. Christmas revelers were scattered around the room, examining the art and taking Kir Royales from the passing waiters. A string quartet in one corner played carols, and the Christmas tree in the center of the room glowed with incandescent lights. Christmas presents were piled up under the tree.

"Who are the presents for?" I watched an arriving couple add two more before melting into the throng.

"They're toys," Will replied. "They'll be shipped off tomorrow to the pediatrics unit at the University of Miami medical center. We do this every year."

"Nice."

"Yeah. Want a Kir? I'll go track down a waiter."

"Sounds great. I'll be here."

Will edged his way into the crowd. My eyes were following him—trust me, your eyes would have followed him, too—when I felt a gentle hand on my arm.

"Megan, darling. Don't you look lovely!" Laurel greeted me. She wore a floor-length black gown and a single strand of pearls with a diamond clasp as large as my knuckle; her blond hair was twisted into a loose bun at the nape of her neck. She had on the lightest application of makeup, just enough to make her skin look luminous and her features flawless. The French really did understated elegance better than any other women on earth.

"Laurel, hi. When did you get back?" I asked.

"This afternoon. I try to be here for all the major events during The Season, but it's difficult. You know about the New Year's Eve ball at Les Anges, of course. The benefit for my foundation?"

I nodded. "I'm looking forward to it."

"Last year we raised two million dollars for women to start their own businesses on the African subcontinent. This year I'm hoping for three. And who is your escort for the evening?"

Remarkable how she could skip from philanthropy to my date without missing a beat.

"Will Phillips," I said, hoping that wasn't a breach of tutor etiquette. "He went to get drinks."

"I knew." Her eyes twinkled. "I saw him pick you up. He is a lovely young man. How goes it with the twins?"

"Improving every day."

She nodded. "I'm sure you expect them to put in some time tomorrow, Christmas or not. The examination test will be upon us in no time, yes?"

"Yes," I agreed. "Absolutely."

Laurel spotted a couple she knew and excused herself, giving my hand a squeeze. "Have fun tonight, Megan."

The twins wouldn't be happy to hear they were working on Christmas. I wasn't, either. How could I fit in a study session and still spend time with James? God. Thinking about him made my insides fold like an origami crane. What kind of girl blows off her boyfriend so she can go to a ball with another guy? Answer: the kind of girl I would not like and certainly didn't want to be—

And then, as if my conscience had willed it, there stood James in the flesh, sipping a glass of merlot and admiring the enormous Christmas tree. I did the only reasonable thing under the circumstances: I fled, scurrying out of the main hall and into the gallery for Chinese art, past the orchestra and the dancing couples, and then out the emergency exit that the party organizers had so graciously left open. I found myself alone in an outdoor sculpture garden, and I hid out behind a well-placed Richard Serra curved metal wall.

Think, Megan, I ordered myself. *Think.*

Will was inside, presumably looking for me. James was inside, not expecting to see me. What could I tell him? Even worse, what if he and Will *met?* It was certainly possible—James would seek out the Baker twins for his own amusement, the Baker twins would find Will, James and Will would—

Breathe. Think logically.

Okay. I'd be safer *inside,* trying to keep them apart, than I was *outside,* where no one could find me.

With a fortifying deep breath, I marched back inside…and directly into James.

"Megan? *You're* here?"

Oh, God. I flung myself into James's arms, doing a quick scan of the room over his shoulder. Where was Will?

"What a great surprise," I whispered in his ear. "But I'm still undercover. You've got to help me out."

He held me at arm's length, brows knit. "You're the surprise. I thought you were sick."

This called for instant improvisation. "I *was* sick. But the twins wouldn't take no for an answer. They're *such* spoiled brats—they practically made me come. So here I am!"

"You don't look sick," he pointed out.

My hands flew to my stomach. "Intestinal thing. One minute I'm okay, the next I'm running to the loo."

The *loo?* I never said *the loo.* The twins said *the loo.* Anyway, no time to dwell on that. Stomach flu would give me a perfect excuse to disappear every few minutes to find my date and keep him away from my boyfriend.

"What about you?" I asked as my eyes darted around, searching for Will. "I thought you were going to hang with your family."

James looked uncomfortable. "I am with my family. My parents are here somewhere, and—"

"James!" a voice cooed. "There you are."

No. Not possible. He'd come with *her?*

"With Heather's family," he finished as he was joined by Heather the Perfect, a vision in peach chiffon and with a glittering silver neckline showcasing that perfect cleavage.

On second thought, maybe I wasn't so fucked. *He* was.

chapter twenty-four

A minute of excruciating small talk later, Heather excused herself, and James walked me into the photo gallery. It had been designated the conversation room by the organizers. There were neither musicians nor a bar, but comfortable love seats had been placed around the room. We found an empty settee under a Maria Magdalena Campos-Pons triptych.

"I can explain," he told me.

"I can listen," I said faux-sweetly. He wasn't the only one hiding information about the evening, but *he* didn't know that.

"First of all, I'm not here *with* her," James offered. "It was her parents who offered us the tickets for tonight."

"You could have mentioned that."

"And I would have, except my mom didn't tell me. I walked into the beach house, and there was Heather in a bikini on the back deck."

Okay, there was really no need for him to hit me with the bikini image.

"She and her folks are staying overnight with us. They're leaving tomorrow for Turks and Caicos. My mom said we should all come."

I could definitely see James's mother coaxing him into going to the ball with Heather. Fine.

James took my hand. "So are we good?"

We were, actually...until I saw Will wander past the entrance to the gallery. He had one empty and one full Kir in his hands, and a big frown on his face. I grimaced.

"What's wrong?"

"Stomach." I grasped my abdomen, praying that Will would not, could not, check this room. "Gotta get to a bathroom." I jumped up. "I'll find you!" I sprinted out of the room, dodging dowagers dripping jewels.

Shit. Which way had Will gone? I caught a glimpse of him just as he stepped into the room with the orchestra. I sneaked up behind him. "Looking for a girl in a lavender dress?"

He smiled. "Where'd you take off to?"

"Oh, you know, dozens of guys asking me to dance. I had to beat them off with a polo mallet."

He handed me the full drink and clinked his empty glass against mine. "Drink or dance?" he asked.

This was so not a night for alcohol.

"Dance. Definitely."

Will handed our glasses to a passing waiter and led me to the parquet dance floor while the orchestra played a version of "Something" that I'm sure made both John Lennon and George Harrison roll over in their respective graves. Dancing proved an exercise in movement anxiety. I kept maneuvering Will so he was between the entryway and me; I was thankful for every inch of his height.

He peered down at me. "You okay?"

"Sure!" I relaxed against him for a moment, then tensed when I thought I saw James. False alarm.

"You seem . . . stiff," Will noted. His right hand slid down my back, dangerously—and amazingly—close to my tailbone. Ordinarily, I would have loved this. However, this was not ordinary. This was a Marx Brothers movie come to life.

Think fast.

"Oh, I have this little stomach thing."

"You're probably hungry. Let's hit the buffet. This caterer is famous for coconut-crusted shrimp. You have to try it."

Though the concept of food was as repugnant as the idea of alcohol, I had no choice but to follow Will to the main room's buffet. The room was so crowded that we took nearly ten minutes to thread our way to the buffet table. I was just about to take the small white china plate that Will was offering me when I saw James get in line at the other end.

It's remarkable how quickly stomach cramps can come on.

After promising that I'd be right back, I hightailed it to the ladies' room, which was almost as crowded as the rest of the party. After a suitable flu-worthy delay, I headed back, looking for James this time.

And now let me wax philosophical for a moment: Some people find it impossible to look away from a car crash. I understand that; I really do. It's horrible, but it's not you, so you can't help but gawk with some kind of sick fascination. Evidently, this can also be true if it's your own car that's heading toward the concrete barrier at a hundred miles an hour.

When I came back to the ballroom, I found myself looking at James. And at Will. Together at the bar. They were clinking martini glasses like long-lost friends.

Will saw me first and waved. "Megan! Come here. I had to battle this guy for the last coconut shrimp." I desperately hoped that Will didn't see James wink as I approached. "Megan, this is James Ladeen. He just graduated from——"

I took a chance. "Yale?"

"How'd you know?" Will was astonished.

James rubbed his jaw. "You look so familiar . . ."

"Maybe you saw me on campus," I managed, offering James my hand. "I'm Megan Smith."

James pointed at me. "Wait. Weren't you in the biology department?"

"Lit, actually. What brings you to Palm Beach, James?" I asked stiffly.

He smiled. "Oh, I've got some friends and family here. How about you, Regan?"

"It's Megan," I corrected, resisting the urge to roll my eyes. Getting my name deliberately wrong was piling it on kind of thick.

For the next ten minutes or so, Will and James chatted while I tried to keep straight whom I was supposed to be and which version of my life was supposed to be true. The two things I had going in my favor were that James knew about Main Line Megan, and that I'd told him I was using my "single" status to get closer to some of the people on the island. When Will explained how we'd met through the twins and how he'd shown me around the island and some of South Florida, James nodded knowingly.

"You know, I have a confession," James said after taking a Kir from a waiter and toasting his new friendship. "I saw you once at a coffeehouse near campus, Regan. I thought you were cute, and I wanted to say hello, but you left before I got the chance."

I searched for something clever to say and came up with the scintillating "Wow."

"Dance, Regan?" James asked. "You don't mind, Will?"

"Go ahead." Will nodded. "Just don't fall in love. Megan, I'll catch up with you later."

"He likes you," James observed as he led me back toward the dance room and took me into his arms. "He's too damn good-looking to like you."

"Don't be jealous. He's just another Palm Beach pretty boy," I lied. I saw Pembroke dancing with Suzanne, who wore a green gown that hoisted her cleavage so far north, I worried that she might inhale her own nipples.

James pulled me closer. I took a deep breath and then let it out again. Okay. The worst thing had happened—James had met Will. And I had somehow survived the crash.

Moments later, I saw James's father and mother near us. She wore a black jersey gown with a low-cut back—very New York—and raised her eyebrows, surprised to see me. Then she beckoned to her son: *Come dance.*

"It's fine," I murmured into his shoulder. "Go. You can explain how I ended up here."

I found an empty bench next to a display case of two-thousand-year-old Han Dynasty jade pieces and started thinking that Jim Morrison was wrong: Some of us really *do* get out of here alive. I was proud of myself for pulling off the impossible.

Of course, as soon as Heather plopped down next to me, I realized that I'd begun celebrating too soon.

"Nice party," she began.

"Uh-huh." I waited for the other Manolo to drop.

"What's up with you and your... *date?*"

"Will Phillips? He lives next door to the twins," I replied. "And it's not a date."

"I saw you dancing." She raised one expertly arched eyebrow at me.

So. There it was. The thud of the spike heel landing.

"Wishful thinking, Heather." I tried to sound much tougher than I felt. "If I were cheating on James, I'm sure you'd love to kiss him and make it all better."

She smiled thinly. "Believe me, Megan: I can get him back anytime I want."

Oh my God, what was this? Middle school?

"He's not a sweater you loaned me, Heather. Tell him whatever you want. Do whatever you want." I got up and walked away. At least Heather knew what—and whom—she wanted, which was more than I could say for myself.

chapter twenty-five

*M*y parents and Lily called me early on Christmas Day from Lily's apartment. My sister couldn't make it home to New Hampshire because of her show, so my folks had come to her. They'd gone to the theater and seen Lily perform, ice-skated at Rockefeller Center, and eaten at a restaurant where reservations would have been impossible but for the great Lily Langley offering the maître d' house seats to her play. Speaking of which, Lily happily reported that Revolution Studios had picked up the movie rights, and Joe Roth himself had promised her an audition when the script was done.

After wishing everyone a merry Christmas, I congratulated her, of course, but what I was thinking was that the real actress in the family had to be me, starring in *The Two Faces of Megan*. She's a tutor—no—she's a journalist! She's Megan Smith, an egalitarian intellectual. No, she's Main Line Megan, an elitist bitch! She loves her boyfriend, James. No, she blows him off to be with another guy! Let the madcap high jinks commence.

I said goodbye, made myself some coffee, and then called Charma at her parents'. She was thrilled to hear from me, demanded the full report on what was going on with the twins, and gave me the happy news that she would be moving back into our apartment right after the first of the year. Yes, she was still working for the children's theater, and yes, she was still seeing Wolfmother. In fact, he was going to help her move back in. When would I be home? On the fifteenth of January, I told her. Okay for him to hang around until then? she asked. Fine with me, I told her. I was just sorry I wouldn't be around to help. What were we going to do for furniture? She told me not to worry. Her grandmother in Levittown was about to enter an assisted-living facility and had a houseful of furniture to dispose of. "I know you're going to miss that futon from Avenue B," she told me. "But you'll have to adjust."

Once I hung up, both my personas and my thighs managed to fit in the shower, after which we—I—got dressed in Ralph Lauren black velvet trousers and a black cowl-neck cashmere sweater. It was almost nine, which was when I was due in the main mansion's Christmas room. I mean this literally. There was a room in Laurel's house that was used but once a year and for this occasion only. It was organized entirely by Laurel's social secretary, a mousy girl named Jillian whom I rarely saw and whose job description focused on gift giving, gift receiving, and thank-you-note writing. Her claim to fame was her ability to forge Laurel's signature so well that that no one knew Madame Limoges hadn't written the card herself.

Work on the Christmas room had begun weeks before the event and was overseen this season by the famous New York interior designer Harry Schnaper. This year Schnaper had chosen a silver-and-mauve theme, a shocking departure from Laurel's normal pink, but his creds were so good that Laurel let him do whatever he wanted, right down to a blue spruce topped with a silver-haired angel that looked remarkably like Laurel herself. Under that tree went the presents, but only if they'd been wrapped in colors complementary to the color scheme. Others ended up in the closet.

When I arrived, Laurel and the twins were already exchanging gifts. Laurel was dressed for another day at the home office—straight black skirt, white silk blouse, and black suede pumps. The twins wore bikini tops and plaid shorts trimmed in lace (Sage) and pink rolled-waist cotton capris (Rose).

It was odd to be celebrating Christmas in air-conditioning.

Laurel had given the girls pearls from Tiffany. They looked less than thrilled. They'd given their grandmother a new coffee-table book about Palm Beach architecture. She thanked them politely. There wasn't one ounce of honest emotion in the room.

I hadn't a clue what would be appropriate to get for the twins, and it wasn't like I had any serious money to spend. For Rose, I burned a CD of my favorite songs that she could transfer to her iPod. For Sage, I bought a gift certificate for skydiving—I'd seen an advertisement in the *The Shiny Sheet* and thought she might like it. Both girls looked surprised that I'd given them anything. To my surprise, Rose handed me the same thing I'd given her——a CD of her favorite alt bands. From Sage, I got a certificate for a spa day at the Breakers.

Then there was Laurel. What do you give an employer who already has everything? I knew that I couldn't go wide, so I decided to go deep. On Craigslist, I'd found a signed first edition of Simone de Beauvoir's *Le Sang des Autres,* her existential novel of the French resistance. It merited a nearly inscrutable "Thank you. This is lovely." Laurel wasn't the warmest person I'd ever met, but if I wasn't mistaken, she did seem touched.

That was Christmas at Les Anges. No carols, no chestnuts roasting on an open fire, and the only thing Jack Frost could nip would be the dimples of Venus on the twins' asses when they dropped trou and headed for the pool. I did extract a promise from them to be ready to work at five, which got an approving look from Laurel.

I'd told James I'd be at his place by eleven, but I arrived fifteen minutes late due to a stuck drawbridge across the Intracoastal. He didn't meet me outside this time, which meant I rang the doorbell with some trepidation, figuring that Her Heatherosity was probably still there. Good fortune fell upon me, though. James explained that Heather and her family had just departed to South Beach, where they'd visit other friends, stay in the Abbey, and then head off to T&C.

It was the best Christmas present I could imagine.

James's parents were in the living room reading *The New York Times*. In keeping with the *Clockwork Orange* interior, their tree was artificial, more an abstract arboreal sculpture than an homage to the season. There wasn't an ornament on it. Perish the thought of strung popcorn.

We sat down on the back patio for Christmas brunch:

smoked salmon on toast points, mushrooms stuffed with crab-meat, cucumbers in dill sauce, and fresh fruit salad. Mrs. Ladeen, who prided herself on being an iconoclast, called it an "anti-Christmas" dinner. At least I could say "Thank you, Marisol" this time.

"So, Megan," Mrs. Ladeen said, taking a seat at the head of the patio table. "Last night James filled us in on the real reason you're living with the Baker twins. Why didn't you tell us you were there to write an exposé? At least that makes sense!"

My eyes cut to James across the table. "I had to explain why you were there," he told me quietly.

"And we hate Palm Beach. Everything about it," his mother chimed in. "So we're thrilled that you're writing this story. Really."

"I second that," Dr. Ladeen added, serving himself another crab-stuffed portobello.

I was just about to point out that they'd attended one of the premier events of The Season the night before when Mrs. Ladeen held out her glass of chardonnay. "Marisol, a refill? Anyway, we met the twins at the ball. Did James mention that?"

Gee, he certainly had not.

"Overdressed and undereducated and empty as the day is long." Mrs. Ladeen sipped at her wine.

"There's actually more to them than you might think," I told her.

"Really? The contents of their Prada bags?" Mrs. Ladeen smiled at her own witticism.

"To be honest, they're not stupid. It's just that growing up, they were supposed to be beautiful and rich and dumb, so they lived down to every expectation." This made me think of one of my favorite quotes. "'If men define situations as real, they are real in their consequences.'"

"W. I. Thomas, *The Unadjusted Girl*, and I think the publisher was Little, Brown." Mrs. Ladeen sneered at me. "He was overrated even when I was at Yale. They still teach him?"

James cleared his throat, but I went on. "They do. I'm sure they teach him at Duke as well, which is where the twins will be next year."

What can I say? I've never been someone to back down.

Mrs. Ladeen laughed. "Come on, Megan. The tutoring is only a ploy, isn't it? I don't think less of you for it, dear. On the contrary, I admire your game plan. It's fiendishly clever. And if you can make it work, your article will be the better for it. You're surely not counting on it, though. Are you?"

James knew me well enough to understand that a departure would be wise; he asked if I wanted to go for a walk on the beach. Believe me, we had no lack of things to talk about, but I couldn't stay. I had to get back to Les Anges and the girls.

But as I drove north on the Florida Turnpike toward Palm Beach, I couldn't get the things Mrs. Ladeen had said about the twins out of my mind. A month earlier, I probably would have been laughing with her. Instead, I'd defended them. In fact, I'd promised that they'd get in to Duke.

Yes, I badly wanted the seventy-five-thousand-dollar bonus if they succeeded. But it was more than that. Somewhere along the way, little by little, I really had become their teacher... and maybe even more.

Models may have to resort to _____ measures to maintain their figures for fashion shows.

(a) drastic
(b) bulimic
(c) acceptable
(d) reasonable
(e) appalling

chapter twenty-six

Give a turn, Megan," Daniel Dennison said in his musical Australian accent. "Just a bit to the left, please."

I stood on a wooden platform not much larger than the top of a chair and shuffled my feet to the left. It felt very odd to have a guy whose rugged good looks had recently graced the cover of *Time* magazine with the headline "The Savior of Fashion?" looking up my dress. Actually, *his* dress, one of the two he had designed for me to wear in the charity fashion show for the Heavenly New Year's Eve ball at Les Anges.

The charity fashion show was a centerpiece of the event. A stable of famous designers who just happened to be friends of Laurel—Vera Wang, Donatella Versace, Anna Sui, and more—were pleased to participate, as were famous actresses, models, and Palm Beach princesses. After the show, there would be a silent auction for these one-of-a-kind gowns, all proceeds benefiting the Heavenly Foundation. As a rule, the auction netted upward of two million dollars.

It was two days after Christmas, and I was with the twins on Grand Bahama Island at the vacation home of this Australian couturier Daniel Dennison, once the youngest designer in Chanel's history and the current darling of the fashion world. Daniel was Laurel's must-get for this year. She had succeeded, which was why we were being fitted for gowns in his basketball court–sized studio with one glass wall facing the beach. There were six small platforms for pinning dresses on models, bolts of fabric everywhere, a huge table used for cutting, and a wall of fashion sketches pinned to an enormous corkboard.

The twins and I had flown in from the mainland on Laurel's jet, a puddle hop that had taken all of twenty minutes. After clearing customs, we were met by one of Daniel's flunkies, an overly solicitous young woman named Nance. She drove us in Daniel's Land Rover to his "cottage"—that's what she called it—for our fitting.

To give the girls credit, they'd worked all morning on math and science. Their first-semester report cards had arrived from Palm Beach Country Day in the morning mail. Sage received several C+'s and one B–, which might not sound like much, but it was a quantum leap from her previous semesters. Rose did even better, earning near-straight B's, save a C in Bio. Admittedly, these were not "We'd like to welcome you to the freshman class of Duke University" grades, but they did demonstrate significant improvement. Almost as encouraging was that there'd been no bickering, sniping, or cattiness in days, especially from

Sage. I had them right where I wanted them. All I needed to do now was keep listening and taking notes for my exposé. I tried to crush the feeling that my note-taking felt more and more like a betrayal of a sacred trust, but every so often the guilt would bubble up again.

Daniel instructed a young woman, lips full of pins, to do his bidding: "Right here, Marie."

Sage was to my right and Rose to my left, each being fitted by other assistants. Daniel bounced back and forth among us, guiding and instructing, cajoling and reprimanding, even occasionally redraping fabric to his exacting standards. The twins looked a little bored. This fashion-show thing was old hat to them, unlike me—when I was asked to participate, my initial reaction had been a horrified and succinct "Hell, no!" I'd instantly pictured all those size twos and fours stalking gazelle-like down a catwalk followed by yours truly, queen of I-want-to-observe-and-not-be-observed, rattling the floorboards at size eight. On the top. On the bottom, after my time enjoying Marco's cuisine, I was having a serious flirtation with a double-digit experience where both of those digits were real numbers. There was only one person in my family born to grace a catwalk, and it definitely wasn't me. In family photos, Lily was always out front, smiling into the camera. I was the one edging my hips behind another family member or a well-placed pillow.

Yet here I was, on a foot-high block with a world-famous designer working his magic on me.

"Hold still, Megs," Daniel cautioned as Marie inserted a straight pin into the material just under my breasts. "You don't want to be impaled."

The gossamer fabric being pinned to me was white, and the

neckline was so sheer that it appeared as if I wore nothing but a veil until it reached where skin ended and nipple began. The bust was heavily beaded in white and silver, which then faded into the skirt, draping in long, elegant folds to the floor.

"Turn again," Daniel commanded. "Toward me. Now bend forward." I did, feeling like I was in a bad exercise video. "Hold." He was gazing straight into my cleavage, wrinkling his nose. Either he wasn't impressed, or he was playing for Marco's team. Probably both.

In went a few more pins. "Okay, we're done with this one. Rose, it looks like you're finished, too. Sage, I'm going to intervene personally with you. I don't like the way the zipper is falling, and I know just how to fix it. Marie, get robes for Megan and Rose. You'll find refreshments out on the deck. Sage, do not move, under penalty of death."

"No worries," Sage told him. "Rose, Megan, I'll be out in a few. Do not drink all the champagne!"

Rose and I put on our robes and moved out to Daniel's back deck. As Sage had predicted, he'd put a bottle of their beloved Taittinger on ice. A statuesque Bahamian woman brought a tray of crudités and sliced tropical fruits.

I thanked her, sipped the champagne, and tilted my face up to the sun. "Did you get to see Thom last night?" I asked Rose.

She shook her head. "He had another catering gig. I haven't seen him since the Christmas Eve ball, which was just really weird. I barely got to talk to him. I mean, there he was, and there I was, but we couldn't be together. So *tragic*!"

This was a little too *Romeo and Juliet* even for me, lover of all tragic romances. "I don't see why not. I'm sure he would have enjoyed the company."

"All my friends were there," Rose protested. "It's not so simple."

I drank more champagne and took in the way the sun glinted in her hair, her luminous eyes, her sculpted cheekbones, and the tiny cleft in her delicate chin. She was incandescently lovely. "What's the worst thing that could happen if you and Thom just told people you're a couple?" I asked her. "You wouldn't have to even say it. Just *be* it."

"You must be joking."

"Assume for a moment that I'm serious," I said dryly.

Her eyes darted toward Daniel's atelier, as if to make sure Sage wasn't going to walk out onto the deck. "Well, for starters, Sage would ruin it."

"Seriously, Rose. What is it that you think she could do? She'd bust your chops for a while. BFD."

Rose drained the champagne and placed the flute on an end table. Then she stared out at the sea in silence. It reminded me of the first time we'd really talked at Les Anges, after Zenith's visit and the collapse of Sage's plan for independent prosperity. We sat in silence for a long while. The lapping waves below were the only sound. Then, still staring straight ahead, she spoke so softly, I could barely hear her.

"I remember the flight from Boston to Palm Beach after our parents died. We were in Grandma's old plane. The flight attendant brought us ice-cream sundaes, like somehow that was going to make us feel better. I remember watching the ice cream melt." She wrapped her arms around her slender torso. "I remember thinking that I should feel something, but I didn't feel anything. Not scared. Not sad. Just...nothing. Then the pilot started the engine, and all of a sudden it was real. And then Sage...she put her hand in mine and said, 'As long as we have each other, we're not orphans.'" Rose turned to look at me. Her eyes were glassy with unshed tears.

Whoa. All I could think was: Who was I to push her about this? It wasn't like I'd had to face that kind of tragedy. It wasn't like all I had in the world was my sister. I reached out and squeezed her hand. "I think I understand, Rose."

"Gee. Are we bonding?" Sage stood behind us, her hands on her robed hips. Her tone was decidedly nasty.

Rose snatched her hand away from mine as if we'd been caught cheating. "You're finished with Daniel?" she asked her sister.

"No, I came out to share in your *Seventh Heaven* moment." Sage tightened her belt and took a healthy swig of champagne directly from the bottle. "What's so touchy-feely out here?"

Rose's eyes flashed a warning at me. She obviously wasn't supposed to have told me quite so much about her sister.

"It's personal," I said.

"Ooh. A little prickly, are we?" There was nothing on Sage's face but disdain. Where was the girl who had been so nice to me before the Christmas Eve ball? She turned to her sister. "You don't really think she *cares* about you, do you?"

"Actually...yes, I do," Rose told her, squaring her tanned and freckled shoulders.

"Don't be dense, Rose," Sage told her sister pityingly. "She just wants the money Grandma promised if we get in to Duke."

Rose looked confused. "What are you talking about? Megan is *rich*."

"She told me that her mother cut off her allowance because she pulled a Precious, and she doesn't get her trust till she's thirty or something."

Actually, I hadn't told Sage any of that. But I hadn't done anything to dissuade her from the notion when she'd "figured it out," either.

Rose took the revelation in stride—thank God—and didn't back down. "That's her, not us. If you fuck this up, *we're* the ones who are going to need money."

Sage got up so abruptly, she almost knocked over her chair. "You know what, Rose? You're right. If I fuck this up, you can score twenty-four hundred on the SAT and still not get the money. My advice would be: Suck up to me instead of her. Because right now you can bite me."

She took the stairs two at a time down to the beach, then stormed off.

I turned to Rose. She looked miserable.

"Relax, sweetie." I patted her hand. "The money thing just flips her out." I leaned forward, picked up the fruit tray, and offered it to her. "You should eat—"

"You just don't get it, Megan." Rose stood up. "She's all I have."

I watched her run down the stairs and up the beach after her sister.

The dramatic unraveling of two romantic relationships in one day is something that:

    (a) happens only in movies.
    (b) happens only in Palm Beach.
    (c) happens only to assholes.
    (d) happens only in situations of extreme misunderstanding.
    (e) cannot be endured without booze.

chapter twenty-seven

*S*age turning on her sister at the fitting should have been fodder for my editorial saga of all things Palm Beach. I should have been at my computer, pounding in my delicious word-for-word recollections. I should have felt motivated. But all I felt was sadness. Not just about Sage but about myself.

Who was this girl I had become, who was ready to benefit from the misery of two girls still wounded by their parents' deaths? How could I tell so many self-serving lies to so many people to get my story? At least Sage had an excuse: Her emotional growth had ended the moment that plane plunged into the ocean. But I'd had a perfectly normal upbringing—compost-heap-obsessed parents aside—and was supposed to be an adult. What was my excuse? Especially when I sometimes got the sense that I was the closest thing they had in their life to a surrogate mom.

That was what I went to sleep thinking about the night of the fitting, and it was what I was still thinking about the next morning when James called. There was some crisis at *East Coast*. He'd have to return to New York that afternoon. Could we meet for a drink before he went to the airport?

We met on the front patio of Le Palais D'Or—the Golden Palace—on Worth Avenue, a restaurant that went heavy on the gilt or, in my case, the guilt. I wore an outfit in which I could actually breathe: Chloe tab-waist gray pin-striped trousers and a black vest over a soft gray Imitation of Christ T-shirt. More from Marco's suitcase. He was a transvestite with great taste. A truly great guy, a wonderful friend. And just another person I'd be using in my story.

James had already arrived. He rose to hug me, but it felt awkward. I slid into the seat across from him. He ordered us Stoli Bloody Marys, then reached across the table for my hand.

"So what's the crisis?" I asked.

He sat back and ran his free hand through his hair. "Explain to me why it is everyone thinks they can write fiction. Another songwriter's story came in. Worst yet. Unsalvageable. So now I'm supposed to find some *other* songwriter who can deliver in a week."

"Jimmy Buffett can write," I suggested.

"Has to be someone fresh and younger than Jesus. " James sighed.

The waitress, a basic Palm Beach blond lollipop with expertly streaked hair, put our drinks and a basket of fresh bread on the table. James sipped his drink. I sipped mine, too, just for something to do.

"So, how do you feel about things?" he finally asked.

What? Did he, too, sense that something was off?

"Your article," he prompted. "You must have a lot of material by now. You should probably start thinking about form and bang out a first draft. You can fill in the rest of the material later, when you come home, and—"

"No," I blurted.

He smiled. "You want to wing it? Living dangerously. You know it's better in the long run if you outline and—"

"That's not what I meant, James. I meant no, I'm not writing it." I swear, I almost turned around to see who was talking. Yet with the words out of my mouth, I knew it was the right thing to do.

He actually snorted a laugh. "No. Seriously, Megan—"

"I am serious."

"Well." He folded his hands together and placed them on the table. "Can I ask you something?"

"Sure." I leaned forward.

"*Have you lost your mind?*"

"I like them," I said lamely. "The twins, I mean."

"You like them." He stared at me as if I had grown a third eye on my cheek. "You're not going to write about them because you *like* them?"

"Something like that."

He shook his head, crossed his arms, and regarded me as if I were a stranger. "Jeez, Megan, you're a journalist. At least I thought you were."

"I am a journalist," I defended myself. "You should see my notes. You should see what I went through to get what I got.

When I first got here and was pumping the cook about the twins, he told me—no lie, direct quote—'They're damaged.'"

"Great stuff," James acknowledged.

"No! Don't you get it? How can I take advantage of two teenagers who lost their parents and never recovered? What kind of a person would that make me?"

The waitress came back and asked if we wanted anything else. I waved her off as James put his head in his hands.

"If your brilliant insight is that the Baker twins are scarred by the death of their parents—which isn't exactly a shocker, by the by—find a way to write it and make it interesting. But don't kill the biggest opportunity of your life because you feel sorry for the poor little rich girls."

I looked into his eyes. Really looked. "I can't teach them and write about them at the same time, James. It isn't right."

He drummed his fingers on the table. "I know exactly what's going on here."

"I wish you'd fill me in."

"Look at you." He gestured at me.

I looked down, then back at him.

"The hair, the makeup, the clothes," he listed. "Megan, you've become their *clone*."

"That's ridiculous."

"No, it makes perfect sense when you think about it," he said confidently. "It's Stockholm syndrome, where a hostage identifies with his captors. In your case, it's Palm Beach syndrome, where the writer identifies with her subjects."

"Just because I look different—"

"You've changed." James gripped the edge of the table and leaned in, his expression intense. "The girl I knew was a *real* writer.

She didn't give a shit about fucking designer whatever. And she *never* would have let her feelings get in the way of her story."

"I'm not, I—"

That sentence went on permanent hold, because that was when I saw Will walking down the other side of Worth Avenue.

I'm not big on the power of prayer, but I prayed for him not to see us.

But then Will stopped walking, and I saw him shield his eyes to peer across the street. Then James shielded *his* eyes to figure out whom I was staring at.

It didn't take long for either of them. Will started purposefully down the sidewalk again, his body stiff and angry-looking, and James spun back to me. "You fuck him?" he practically spat.

Does mentally count?

"No." That was the truth. I hadn't even kissed him.

"Christ."

"Nothing happened, James," I insisted. "Nothing."

He stood up. "You better get your shit together, Megan. You're coming home soon. This fantasy will be over. Then what? You think *SAT tutor* on your résumé is going to wow the New York publishing world?"

We both knew the answer to that.

I reached for his hand. "I know you're mad. And maybe I am crazy. But..."

"You're not changing your mind," he filled in for me.

"No. I don't think I am."

"Honestly, Megan? I don't think you've been doing a whole hell of a lot of thinking about anything. Work. Us." He tossed a few bills on the table. "Maybe we need to take a break until you're back in New York. It's kind of weird having a hostage for a girlfriend."

I wanted to apologize, to say that he was right, that I was wrong, and that of course I would be writing my story. But I couldn't. I didn't.

I just watched James climb into his Volvo and drive away.

I stood watching the space where James's car had been for several minutes, wishing I had someone to talk to. Someone to be a real friend. And then my feet started moving toward the Phillips Gallery almost without my realizing it.

Inside, Giselle was talking to a young woman wearing a tiny orange tartan skirt and to a man twice her age whose hair transplant had not fully taken.

"Hi, Megan," Giselle greeted me after the mismatched couple had departed. "Will's in the back. Just knock."

I did. He called, "Come in," without even asking who was there.

"Hi," I said as I opened the door.

His office was windowless and small, with art books open on every available surface. I peeked at the Excel document open on his computer. It meant nothing to me. The quick glance he made in my direction before he turned his attention back to his work said I meant nothing to him, either.

"Hi," I repeated. "Could we talk?"

He regarded me coolly. "I'm kind of busy."

"You're the closest thing I've got to a friend in this town," I told him, meaning it. "So please, just five minutes..."

He closed his laptop and motioned to a folding chair. Then he folded his arms. "So?"

"So...I saw you before," I acknowledged. "I mean, I know *you* saw *me* before."

"With the guy you only knew *slightly* from Yale. Blossoming friendship?"

"It's...complicated." Part of me wanted to just explain everything, but how could I? He'd hate me. The twins would hate me. Everyone would hate me. I'd be totally and utterly fucked.

Will frowned and shook his head. "What is it with you, Megan? I'd really like to know. I mean, every time I feel like I'm getting to know the real you—"

"What about you?" I shot back because, okay, I was feeling defensive and more than a little battered and bruised. "One minute you're the playboy of the Western world, the next you're mister sensitive art guy."

A muscle jumped in his cheek. I figured I'd hit a nerve.

"You done?" he asked.

"I don't want to fight with you, Will." I could hear the exasperation in my voice. "There's nothing to fight *about.*"

"You're right. There is nothing to fight about." He stood and opened his door in one swift motion. "See you, Megan."

Celebrities at a gala fund-raiser fill space at a rate of 0.2 per square foot. How many famous men and women would attend a soiree at a 4,000-square-foot mansion?

    (a) 200
    (b) 300
    (c) 500
    (d) 800
    (e) 900

chapter twenty-eight

*Y*ou know it, I know it, you don't even need to go to Yale to know it—F. Scott Fitzgerald's most famous line from *The Great Gatsby:* "The rich are very different from you and me."

Ernest Hemingway is reputed to have responded, "Yes. They have more money."

Please. Here's what he should have said: "Yes. They have bigger and better parties."

I thought I'd seen extravagance at the Red and White ball and the Norton Museum of Art Christmas Eve event. But compared to what was about to unfold at Les Anges, they were pin the tail on the donkey. I was fast discovering that no one outdoes Laurel Limoges.

My first clue should have been the arrival of Secret Service agents on the property two days beforehand to set up a command post and a security perimeter. I had lunch with Marco and Keith, who had just returned home from New Jersey. Marco made us white-truffle risotto—words can describe neither the dee-lish factor nor the calorie factor—and I joked, "Who are they expecting, the president?"

"Former, darling." He refilled my wineglass. "Two of them."

Also, he told me, the CEOs of several Fortune 100 companies, a handful of heads of state, and a dizzying array of movie, fashion, and sports stars. "So, are you quite ready for your coming-out party?"

"My what?"

"He means the fashion show," Keith explained. "Every beautiful woman should get to model in a fabulous fashion show at least once in her life."

I pictured the risotto applied in lumpy layers to both of my hips. "I'm so much bigger than the other models."

"Just a trend, darling," Keith assured me. "A few years back it was heroin chic—remember?" He shuddered. "Palm Beach matrons trying to look like strung-out teenagers. It was quite the horror show."

Marco clinked his wineglass to mine. "Chin chin, darling. You are gorgeous and fabulous and perfect exactly as you are."

"But... I have no idea how to model," I protested.

"Shoulders back, neck long, head high," Keith instructed me.

"And, of course, there's the strut," Marco added. "But everyone knows the strut."

I blanched. "I... don't know the strut."

"*America's Next Top Model?*" Marco asked. "I know a dozen drag queens who wear clothes and walk the catwalk a zillion times better." He stood, put a hand on his hip, and proceeded to do a perfect model walk. "It's a straight-line thing, darling," he explained as he walked the length of the kitchen, then spun to us. "As if you're on a tightrope. Like so." He flounced back to us. He gestured with a flourish, meaning I should give it a try.

I tried. Felt like an idiot. Lost my balance. "Oh, *that's* attractive," I groused.

"Well, for one thing, you can't look at your feet. Head up. Shoulders back. You own the world! Try again."

Head up. Shoulders back. I own the world. I walked the length of the kitchen again. It was only a marginal improvement.

"The sexiest part of your body, darling, is right here." Marco pointed to his head. "Remember that, and all else follows."

Over the next couple of days, as the decorating and setup kicked into high gear, I practiced walking across my room like a model. I felt like a grace-free donkey each and every time.

The second clue that Laurel Limoges was not to be outdone was the not-so-small army of workers who descended on the property in the days before the event. Several tents were erected around the property. One for the catering service, one as a changing area for the fashion show, one that was air-conditioned and mosquito-netted in the event of a hot and humid night, and one to house the blind auction for charity.

I wandered through the blind-auction tent soon after it was set up. The array of merchandise could have stocked a Neiman Marcus. There were cases of wine, fur coats, world cruises, perfect Tiffany diamond earrings, a walk-on role on *Grey's Anatomy* . . . and that was just one aisle. As for the auction of the gowns we'd be wearing in the fashion show, there were mannequins at the ready with poster-sized framed photographs of the gowns propped against them. The minimum bid for each gown was five thousand dollars.

Every contingency for the party had been covered. Temporary moorings had been sunk in the ocean so guests might arrive by boat. In an effort to deflect traffic, only a limited number of parking passes had been issued to the crème de la crème of Palm Beach society, plus the majority stockholder of a company that Laurel was considering acquiring. Otherwise, limousine shuttles would run from the Breakers, Mar-a-Lago, Bath & Tennis, the Colony Hotel, and the Ritz-Carlton. There was a helipad, and a LifeFlight chopper was on duty in case any octogenarian Palm Beacher found the flesh around the twins' pool too much for his or her heart.

The third clue that Laurel's New Year's Eve bash was *the* event of The Season was seeing it before my very eyes.

I came downstairs at nine-fifteen, and things were already rocking. The property was crowded with beautiful and famous and beautiful and not-so-famous revelers. I made my way down the pathways crowded with partyers, keeping a lookout for Will. We hadn't spoken since I'd left him at the gallery. Maybe he wouldn't even come. I did move aside for one person who stopped me in my tracks—the guy I thought of as *the* president walked past me with his daughter, preceded and trailed by Secret Service agents.

And they say Democrats don't come to Palm Beach.

The fashion tent was already fairly crowded, though it was forty-five minutes before the models were due for hair and makeup. *Scoop* had covered the New York fashion scene extensively, so some of what I was seeing was familiar. There were steps leading up to the runway, its entrance masked by pink velvet curtains. To the left were the racks of gowns; a beefy woman in a security uniform stood over them. There were sixteen models in all—the twins and I were in group three. I noticed Faith Hill having false eyelashes glued on, Kate Bosworth under a hair dryer, and Julie Delpy talking away in soft French on her cell phone.

I was modeling with them. Me. Megan Smith. Oh *God*.

I sidled over to the clothes rack, smiled at the security guard—she didn't smile back—and found my gowns. They were bigger than the others; I could tell even with them on their pink velvet hangers.

Was I insane? Why had I been eating Marco's risotto? What if the gowns didn't fit anymore? I took the hanger from the rack and held the first of the two dresses up to myself as if I could somehow tell whether I could get into it and zip it by just looking at it.

"If you're wearing that, it's going to look great on you."

I whirled at the sound of the voice. I knew that—

Lily. She wore a shoulder-baring charcoal-silk column with her hair tied back in a simple and elegant ponytail. "Anna Sui." She twirled for me. "Isn't it to die for?"

I flung myself into her arms. It was so good to see her. "Oh my God, why didn't you tell me you were coming?"

"One of the models got the flu this morning, and they had to find someone with her exact measurements. They found me! I wanted to surprise you." When she pulled out of my embrace, she took a good look at me. "God, Megan. You're *gorgeous*."

The heat rushed to my face happily for once. "Really?"

"Your hair, your face, that dress . . . you're beautiful."

"I made a few changes," I admitted. "And . . . I think I like it."

She grinned and took my hand. "Me, too. Come on, I want to introduce my baby sister to my friends—"

I hung back. "Wait."

"What? You have to meet Drew; she's such a riot, and—"

"Lily," I hissed, the reality of my sister's arrival in Palm Beach dawning on me. "*Listen* to me."

"What?"

I dropped my voice practically to a whisper. "The girls I tutor don't know you're my sister."

"Why not? That's crazy."

Right. Even if I hadn't told outright lies about who I was and where I came from, I definitely had used every misimpression to my advantage. Plus, I could not recall what, if anything, I had said about having a sister at all. I didn't have time to fill Lily in, much less expect her to play along. People knew Lily. That was why she was here. If I said she was my sister, it was game over.

I tried to explain it in a way that wouldn't make her hate me. Which is so self-serving. But I was in too deep to dig my way out.

"The twins have a lot of sister issues," I explained. "I didn't want to complicate things."

Lily rubbed her chin but finally nodded. "Oh, Megan, I think I get it."

"Not all of it. They think I grew up rich." Okay, that one just came out. I wasn't used to lying to my sister. Which is a good thing.

I'd like to take this opportunity to say one more time that my sister is, and always has been, nice. If *slightly* condescending.

"Okay, no problem, I'll be Lily Langley all night. So how do we know each other, then?"

I saw Sage and Suzanne enter the tent.

Oh, no. I couldn't even think straight.

Lily must have registered the look of horror on my face, because she leaned in and grabbed my arm. "We both spent a summer studying French at the same girl's school. In Switzerland."

"We *what?*" I looked at her, wide-eyed.

"Megan, hi!" Suzanne called, then made a beeline for my sister. "Aren't you Lily Langley? I was in New York over Thanksgiving with my parents, and we saw your play. You were *so* amazing."

"Thanks," Lily said to her. "Who are you modeling tonight?"

"Versace. She knows how to make the most of my assets. I already bid ten thousand for my first gown so that no one else will get it."

Sage tapped a finger against her pouty lower lip and looked from me to Lily and back to me again. "Okay, how weird is this? You two look kind of like each other. And you have the same name as her sister."

I laughed a little too heartily. Evidently, I *had* talked about a sister named—

"Oh, sure, I met that Lily once. Megan's probably already told you, but..." Lily leaned forward confidentially. "She is such a *loser.*"

Choose the word that is most closely related to the following word:

PINK

(a) chartreuse
(b) rouged nipples
(c) blush
(d) cerulean
(e) *M!ssundaztood*

chapter twenty-nine

I could not feel my hands. Or my feet. Either I had just come down with a terrible circulatory disease, or I was so nervous about stepping onto the runway that I had simply lost all blood flow to my extremities.

I stood between the Baker twins backstage, where several big-screen monitors had been erected so that the models and show personnel could follow what was happening on the other side of the curtain. Right now the last of the plastic sheeting was being removed from the temporary catwalk.

There were only two rows of chairs ringing the T-walk of the stage, for those guests whose age or status merited sitting. Everyone else stood, movie stars shoulder to shoulder with athletes, entertainers, and trust-fund kids. One special seat—large, regal, and pink—had been reserved for Laurel, and the crowd applauded as she took her place. She was dressed in a white satin evening shirt with a portrait collar and a long black chiffon skirt. As I watched her on the monitor, her shoulders and head held high, the queen of everything, I wondered if she ever thought of the poor Parisian girl she once was.

All at once, the lights that had been set up around the property popped off, and spotlights hit the runway. Celestial instrumental music streamed from large speakers on either side of the stage. Two assistants opened the pink velvet curtains to reveal the first model. The crowd oohed and applauded when they saw who it was. Kate Bosworth began to strut down the catwalk.

"Our first gown is modeled by actress Kate Bosworth. It was designed by Vera Wang," said the voiceover. "The sheer silk chiffon has horizontal pin tucks across the chest and skirt and raw chiffon ruffled shoulder seams."

Kate stopped at the top of the T, one hand on her hip, then spun full circle and strutted back as if she'd been doing it all her life.

The numbness reached my wrists and ankles. This was insane! I was a writer, an *observer*, dammit! What the hell was I doing in a fucking fashion show? Models were about as observed as you could get.

"Our next gown was designed by Ralph Lauren, and it's modeled by the new toast of New York theater, Miss Lily Langley."

My sister hit her mark as the curtains parted, and the crowd applauded even louder than they had for Kate in an apparent effort to prove that they were in the New York know. Lily floated gracefully down the catwalk. Piece of cake.

One by one, names were called, and one by one, models paraded onto the catwalk. The ones who had just come offstage were hurriedly changed into their second gowns by a pit crew of assistants. The stage manager was waving three fingers over her head, which meant that all the models in group three had to get in line. That included the twins, Suzanne de Grouchy, Precious, and me.

I really, really, *really* had to pee.

"Next, the lovely young women of Palm Beach..."

Rose eased over next to me. "Megan?"

"Yeah?"

As discreetly as she could, she pressed something into my right hand. I looked down...and felt that familiar flush work its way up my neck to my jaw. She'd given me a pair of panties. They were utilitarian and flesh-colored—the opposite of the pink mesh La Perlas I was wearing.

"That gown is kind of sheer. Sage and I think it would be smart for you to wear these. You don't want to draw attention to..."

I got it—I most certainly didn't want to draw attention to that particular uncoiffed part of myself. I whipped on those panties in record time and thanked her profusely.

The pink curtains parted. Sage stepped forward, clearly in her element. Once she cleared the curtain, she thrust out a hip bone and threw one hand over her head as if to say: *Hello, world! Here I am!*

"Modeling a Daniel Dennison for Chanel gown is the lovely Sage Baker. Sage's gown is sheer lemon polka dot over aqua silk, shirred under the bust. The hem and bodice are raw-edged."

Sage came off to huge applause. Rose was next. After her would be Suzanne and then me. I saw Suzanne adjust the cleavage of her electric-pink Betsy Johnson creation.

"I'm so nervous," I whispered to her. "Any last-minute words of wisdom?"

Suzanne smiled. "When you hit a pose, do it at a slight angle, and put one hand *above* your hip bone with your palm open. It'll take ten pounds off."

Like *that* made me feel better.

Rose finished, Suzanne stepped out, and I was next. Oh God. I felt a warm hand on my forearm. It was Lily, already dressed in her next gown of copper sequins. "Break a leg," she whispered.

Yeah, I know this is the way you're supposed to wish someone luck before she goes onstage. But in my current state, I didn't need the subliminal suggestion.

Suzanne came back through the exit curtains and placed her open palm just above her hip bone, reminding me about the look-ten-pounds-thinner thing. Way to screw with my already nonexistent self-confidence.

"And now please welcome someone new to our community, the lovely Megan Smith, in a gown by Daniel Dennison!"

The curtains parted. Bright klieg lights hit my face; I hadn't been prepared for that. They made it difficult to see the audience at first, but maybe that was a blessing. I didn't even attempt the walk-a-tightrope-strut that everyone else had made look so effortless. Instead, I just tried not to lose my balance in my three-inch Manolo heels.

It was only when I reached the T that I could see the people seated below. Laurel sat next to my favorite ex-president and his wife. All three of them smiled at me. Maybe models are supposed to look as if they're floating in a sea of ennui, but seriously, how could I not smile back?

I turned—there was only eighty-five feet between me and

backstage, also known as survival. Then, just beyond the seated dignitaries to my left, I spotted Will. Unlike the other encouraging expressions in front of me, his was icy.

That was all the distraction I needed. I felt my ankle start to turn, and I heard a gasp from the audience. It was sheer will that kept me from falling. It's amazing what a great motivator fear of public humiliation can be.

"Are you okay?" Rose asked as I wobbled through the curtain. Sage was beside her, and if I hadn't known better, I would have said she looked concerned, too. They'd already been zipped into their second outfits—teal-blue silk chiffon with a fitted bodice and a full flouncy skirt. Sage's was covered in sparkly skulls; Rose's was adorned with hearts and butterflies.

"I'm fine," which was true, in that I was still mobile.

A dresser carefully unzipped my gown while another set black velvet Laboutin open-toed pumps at my feet.

Sage nudged me. "So it was fun, right?"

"Actually, it was terrifying."

Sage sighed dramatically. "You cannot be a wuss your entire life, Megan. I mean, think about it. You just strutted your stuff with some of the most gorgeous and famous women in the world, including me."

That made me laugh. A short, squat dresser held my hand as I slipped into the new heels.

"You know that bar in New York—what's it called—where girls take off their bras and dance on the bar?" Sage asked.

"Hogs and Heifers," the dresser filled in. "I left my bra there once." She moved off to help another model.

"Right," Sage agreed. "Well, see, even girls like her lose their inhibitions at that place."

"Is there a point here?" I asked as I smoothed the skirt of my gown.

"Yeah." Sage took me by the shoulders. "For the next ten minutes, stop worrying about whatever the hell it is you're always worrying about, and go out there and be hot, you asshole! You're a fucking supermodel now!"

The assistant stage manager was motioning frantically for us to get in line for our second runway walk. Right before Sage and Rose went out onstage—they would model their similar gowns at the same time, per Daniel's instructions—the music changed to Justin Timberlake.

Rose and Sage made their entrance. I watched them strut to the music on the monitor, blowing kisses to the whooping audience at the end of the runway.

Then it hit me: I could go out there and do what I always did—watch myself rather than be in the moment. Or I could go out there and enjoy it.

The next thing I knew, I was out on the stage. The music was pulsing. I threw my shoulders back and thrust out my chest. I did the tightrope walk, one foot in front of the other, head held high. I threw my hair around as I did a turn, and let it brush over one eye sexily before I shook it off my face again.

For the next thirty seconds, I *was* a fucking supermodel. I didn't even look for Will. I was too busy seducing the entire audience with my fabulousness. And Sage was right; it was unbelievably, fantastically, once-in-a-lifetime fun.

When I came off the stage, I felt euphoric. Rose threw her arms around me. "Oh my God, you were amazing!"

I hugged her back. "I was, wasn't I?" I cried gleefully.

"Curtain call!" the stage manager shouted, making huge waving motions with his arms.

All the models were hustled out onstage first; the designers followed. The audience stood and applauded. I was between Sage and Rose. We put our arms around one another's waists and started an impromptu cancan as the audience cheered.

"Remember, ladies and gentlemen, all these clothes can be viewed in the auction tent in twenty minutes. Happy New Year, everyone!"

Backstage, I carefully handed my gown to a dresser, who would take it to the auction tent. Still on a high, I changed back into the pale pink tea-length dress I'd been wearing before. I, Megan Smith, had modeled with the rich, famous, and infamous and lived to tell the tale.

Lily ran over to me. "How much fun was that?" she exclaimed happily.

"I *loved* it!" I said, hugging her. "Let's go have some more fun."

When we exited the tent, the first people I saw were the twins laughing with Will. His eyes met mine briefly, then went back to Sage and Rose. Well, I wasn't going to let seeing him ruin my mood.

"Who's that with the Baker twins?" Lily asked, taking my arm.

"Will Phillips. He lives next door."

"Hot," Lily decided. "Right?"

Ah, the irony.

"He's okay."

"Is he seeing anyone?" she asked.

And the irony just kept on coming.

"Not that I know of."

"Great." She tugged at my hand. "Introduce me."

We joined the trio, and I quickly introduced Will to Lily Langley, who knew me from our *séjour linguistique* in Switzerland.

"You're in New York now?" Will asked. "My mom lives in the city. Next time I'm up, maybe I can see your play."

"If it hasn't closed," Lily quipped.

Damn. These two were chatting like the two confident, eleven-on-a-looks-scale-of-ten people they were.

"I saw the *Entertainment Tonight* thing about you," Rose said to Lily. "You got cast in the movie version of your play, right?"

Lily smiled. "*Cast* might be too strong a word. But I know they're going to look at me for the part. Then all I have to do is beat out Natalie Portman." Lily rolled her eyes. "As if that'll happen."

Sage sniffed. "She's totally overrated."

"So you two know each other from way back," Will remarked, looking from Lily to me. The mere idea of me made him sound stiff. "Small world."

Lily gave him a flirtatious look. "You seem to know a lot more about me than I know about you. Megan said you live next door."

"That's all she said?" Rose asked, looking at me like I was crazy.

"And that we're friends," I added. My voice, I realized, sounded as strained as Will's.

"Well, I hope we can be friends, too," Lily told Will. "Maybe we'll catch up later?"

"Sure," he allowed, with another quick glance at me. "That sounds good."

"Hot guy," Lily observed as Will and the twins headed off toward the bar for refills.

The best I could muster was a very weak "Yeah."

chapter thirty

I walked with Lily to the food tent, which had been divided into three different catering areas. There was French for the foodie types; organic vegetarian for the Hollywood types; and Brazilian churrasco for the Atkins types, with all manner of meat being roasted on an open pit. The aroma wafted to me like a come-hither signal. All at once, I was starving.

"You're Lily Langley, right?" A sixtyish, stick-thin woman in candy-cane-striped silk grabbed Lily's right hand as we stepped into the tent. "Darling, you are a gift to the American theater!"

"Thank you so much. This is my sis—friend Megan Smi—"

"Lovely to meet you," the woman trilled, but she was already brushing past us, her gaze scanning the area for more important people.

"Pick a line," Lily said. I pointed to the meat. As we were heading for it, one of Lily's actress friends from New York ran over and grabbed her arm. "Lily, Dominick Dunne is holding court by the blind-auction tent. He wants to meet you."

Lily looked at me, hesitating.

"Go," I insisted. "You can eat later."

She gave me a hug and whispered, "I'll call you right after midnight, and we'll meet on the beach."

Frankly, it was easier this way. Pretending that my sister wasn't my sister was a new low, even for me. I got some succulent-looking slices of grilled steak and ate them standing in a corner, watching the parade passing by. I saw a model from the fashion show with her boyfriend. He was gorgeous, but even in her velvet ballet flats, she had four inches on him. There was a ninety-something couple swaying to the big-band music coming from the speakers. The only person I really wanted to be with tonight—Will—didn't want to be with me.

I passed dozens of people on the walkway from the tennis courts down to the ocean; I didn't know most of them. I heard a couple "Lovely job in the fashion show" and "Fantastic dress!" comments, but already, the me who had flirted with an audience while strutting in a ten-thousand-dollar one-of-a-kind dress had crawled back into her shell.

As I approached the twins' pool deck—the rock wall was beyond it—I saw Sage striding past the steps down to the beach. She was heading for her friends at the bar near the stage. Suddenly, Thom, who was dressed in his *Heavenly* deckhand outfit, bolted up the steps from the beach three at a time, slung his arms around her from behind, and planted a steamy kiss on the back of her neck.

Sage screamed. Then she spun around. "What the fuck do you think you're doing?"

Thom staggered. The kiss obviously had been intended for her sister. "Sage! Shit! I am so sorry," Thom apologized breathlessly.

I saw Rose and the usual suspects—Suzanne, Precious, Dionne—come running, drawn by Sage's scream.

"I'm so, so sorry, Sage," Thom hastened to explain. "I thought you were Rose."

"Rose? You thought I was *Rose?* What kind of bullshit excuse is…" All that SAT training paid off as she made the intellectual leap. Her jaw fell open. "Oh my God. Rose, you're doing the *cabin boy?*" She threw her head back and laughed into the night. "That is so…*desperate!*"

I looked at Rose, whose face had turned a shade of red that was usually reserved for me.

"Look, no offense, Sage," Thom said. "But what Rose does and who she does it with really isn't any of your business."

"Listen, you little leech. *Everything* my sister does is my business. Have you been fucking my sister while you're supposed to be working?"

"I'm not even going to dignify that with a response," he replied, looking genuinely offended.

Sage's smile was lethal. "I'm going to bury you."

"Go for it, Sage," Thom encouraged her, then held out a hand to Rose. "Come on, Rose. Let's get out of here."

With everything in me that still believed in love, if not for myself then certainly for her, I rooted for Rose to take his hand. *Come on,* I thought. *Come on. Take his hand and walk away. Please, Rose. Take his hand.*

Instead, she stepped backward. "I don't know what you're talking about."

That was all it took. Thom shook his head, not taking his eyes off her. "I can't..." But he never finished his sentence. I could only imagine the betrayal he felt as he walked away alone.

"What'd you do, Rose? Flash him and he fell in love or something?" Precious asked. "That's so pathetic!"

Rose smiled and excused herself. I headed after her, hoping the others didn't see me, but she was hard to find on a beach crowded with revelers. It was only when I got to the thin nautical rope on the beach that marked the dividing point between Les Anges and the Phillips' property, Barbados, that I saw Rose sitting in the sand near the waterline.

I dropped down next to her but didn't say anything. She lobbed a few pebbles toward the incoming waves. I did, too. Then she skimmed a few small stones into the ocean.

"You hate me," she said finally.

"No."

"I hate me. I can't believe I ruined things with Thom."

"Maybe it's not too late?" I offered. "You could apologize, you know."

"And how would I do that?" she asked, lobbing a bigger rock into the water.

"Throw your arms around him, plead temporary insanity, and ask if he wants you to put up a billboard on Worth Avenue announcing that you're a couple," I advised.

She looked cockeyed at me. "Worth Avenue doesn't allow billboards."

I smiled and smoothed back her hair. She leaned against me,

almost the way a child would against her mother. "You'll figure it out," I counseled. "Skywriting?"

"That's a thought."

We headed back, holding our heels in our hands and silently walking in the waves. By the time we'd reached the bottom of the steps, it seemed like the entire party had gathered on the beach to count down the final seconds of the year.

"Ten, nine, eight..." More and more people joined in, counting down to midnight.

"Five, four, three, two, one. Happy New Year!"

The noise was deafening as the sky filled with a fabulous fireworks display, color bursting upon color, ruby bleeding to emerald and then to silver and gold. The beach lit up as the show glowed overhead. I looked around at the crowds watching the sky, at all the couples embracing to welcome in the new year.

And that was when I saw Lily in Will's arms. He was kissing her the way I'd dreamed of his kissing me. I felt my heart ache. The year was ruined, and it was only a few seconds old.

c h a p t e r   t h i r t y - o n e

*O*h, what a tangled web we weave, when first we practice to deceive!

No shit.

Most people think William Shakespeare is responsible for that pithy truth, but it was, in fact, Sir Walter Scott. I think when a person (meaning me) ends up being the walking definition of such a quote, she should at least know who the hell is responsible for it.

It was a simple case of anesthetization, Palm Beach–style. After seeing Lily in a liplock with Will, I stumbled to the nearest bar, grabbed a bottle of Cristal, and spent the first half hour of the New Year guzzling it, hiding out in my suite.

Lily called me around twelve-thirty, by which time I had

made a serious dent in the bubbly. I told her I wasn't feeling well—true enough, though not for any physical reason—and was going to bed. She wanted to come up and give me a hug, since she'd be jetting back to New York in the wee hours of the morning. I put her off. I was going to sleep. She should stay at the party. Have fun. Keep kissing Will.

Okay, I didn't say the last one.

Personally, I've never been a big believer in karma. When the distraught woman on the evening news thanks God for saving her, her family, and her home from the terrible tornado, I always wonder about the family next door who lost everything. So was God, like, really pissed off at *them*? The whole what-goes-around-comes-around thing is simply our way of trying to make sense out of things that make no sense. Great stuff happens to bad people. Bad shit happens to good people. This is just the way it is.

But if I *did* believe in karma, I would say that watching my sister kiss Will was exactly what I deserved. I couldn't blame Lily. She had no way of knowing how I felt about Will. I couldn't blame Will, either, because there was this little thing called a *boyfriend* I'd hidden from him. All I could do was blame myself.

I pounded the bottle and fell asleep; I didn't wake for hours. I squinted at the luminous hands of the clock on the nightstand. It was just past five. I sat up. I felt as if a football team were doing up-downs inside my head. I sat up and turned on the lamp. My eight-hundred-thread-count Egyptian-cotton pillowcase was now adorned with a Jackson Pollock–esque mini-canvas of mascara, lipstick, and drool.

There are few things as awful as a champagne hangover

at five-thirty in the morning. One of the few is said champagne hangover compounded by an awful memory of what prompted the drinking bout in the first place. The thought of Will doing things to Lily that I had imagined him doing to me made me run to the bathroom and puke my guts out. Interestingly enough, barfing in a mansion after chugging Cristal is just as nasty as barfing in a fifth-floor East Village walk-up after downing too many Long Island iced teas, an experience I'd endured at Charma's summer tar-beach birthday party on our roof, my only other up-close-and-personal visit with the porcelain throne.

I showered, brushed my teeth, and, feeling only marginally more human, decided to go out on my balcony to get some fresh air. The torchlights by the pool below were still burning, though the party was long over. But that wasn't what caught my attention. It was Sage and Rose. They were going at it. Big-time.

"Why do you ruin everything for me, Sage?"

"I don't know what the fuck you're talking about," Sage responded. She was stripping out of her clothes as she spoke.

"Thom!"

"Who the fuck is Thom?" Sage asked, yanking off her shirt. And then derisive laughter. "You mean the cabin boy?"

"He's not *just* the cabin boy," Rose told her sister.

"Oh my God! You really *do* like him!" Sage stepped into the shallow end of the pool. "Well, don't blame me, *you're* the one who let him walk away. Oh my God. This feels great. Hey, get some champagne from the cabana."

Rose didn't move. "What's it like, Sage?" Her voice was low now. I had to strain to hear.

Sage slid into the water, grabbed a floating noodle, and rolled onto her back. "What's *what* like?"

"To be you. To always be so sure about everything."

"It's great, Rose." Sage pulled herself up on the opposite side of the pool and sat there, looking as perfect as a human can look while clad in nothing but youth, great genes, and nipple piercings. "Maybe your taste in guys just sucks, Rose. Ever think of that?"

"Oh, so I should be like you? Fuck whoever I want and never care about anyone or anything?"

"Whatever." Sage got up and padded over to a pile of fluffy, oversize pink and aqua towels. "Go get the champagne, Rose. Seriously."

"I can't believe you sometimes." I heard the tightness in Rose's voice. She was close to tears.

"Boo-hoo, poor you," Sage sang out.

"I *hate* you!" The ragged sound was torn from someplace deep inside of Rose.

"Like I fucking care," Sage jeered.

"You guys, you guys, stop!" It was out of my mouth before I had considered whether or not I should intervene.

They looked up at the balcony, shocked that I'd overheard them. I pulled on a robe and ran downstairs. When I got there, Rose was sitting alone at a table, and Sage was wrapped in a huge towel, lying on a chaise longue and guzzling the champagne she'd retrieved from the cabana.

"Go away," Sage told me.

I ignored her and sat on the end of her chaise. "You're saying things you don't mean because you're upset."

Sage balanced the champagne bottle on her stomach and eyed me around it. "They teach you that at Yale?"

"No," I replied. "My parents taught me that. God knows I've made a lot of mistakes anyway..." I stopped myself. This could not be about me. "Maybe Rose should have told you about Thom, but you have to understand why she didn't. She cares so much about what you think."

"That's bullshit," Sage muttered.

I looked over at Rose, who wasn't saying a word. Her head was tucked into her chest, and she had wrapped her arms around herself as if she could physically bind in her own pain.

I turned back to Sage. "Rose told me a story. About the day the two of you left New York after your parents died. How scared she was on the plane. You know how she got through it, Sage? She got through it because of you."

Sage smiled in an unamused way. "I know. I heard her tell it to you. When you two were out on the deck in the Bahamas." Sage turned toward Rose. "You had no right to tell her that. No right at all."

Rose nodded mutely.

"You're such an asshole." Sage's words to her sister were as stinging as ever. Then she was silent.

I was looking out toward the water, trying to clear my foggy head and decide what else I could say, when I heard a sniffle.

"How do you think I got through it, Rose?" Sage asked her sister, tears in her voice. She put down the champagne bottle and sat up, swinging her legs toward Rose. "Do you think I held your hand just for *you*?"

I saw the realization dawn on Rose's face. "But you didn't seem scared."

"Don't let it get around." Sage reached out and took her sister's hand, as she had all those years ago. "I . . . don't want to lose you to anyone, okay?"

Rose sniffled loudly and nodded.

I stood. "I'm going to the beach to watch the sunrise. You guys should be alone." I headed down the stone staircase and across the planked walkway to the temporary dock. I walked out to the very end. A minute later, I heard two sets of footfalls as the twins joined me. We stood together for a long time in silence, as the first shards of daylight pierced the sky.

"Sage?" Rose asked.

"Yeah?"

"As long as we have each other, we're not orphans."

They cried. I cried. The sun rose on all of us, all cried out.

When we finally went back inside, I hugged them both, then headed back to my suite. There was one more thing I had to do. My iBook was on. I clicked on the folder labeled TWINS, the one filled with notes I'd kept so diligently for my exposé. There was so much I could write if I wanted to, because at last I had it figured out.

Every time it had looked like Rose was growing close to me, Sage had freaked out. It had happened in the Bahamas, it had happened on the pool deck when Sage had oh-so-maturely thrown the pencil at her sister, and it had happened—albeit briefly—when Sage had realized that Rose knew more about my trip to Clewiston with Will than she did. Rose had told me that Sage hated all her boyfriends. But Rose could have hooked up with Orlando Bloom plus Bill Gates's bank account and Sage would have had the same reaction. The equation was simple. Rose + anyone = the possibility of Sage without Rose.

So much crap to cover so much insecurity, I mused. But maybe that's what happens when your parents die young, and all you have left are your sister and your bravado to get you through the scary moments.

I clicked on the TWINS folder and held my finger over my keyboard. And then I pressed "delete."

chapter thirty-two

*N*umber eight," I read to the twins. "Who wants to take number eight?"

In an effort to jump-start their brains, we'd changed study environments and settled down for the morning in my den instead of on the pool deck. I was stretched out on my couch. They were sprawled on a floor that was already a mess of papers, books, calculators, notebooks, half-eaten bags of Healthy Pop microwave popcorn, and half-consumed bottles of FIJI water.

It had been a week since the long day's journey into the endless night of New Year's Eve. The twins hadn't spoken with me about it, hadn't even mentioned it. If they'd talked about it with each other, they certainly hadn't shared that with me. But the result was impossible to miss—they were kinder to each other now. Sage didn't jump to the bitchy quip as often. Rose didn't look to Sage so much for approval.

I was proud of them, and I felt pretty good about how I'd

helped. I'm sure you'd guess, what with my sensitivity and maturity and everything, that all this would have been the catalyst I needed to pick up the phone and call my sister. But I didn't.

It's *so* much easier to be wise and mature on behalf of others.

Rose called Thom to apologize. When he didn't answer, she left a heartfelt message on his voice mail. When he didn't call back, she wrote him a letter (we're talking snail mail here, so this was perhaps a life first for her), which she'd asked me to proofread so there wouldn't be any embarrassing errors. She'd misspelled *psychological* and misused *vilify*, but otherwise, it was sensitive and self-aware.

I only wish her efforts had paid off. Thom imposed a total blackout. Oh, sure, Rose knew she could go out on the *Heavenly* and talk to him face-to-face, but personal progress did not equal personal transformation. I couldn't blame her. I mean, did you see me heading over to Barbados for a little face time with Will? Ha.

"I'll read number eight," Rose volunteered. She picked up the test booklet, where we were working on grammar. "'Some Italians consider Americans to be overweight, wasteful, and they don't understand international politics.'"

"Who wants to correct the grammar in this part of the sentence?" I asked. "'*To be overweight, wasteful, and they don't understand.*'"

Rose pointed to her answer key. "I'd say E: 'Overweight, wasteful, and ignorant of.' It's that parallel-structure thingie that Megan was talking about last week."

"Fuck," Sage said.

"Too bad they're not testing you on that," Rose joked. To my surprise, instead of getting pissed, Sage managed a half-smile in response.

"Review it later, you'll get it next time," I encouraged Sage.

I hoped that my voice belied my concern. We had only seven days to go before the SAT, and we were running out of time for "next time." Their academic progress had stalled at the worst possible point—just below where they would need to be to get in to Duke. They'd improved so much, but it still wasn't enough, and I was at a loss as to what I should do.

Rose admitted to being stressed about the SAT; Sage didn't. But I noticed that her nails, normally in a state of constant manicured perfection, had been picked and bitten to the nub. She'd taken to curling her fingers under so that no one would see.

"Okay," I told them. "Let's try the first math problem in the next section. Rose, want to take a crack at it?"

"My brain doesn't work this way," Rose groused, trying to make sense of the equation.

"You can do it; I know you can," Sage encouraged.

That made one of us. To see them working together was a thing of beauty, but between Sage's work on the qualitative side of the ledger and Rose's on the quantitative side, my optimism was dissipating like beach fog under the hot sun.

Rose knocked her knuckles against her forehead. "I can't concentrate!" she lamented. "I keep thinking about Thom."

"Honey, no love is that blind," Sage stated. "You were the one who kept telling me not to fuck us out of the eighty-four million. Take your own advice."

"I know," Rose agreed. "But it's hard. I need a break." She pulled the most recent issue of *Scoop* from underneath her books. I half expected to see a photo of Lily Langley with her "new mystery boy toy" or whatever my replacement had decided to call Will.

"Rose, put away the magazine," I said gently. "We've got seven days. If you get up at seven and work until eleven-thirty at night, that's more then sixteen hours a day. Times seven, minus short breaks to eat and pee. Whacked up three ways between math, humanities, and writing."

The girls groaned in unison.

"Okay, so we know *you* won't take it for us," Sage mused. "But how about Ari? Seriously, the guy is walking brain cells."

"Even Keith can't dress Ari to pass for you," I told them. "How about you decide you're willing to kick your ass and do everything I say, and *only* what I say, for the most important week of your life?" I looked at Rose. "And you, too?"

When I was little, my father had taken Lily and me up to Mount Washington one June. He was a skier, we were both snowboarders, and he wanted us to hike up Tuckerman Ravine with him—it was still full of snow—and ride down as he followed us on skis. There is no chairlift at Tuckerman. To get to the top, you climb. Both Lily and I were dying when we reached the last five hundred feet. I was only ten years old.

Lily quit. She threw both her board and her body down in the snow. But I did everything my dad told me to do, listened to every direction. And then I was up and over the last steep incline. At the summit, I buckled onto my board and took that first reason-defying plunge over the lip of the headwall.

And then I was flying. It took only thirty seconds to carve sweeping turns to where Lily was still waiting.

"You did it," she said admiringly.

"I just listened to Dad," I told her.

Why did I remember that now? I always thought of Lily as doing everything better than me. But that time on Tuckerman she'd given up, and I'd gone the distance. Memory can be so selective.

Sage got a cunning look on her face. "Tell you what, Megan. If you do something for us, we'll do something—"

"Oh, no, you don't! I've been down this road, remember? Nude swim?"

"Actually, what we want you to do is a matter of . . ." Sage leaned over and whispered in Rose's ear.

Rose grinned and then nodded. "Sage is right. Something has to be done. About the hair."

This was the last thing I expected. "But Keith cut it!" I protested. "*The* Keith!"

The sisters traded looks. Sage folded her arms. "Let me put it to you this way, Megan. Remember the fashion show? Rose lent you some panties?"

"You are, in a word, hirsute," Rose explained with great dignity.

I laughed. *Hirsute* had been a recent vocabulary word.

"I would not laugh if I were you." Sage sniffed. "Hirsute is a plus only on *her-head*."

I blushed, of course. "It's not that bad."

"Excuse me," Rose intoned. "Nude swim? You were standing fifty feet away."

Sage made a chopping motion at her midsection. "Waist." She chopped two inches lower. "Bush."

"It's physics!" I protested. "Water magnifies!"

"Remember that gift certificate I gave you to the spa at the Breakers?" Sage asked with unaccustomed sweetness. "There was a reason for it. It's time to put it to good use." She stared pointedly at my crotch.

"We're not talking bikini wax, either," Rose added. "And we're not talking landing strip."

Which could only mean...I was aghast. "No. Oh, no."

"Oh, yes," Sage said gleefully.

"Do that, and we'll do what you asked us to do," Rose said.

Sage nodded. "Twenty-four/seven for the next seven days."

Seven weeks ago, they'd offered me a bargain and used it to humiliate me. Now they were offering me another one. But this time it was different. They were different. Maybe even I was different.

Whatever look was on my face, they took it as a yes.

Three minutes later, the appointment was made. One hour later, I was on Jinessa's table at the Breakers. One hour and five minutes later, Jinessa was wielding a set of scissors, and I was keeping my eyes closed for dear life. Ten minutes after that, a spatula of liquefied wax came dangerously close to a spot where few—none of them female, unless I counted myself—had gone before.

I have heard that childbirth is excruciatingly painful. But I sincerely doubt that it hurts more than what the spa menu so delicately—but accurately—described as Surrender the Pink.

chapter thirty-three

*P*romptly at seven, please, Megan," the Skull had intoned when he'd summoned me to dinner with Laurel.

Mr. Anderson spoke in the same sonorous tones he'd used for the past eight weeks; however, progress had been made—he'd finally called me by my first name.

That made me smile, as did the fact that the twins had been true to their word. For the past seven days, they'd been Yale-quality students, in effort if not in achievement. I had tried to make it bearable, but studying for the SAT can be mind-numbing. Even so, there'd been a minimum of bitching and moaning. They'd made a deal and stuck by it.

I was reminded of my end of that bargain every time I peeled down. The exquisite La Perla thongs that the twins had delivered to my suite while I was under Jinessa's ministrations were so beautiful that anything inserted into them would have to be considered a work of art. Not that anyone was appreciating my art these days. I hadn't heard from either James or Will. This, of course, reminded me of the age-old philosophical question: Is art still art if no one sees it? Or something like that.

Anyway, back to the twins. Every day we'd worked for three hours in the morning, four in the afternoon, and three in the evening. Their practice test scores were in the low—*really* low—range of what Duke required. But they were in the range. I couldn't have been happier.

On this last morning before the SAT, we'd done a review. Then I'd told them that they were as prepared as they were ever going to be; they should forget about the test that afternoon and engage in their favorite activity: shopping. There are few things in life a Baker twin loves more than Worth Avenue and a coveted no-credit-limit black AmEx card.

So. What to wear to dinner with Laurel? I stared at my considerable assortment of Marco's designer hand-me-downs. I now knew that I looked best in peach, which brought out the green in my hazel eyes, and that beige washed me out. I decided on a simple peach Vera Wang cotton Empire-waist dress that wasn't too fussy or low-cut—but then, her stuff never is. I now knew that, too. I took a long, hot bath, washed and flatironed my hair, and applied subtle and flattering makeup.

I arrived at the main mansion at seven on the dot. The Skull was waiting for me. "Good evening, Megan. You're looking well. Follow me, please." Coming from the Skull, "You're looking well" was the equivalent of "Damn, girl, you're smoking."

I thought he would take me to the formal dining room on

the main floor. Instead, we went downstairs, toward the wine cellar.

"Um, didn't Madame say dinner?" I asked.

"Yes. This way, please."

At the far end of the wine cellar, he opened the door to a room I hadn't even known existed. It held a single table carved out of a massive block of granite. The eight chairs surrounding it were rough-hewn wood. The walls featured frescoes of rural scenes from the French countryside.

There, Laurel was sipping a glass of wine at the head of the table, which was set for two. She looked the way women her age dreamed they could look. She wore a fitted gold and black glazed-linen sheath. Her hair was swept off her face in a French twist, tendrils falling artfully around her face. Her blue eyes, fringed with long dark lashes, looked even more enormous than usual. Once again, Laurel was a walking advertisement for her own products.

As Mr. Anderson took his leave, Laurel gestured to the empty place setting. "Please."

I sat.

"Join me?" She motioned to a carafe of wine and then poured some into my water glass. It was odd. She had the market cornered on crystal. Why were we drinking from water glasses? I noticed that the earthenware dishes set before us were more utilitarian than elegant.

Laurel entwined her fingers. "I reviewed the twins' most recent practice tests today. They've improved a great deal."

I smiled. "Yes. They have."

She took a sip of her wine. "I admit, Megan, there were times when I doubted you were up to the task of tutoring these girls. But you have proved me wrong."

Compliments from the Skull *and* Laurel Limoges in the same evening? This was either shaping up to be an amazing evening or a sign that the apocalypse was imminent.

"Thank you. I appreciate that," I said.

"I don't know if my granddaughters are going to succeed tomorrow," she continued. "But I do know that Debra Wurtzel steered me correctly when she suggested you." Laurel lifted her glass. "To you, Megan Smith. You have accomplished a great deal in your two months here. Congratulations. *À ta santé.*"

I clinked my glass against Laurel's, startled that she'd used the familiar French word for *you* instead of the more formal and distant *à votre santé*, then I sipped the wine. It was earthy and biting, unlike the vintage Bordeaux that I knew she usually preferred.

"To tell you the truth, Madame Limoges, I've learned a lot since I've been here."

Laurel's eyes twinkled. "I think perhaps you've learned to appreciate your own beauty, no?" I had no idea how to reply to that. She patted my hand. "Beauty is a gift, dear. It is meant to be enjoyed." She shook out her napkin and placed it in her lap. "And now, Megan, we shall see whether you've learned to appreciate the best meal that Marco can prepare."

"And serve," Marco chimed in from the door. "I will be your garçon for the evening, darling. And might I add that I don't respond well to finger snapping as a means of getting my attention."

"Perish the thought." I winked at him. He was one of the aspects of Palm Beach I would miss the most.

"The menu, Marco?" Laurel queried.

"Very *campagne*. You'll begin with pâté de foie gras. The

main course will be cassoulet, followed by a peasant salad of field greens, flowers, goat cheese, and pine nuts. The wine, true French plonk, *le pinard* like the peasants drink. And for dessert, my petite doughnuts."

Laurel leaned toward me confidentially. "I don't allow him to make them very often. They are so fantastic that I simply cannot resist."

"Each has a different filling—hazelnut crème, dark chocolate orange peel, Grand Marnier, et cetera." Marco kissed the tips of his fingers and left to get the first course.

"The twins will join us for dessert." Laurel broke off a small hunk of the baguette.

"They didn't mention that."

"I've asked Mr. Anderson to summon them. But I wanted to talk to you first." She stopped as if deciding exactly what she wanted to say. "Eight weeks ago I created . . . I suppose you could call it a trial for my granddaughters. Now that your work is done, surely you have questions about it."

Once a journalist, always a journalist. She was about to give me the inside scoop. I could feel it. Even if I wasn't going to write my article, at least my curiosity would be satisfied.

Marco brought in the pâté. Laurel spread some of it on a chunk of baguette, then waited for him to depart before she spoke again.

"The worst thing in the world is to have your child die before you," Laurel continued. "You cannot imagine it, and I hope that you never experience it. Two years before I lost my daughter, my husband died after a sudden *crise cardiaque*." She sighed. "Loss changes a person. You don't know that, cannot know that, unless you are forced to live through it."

I nodded and waited for her to go on.

"When the twins came to me, I am afraid I was quite unready to care for them. I was too deep in my own grief." She gave the smallest of shrugs. "I have so many regrets. But we cannot go backward. We have only to move forward." She drank a healthy swallow of her wine. "By the time I was ready for them, they had put up a wall that I did not know how to climb. Then I saw that execrable magazine story about them, and the truth of who they had become—the result of what I had *failed* to do—was staring me in the face."

She looked into her glass as if the wine were some kind of oracle. "That is why I came up with this *défi*—this test—where their beauty would not help them and where they would have to depend on each other. I hoped and prayed that this would lead them back to the girls they would have been had tragedy not so deeply touched their lives. And that, my dear, led me to you."

There were so many questions that the writer in me wanted to ask. For starters, had it never occurred to her that she and the girls were a family therapist's dream? Why was her grief an excuse for neglecting her own granddaughters? And how about: Once she realized that she'd made a mistake, *why didn't she just tell them the truth?*

Me. Me! Wondering why someone else didn't just tell the truth. I'll pause here while you laugh your ass off.

Here's all I did ask. "Sage and Rose—did you want them to hate you?"

"No. But if they needed to hate me to learn to love themselves and each other, then so be it."

Marco returned, took the appetizers' dishes, and set redolent plates of mouthwatering cassoulet in front of us. As we ate, Laurel recounted stories from her childhood—there'd been an uncle who lived in the Morvan district between Autun and Nevers and cared for the Charolais cattle of a wealthy landowner. His patron had rewarded him with a small stone cottage whose kitchen looked very much like this room.

"And so I re-created it here. It is why we are drinking this rough wine and eating this cassoulet. It is his recipe. I bring few guests to this room."

I smiled. "Thank you, Madame." I wasn't sure what else to say.

"So, Megan. What will you do when you return to New York?"

Talk about an appetite killer. I put down my fork and wiped my mouth with the rough muslin napkin. I hoped that the twins would get in to Duke and my college debts would be gone. I wouldn't know that until the SAT scores were reported online two weeks after the test. Other than that, I had no idea.

"Look for a job, I guess."

"Like the one you had before at Debra's magazine?" She smiled, and I realized that Debra must have told her about the fit between *Scoop* and me. That is, nonexistent.

"I hope for something…more substantial," I suggested.

"Perhaps I can help you to realize your lofty ambitions. I know several people in the publishing world. Some of them are at…*substantial* magazines. I can make some calls on your behalf. And in the meantime…" She reached into a pocket of her sheath dress and extracted a small envelope. "For you."

I opened the envelope. Inside was a business check for seventy-five thousand dollars. "Your bonus," Laurel explained. "You worked hard, Megan. You have prepared the girls. There is not another thing you could do."

I stared at the money. The right thing to do would be to protest, to say that I hadn't earned it until the twins were admitted to Duke.

Oh, *please*, of course I took it. What am I, a saint? "I wanted to offer you another observation," Laurel said. "It makes more sense in French than in English, if you'll allow me. *Tu es une jeune femme très débrouillarde*."

I blushed. In French, the word *débrouillard* is about as high a compliment as one can pay. It means a combination of smart, thoughtful, practical, and above all, resourceful.

"Thank you. Really."

"When I was just starting out in Paris, it was not easy. Few salons were willing to try the new beauty products of a French girl with an address in the *dix-huitième arrondissement*. I mixed these products in the sink of the common bathroom of our building—though I did not share that at the time. It took every penny I could beg, borrow, or steal." She entwined her elegant fingers. "So from time to time it was incumbent on me to embellish the truth a bit. A generous backer bought me an expensive gown, and I wore it when I made my sales calls so they would think I was an upper-class girl. It was a means to an end."

Her eyes twinkled as she looked at me. And then I knew that she knew.

"I'm sorry," I managed.

She waved her hand dismissively. "The Main Line of Philadelphia story was your means to an end," she said with a half-smile. "In a way, you were emulating me without even knowing it."

"I'll tell the girls the truth," I volunteered. "After they take their test tomorrow."

Laurel nodded. "That sounds like the right timing."

I looked down again at the check in my hand. "This is so generous of you—"

"What's generous?" Sage asked. She and Rose were standing in the entryway.

"Mon dieu," Laurel exclaimed. "Rose, what have you done?"

Rose grinned, then twirled. "Do you like it?"

She'd cut off her glorious hair. It was now nape-of-the-neck short with choppy bangs that drew attention to her enormous eyes.

"I love it!" I exclaimed, not only because that was the truth, but because the sparkle in Rose's eyes made it clear that she loved it. She didn't look like an imitation of Sage anymore. She looked like herself.

"It's...a departure," Sage allowed.

"Jean Seberg, *À Bout de Souffle,*" Laurel observed as Marco brought in a carafe of coffee and a platter of his tiny doughnuts. "*Breathless*. With Belmondo. You must see it sometime. Yes, Rose, I quite like it. Sit down, girls. It is time for dessert. And for me to congratulate you on a job well done."

Sage lowered herself slowly into a chair, staring at her grandmother as if she'd just grown horns. "Did you just say something nice to us?"

"Yes, Sage," Laurel confirmed. "I did. I think you have worked very hard. But what is more important is that *you* now see you are capable of working very hard. And when you work hard, there is success in the effort. That is why, whether or not you succeed tomorrow—"

"You're giving us our money anyway!" Sage squealed. She

jumped up and began a happy dance. "It's my birthday, it's my birthday, not really, party anyway—"

Laurel held up a palm. "*No.* Nothing motivates like motivation. Sit."

Sage slunk back to her seat.

"Your incentive to do your very best tomorrow remains," Laurel decreed. "However, Megan's debt has been retired. In full. I think all three of us can agree that she more than earned it. Yes?"

"Yes," Rose agreed.

"Definitely," Sage conceded.

"Very good," Laurel approved. "Girls, your grandmother is proud of you. Megan, I think you've done everything you could."

"I don't," Rose said softly. "There's something else she could do if she really wanted to."

Laurel frowned. "What is that?"

I saw tears well up in Rose's kohl-rimmed eyes. "She could *not* go back to New York. She could stay."

"Everyone must move forward, my dear," Laurel explained. It made my heart ache. "Megan. You girls. Even me." She raised her eyebrows at me. "A small toast would be appropriate? With something special?"

"Small," I cautioned her. "Very small."

"Some thimblefuls. I have cognac, from my great-uncle, in my office. Camus jubilee. Very special occasions only. I'll get it."

She departed, leaving me with the twins. Of course, knowing what I did about her now, I understood that she could have called any one of a dozen minions to fetch it for her. She was getting it herself to leave Sage, Rose, and me alone together.

"I just want to say—" I began.

"Don't even *think* about vocabulary," Sage warned.

"I won't. You're ready. No more work, I told you."

"You really like the hair?" Rose asked me.

"I really do," I assured her.

Sage pulled out her new cell phone from the back pocket of her jeans. "While I'm thinking about it, give me your parents' number in Gladwyne."

I gulped the rough red wine to bide for time. What parents' number in Philadelphia? I didn't even know the area code for Philadelphia.

"Why?" I asked, trying to sound casual. "You've got my cell."

"In case you move or you go to Europe or something," Sage explained. "Your parents will always know where you are. So what is it?"

It was one of those life-passing-before-your-eyes moments. And then I was saved by fate.

"Oh, shit, it's not charged," Sage groused. "Remind me to get it later."

"Sure," I quickly agreed. *Tomorrow*, I told myself. *Tomorrow after the test. You'll tell them the truth.*

I was limp with relief when Laurel came back with the Camus jubilee.

"To tomorrow," she toasted.

I had seventy-five thousand dollars in my pocket, which made me feel fantastic, but there was a niggling feeling underneath. Eight short weeks ago, I'd hated these girls, and rightly so. But the hate was long gone. They were so much more than they'd seemed at first blush. However, I was so different from the person they thought they knew. How had it happened that they'd grown brave enough to be honest with each other and with me, yet I was still light-years from being honest with them?

"To tomorrow," I agreed. Those two words had special meaning now. The next day, right after they took the SAT, I'd tell the twins everything. "*Chin chin.*"

Choose the pair of words that most closely resembles the following analogy:

MOONLIGHT : CHAMPAGNE

(a) strawberries : champagne
(b) puppies : cuteness
(c) one-night stand : tequila
(d) suntanning : wrinkles
(e) mascara : eyelashes

chapter thirty-four

One last night in paradise. One last walk on the beach.

The cool sand squished between my naked toes. I stared out at the endless expanse of deep purple that was the ocean under a sliver moon. After feasting on Marco's petite doughnuts—trust me, no human, not even the Baker twins, could resist them—the three of us waddled back to their house. I double-checked their alarm clocks, joked about putting them to bed like little kids, and gave them both massive hugs. We'd have breakfast together in the morning, and I would take them to the test center in West Palm. I tried not to think about whether they would hate me when I told them the truth. I held on to this: Once I had a chance to explain, they would understand.

The night was cool and breezy. I pulled my True Religion

jean jacket closer and watched the waves crest against the shore. Once I was back in the concreteness of New York, would I be able to conjure up the colors, relive the bracing bite of the salt air, remember the heady aroma of the flowers that perfumed the air of Les Anges? Would I be able to close my eyes and see how a cruise ship looked, outlined in lights, out at sea? Recall how the faint strains of its orchestra, playing music from a bygone era, wafted all the way to shore?

Starting tomorrow night, all this would be gone from my life. Palm Beach wasn't my home—it was as far from home as I could imagine a place being—but I was sad to leave it all the same. Why is it that for everything you gain in life, something is always lost?

I found myself walking south, toward Barbados. I couldn't say Will was something I'd lost, really, since I'd never had him in the first place. Whatever I felt—*had* felt—for him that day at Lake Okeechobee seemed so long ago and far away, like a dream.

I crossed the nautical rope between Les Anges and Will's family's property. Maybe a thousand feet in front of me was a small structure I'd never noticed before, illuminated by gaslight torches. There was no one else on the beach, so I went to investigate. As I got closer, I saw that the structure was a thatched-roof pavilion with a bar and a few tables randomly scattered across a plank deck. The things Palm Beachers did to re-create a place where the gross national product didn't equal one Palm Beach family's fortune were simply too ironic for words.

I began humming Bob Marley's "One Love."

"Wrong island."

I spun, surprised to see Will stepping through the sand in a black tuxedo minus the tie, his white shirt open at the collar.

He looked like one of those Rat Pack guys from the sixties, like Frank Sinatra or Dean Martin, singers my counterculture parents had loathed. Will's sapphire-colored eyes shone in the torchlight.

"It really does scream Caribbean, doesn't it?" he asked conversationally, as if we were casual friends who'd happened to run in to each other. "It was my stepmother's idea. She and my father went to, you guessed it, Barbados for their honeymoon. I'm sure they never left the resort and saw nothing of the actual island, but it's the thought that counts." He sat on one of the bar stools, his hands shoved deep into his pockets. "So, hi."

"Hi. Long time no see." I winced. Had I really just said long time no see? Me? Miss Wit? "I love a guy who trolls the beach in a tux," I added. There. That was better.

"My dad's giving a thing for some buyers. Black-tie. Very stuffy bunch." He nearly smiled, but not in a happy way.

"Not really Hanan's clientele?"

Will laughed. "My father would die before he'd show Hanan's work."

I kicked a toe into the sand. "But you told her you were going to. She's counting on you."

Will frowned. "Never a wise thing to do." He went behind the bar. "How about a Red Stripe?"

"Aren't we supposed to be in Barbados? Someone has geography issues."

"That would be the stepmother again. It's not her strong suit. So few things are." He took two beers from a small fridge, handed me one, and clinked his bottle against mine. We both took long sips. Will leaned an elbow on the bar. "I was actually about to come see you."

Okay, yeah, I admit it. I got a little thrill. "That's nice."

"To wish the twins good luck tomorrow," he clarified.

Ouch.

"We just got back from London," he explained. "We were there for the winter auctions. Sotheby's, Christie's. Then Tajan in Paris."

"Nice life."

"Someone has to live it." He took another long sip. "So I was wondering how they're doing. If they're ready for their test."

I ran my thumbnail around the beer bottle. "Honestly? I don't know. But I do know they both worked their asses off."

"That's a first."

"I'll tell you something even more impressive. Laurel paid me."

"Wow. That should be on the front page of *The Shiny Sheet*." Will came around the bar. "Walk?"

"Sure."

We headed for the waterline, walking in silence. Something he'd said was bothering me. "Why did you say before that it isn't wise to count on you?"

"Every once in a while I get delusions of independence— forge out on my own with my own gallery, representing the kind of art that I love . . ." He shrugged. "But let's face it, Megan. I'm a rich kid who's never really had to work hard at anything. Why bother?"

"To prove that you're not your father."

He glanced at me. "To you?"

"To yourself."

"Ah."

We strolled on in silence as the waves rushed to shore.

"I have a question, Megan Smith," Will said at last. "That

morning on Worth Avenue. That guy in the café. And at the Christmas ball. Who was he, really?"

A brief editorial comment: Lies are exhausting.

Suddenly, I was overcome with malaise. I wanted to sink into the sand and go to sleep. Which would be one more way for me to avoid telling the truth.

Okay. So, no sand nap. I would tell Will now and the twins tomorrow. But how to start? Where to begin?

"I knew James at Yale," I said carefully.

"Yeah, I kind of got that." I heard the tension in Will's voice. "And?"

"And there was a time when we were … close."

"I kind of got that, too. But why didn't you just tell me?"

"I should have," I agreed. "When I first came here, after the twins pulled that nude-swim thing—I hated them. I hated their friends. And *you* were one of the friends."

"What does that have to do with the Yale guy?"

I sighed. "Just…" I cracked my knuckles, which is not something I usually do. "Stay with me, it's a long story."

"Ooooh-kay." Will knit his eyebrows at me, kicking at the sand as he walked.

"Until we went to see Hanan, I didn't really care who you were or what you thought. But then everything changed."

He stopped walking and turned to me, waiting.

"Because I saw who you really were." I stopped walking, too. "And who you really were—are—is so … so … I thought if you knew—"

In the movies, this is where the girl's great confession grinds to a screeching halt, the guy pulls the girl to him, and then he kisses the hell out of her.

Ladies and gentlemen, welcome to my movie moment.

His lips were on mine, one hand tangled in my hair, the other pressing me to him. Everything I'd ever imagined, including my bathtub fantasies, was left in the dust by the breathless reality of his mouth on mine. My brain flicked momentarily to Lily and how I'd seen him kiss her, too, but then he tugged off my jacket and pulled my T-shirt over my head, and all thoughts of everything and everyone were gone. Then he put his tux jacket on the sand and laid me down on it. Soon I was naked and he was naked and I understood all those movie metaphors about crashing waves.

I'm pretty sure I moaned some things that would indicate I really, really liked what was happening. I was even happy that I'd surrendered the pink—and that Will was the one who would see my, um, art.

It turns out that sex on the beach really is hot. I mean, the sand thing does add a certain...tactile element that you're not necessarily looking for, but it couldn't have bothered either of us very much, because we went back for seconds. What can I tell you? I had a lot of sexual tension built up.

I think we fell asleep briefly, what with all the fresh air, deep breathing, and aerobic activity. I woke up in Will's arms. He kissed my forehead. Then his lips started heading south. I tugged him back up to me.

"Let's go to my bed," I whispered to him. "I'll sneak you in."

"How high school," Will teased. He rose and hoisted me up. I pulled on my T-shirt and jeans but balled up my La Perlas in my jean jacket. Hand in hand, we headed for Les Anges. Every few feet he stopped to kiss me, to whisper my name in a throaty voice.

We climbed the stone steps and padded across the pool deck, then tiptoed to the front door of the twins' manse. He pinched my ass on the way up the grand curving staircase. I swatted at him and put a finger to my lips, warning him to be quiet. At the top of the stairs, he pulled me to him again and gave me another sizzling kiss.

Something between a groan and a sigh escaped from my mouth. If my IQ hadn't dropped to somewhere south of my navel, I probably would have been embarrassed. But it had, so I wasn't.

I was about to point the way to my suite, when the lights snapped on. There were Sage and Rose, blocking the way. They both wore Juicy Couture sweats. There was a hard darkness in their eyes that said something was terribly wrong.

"What's the matter?" I asked. "Why aren't you—"

"How could you?" Rose asked, her face gray under her tan.

"We know everything." Sage stared at me with pure hate.

chapter thirty-five

Rose took in the sand in my hair, the sand in Will's hair, the La Perla thong sticking out of my jean jacket pocket, and made the obvious leap. "You two were doing it on the beach."

Will and I stood there. The visual clues were kind of hard to deny.

"Would you like to know who you just fucked?" Sage asked Will savagely. "Or should I say, who you're getting fucked by?"

That was when I saw what was dangling on a cord from Sage's left hand.

My flash drive. Oh God. My flash drive. How could I have been so stupid? I had erased all my Palm Beach notes on my computer after we'd watched the sunrise on New Year's morning. I'd even wiped out my computer's trash bin. But I hadn't thought about the backup on my flash drive. They must have read every damning note I'd taken over six weeks here in Palm Beach.

"What's she talking about?" Will asked me.

Sage smiled coldly and twirled the flash drive. "Do you want to tell him, Megan? Or should we?"

I wanted to barf, or run away, or fall to my knees and plead for mercy. But of course, I couldn't do any of that. Instead, I stood there while the twins launched into the story of how they'd found me out.

After I'd left to walk on the beach, they'd been too nervous to sleep, they explained. So they'd come to my room to talk. Since I wasn't there, they'd decided to review a few practice SAT problems for the hell of it.

"We booted up your iBook to look for some examples," Rose told me. "We couldn't find any files, and then we saw this."

Sage held up my flash drive. "So we plugged it in, and what do you think we saw, Will?" she asked him. "Files. With our names on them."

"Your name, too, Will," Rose added.

I looked at him for the first time. His face was torn by emotions, and I could read them all. Suspicion. Doubt. Hope that this wasn't true. Fear that it was.

"Ask her what's in those files," Sage urged him.

"You don't have to ask, Will. I'll tell you." My knees were weak, but on I went. "They're notes. For an article I was going to write about Palm Beach. But I changed my mind and decided not to write it. I deleted them from my hard drive. I guess I forgot to get rid of the backup."

I saw Will's expression change from confusion to anger. "You really expect us to believe that, Megan? A girl as smart as you are 'forgot' to erase her backup?"

"It's the truth," I insisted.

"*Truth?* Jesus, Megan." Sage laughed bitterly. "You pretended to tutor us, pretended to be our friend, when all the time it was a big act to fuck us in print."

"And do you want to know what she said about you, Will?" Rose asked with cold fury. "That you're a pathetic former frat boy who hangs out with high school girls. That what others would call statutory rape, you call getting lucky."

"You wrote that?" he asked me.

"I can explain," I said in the timeworn fashion of those caught in the act. "I made those notes before I really knew you—I was being flip because I was angry, like I told you on the beach." I turned back to the twins. "When I first came here, I really did come as a tutor. I didn't have any other agenda."

"Oh, please," Sage scoffed. "Who the hell are you? What's your name? And don't tell us it's fucking Megan Smith."

"But it *is* Megan Smith," I said miserably.

"Yuh," Sage scoffed. "I bet. So where are you from, Megan Smith?"

I gulped hard. "I was raised in Concord, New Hampshire. I went to public school. My dad's a professor at the University of New Hampshire. My mom's a nurse-practitioner."

"So you're not from Philadelphia," Will stated. Then he swore under his breath. "I knew there was something off."

"I never said that I was from Philadelphia, actually," I pointed out in a lame attempt to explain myself. I turned to the twins. "You guys did a Google search and decided some rich girl from there was me. And okay, I let you think it. But if I hadn't, you never would have studied with me."

"But once we were studying, you didn't correct the record, did you?" Sage challenged.

"No," I said miserably. "I didn't."

"Not even after you allegedly wiped out your notes?"

I shook my head. The facts were the facts. I sneaked a glance at the twins. Rose looked like she was ready to cry. Sage, on the other hand, was obviously prepared for first-degree homicide.

"Megan, there's one thing I don't understand," Rose murmured.

"Yes?"

"If you're not the girl from Philadelphia, and you're not rich—where'd you get all the clothes?"

"Marco. He helped me."

"We'll be talking to Grandma." Sage sniffed, her eyes narrowed.

There was no sense in telling her that Grandma already knew. She'd find out soon enough.

"Why'd you do it?" Will asked, bewildered. "Why did you lie about everything?"

"I tried to tell you before . . . on the beach. That's what I was trying to say before we—you know." I shook my head, trying to remove my momentary mental lapse into beach ecstasy from my brain. "When I first came here, I didn't even know why I was here. But then that first night, when they played that trick on me and—"

"Hold on," Will ordered. "You're blaming this on the twins?"

"No," I said. "I mean . . . Yes, I did the research. Yes, I took notes. But——"

"You changed your mind about writing it," Rose finished the sentence for me in a jeering singsong.

"I'm telling you the truth, Rose," I insisted, hearing my voice shake. "And I just wish . . . I wish you could find it in your heart to believe me."

Sage made a face. "Why should we? You lied about everything."

"Because if you look at my iBook, the files are gone. And I haven't taken a single note in two weeks!"

"She fucking used us, Rose," Sage concluded. "And she wanted to make money for doing it."

"But look at all the work I did with you," I pointed out. "That was real!"

"Anyone could have done that," Rose said, her voice flat. She took the flash drive from her sister and tossed it at me. "I *trusted* you."

What could I possibly say? "I'm so, *so* sorry." I reached for her hand, but she jerked it away from me.

"Tell it to someone who cares," she spat.

"Megan?" Will asked, chewing on the inside of his cheek. "That guy James? Was he in on this, too?" He saw the answer in my eyes. "Holy shit," he muttered, as much to himself as to me. " He *was*."

"Who's James?" Sage demanded.

"Ask your tutor," Will told her.

There was nothing I could say or do, no explanation I could

give, that would make the three of them understand. It was a lost cause. But I didn't want the girls to hurt themselves any more than I'd hurt them.

"I'm so, so sorry for any pain I caused you," I told the twins. "Don't let hating me screw up your test tomorrow."

"Like you give a shit." Rose snorted. "We'll be reading about ourselves in fucking *Scoop*."

For a second I wondered how much more they knew about me. Had they made the *Scoop* connection, too? "I know you don't believe me, Rose, but I do care about you. So much. And Will—"

He shook his head. "Megan—if that really is your name— don't. Whatever you were going to say, just . . . don't."

He turned and headed down the stairs. I didn't even think about following him.

"We're going to our rooms now," Rose said. "When we get up in the morning, I strongly suggest that you be gone."

That was it. I went into my suite and shut the door behind me. Numbly, I called a cab to the airport, rinsed myself off in the shower, changed into ugly Century 21 outfit number two, and packed my stuff. It didn't take long, since I was taking back to New York only what I'd brought from New York. Everything else—the clothes from Marco and the girls, the makeup, the gear, the bling, even the flatiron—I piled neatly on the bed. On top of it all, I put the check from Laurel, the ATM card to the bank account Laurel had opened for me, and my flash drive.

I wrote a note to Marco, too. He'd befriended me when I'd needed a friend the most. What had I done? I had used him. *I'm sorry* felt grossly inadequate, but I said it anyway.

Then, dressed exactly as I'd arrived at Les Anges, with the same backpack over my shoulder, I headed for the front gate to meet my cab, stopping only to slip my note under the door of Marco's cottage. I was leaving behind everything I'd gotten in Palm Beach—everything, including my heart.

chapter thirty-six

I jammed my hands in my pockets against the biting cold as I trudged up the steps at the Astor Place subway stop on the downtown number 6.

The night before had been the worst of my life. Beavering half of New York and getting burned out of my apartment paled in comparison. I'd huddled in the Palm Beach airport until 6:10 A.M., when I was finally able to get on a flight to La Guardia, and then I'd been shoved into coach purgatory between a crying baby and a hygienically challenged guy. It reminded me of one of my earlier vocab lessons with the girls—a thought that made me smile before I found my chin trembling.

There was DIRECTV on my seat back, but I couldn't watch. All I could do was think of how I'd made a mess not just of my life but of a lot of other lives, too. I willed Rose and Sage to be at the SAT testing center in West Palm. I hoped with everything I had that they would put aside last night and do their best.

The weather in New York was gray and fifty degrees colder than in Palm Beach. I was surrounded by the pasty faces of an urban workforce who didn't get much sun. When I reached the top step of the Astor Place station, the winter storm that had been in the offing since I landed smacked me like a slap of reproach. Icy wind bit my face; slanting snow gathered on my eyelashes. I had no gloves, boots, scarf, hat, or jacket. When I'd departed in such a hurry from New York two months ago, I hadn't given a thought to the fact that I'd be returning in the middle of winter.

A middle-aged man in a long coat racing for the subway steps jostled me; I slipped on the icy sidewalk. Out went my feet. I fell heavily to the ground, my ass landing in one of those snow/slush/dog pee puddles that just scream *winter in New York*.

Welcome home.

Thoroughly soaked, teeth chattering, I slogged east past the cheap-chic shops and restaurants of St. Mark's Place. When I got to East Seventh Street, the bells of St. Stanislaus began to chime as I let myself into my old building. It no longer smelled of smoke, but of the ethnic dishes cooked by its residents: stuffed cabbage from the Polish lady on the ground level, kimchi from the Korean couple on two, homemade borscht from the Russian family on three, serious cheeba from the Rasta on four.

And then, finally, I was at my door. It was a good thing, too. My ass had frozen into an ice sculpture.

I'd called Charma from La Guardia to warn her that I'd be home a little bit early. There'd been no answer, which had led me to think that she was out doing one of her children's theater tours. But when I unlocked the three locks and opened the door, I found Charma oh so naked and oh so *entwined* with the guy in the Wolfmother T-shirt from the park that Sunday from so long ago, when I'd first lost my backpack.

I stumbled back into the hallway and slammed the door shut. "Ohmigod. I am so sorry!" I yelled through the door. "I'll be back!"

"No, wait, don't go! We'll get dressed!" Charma yelled back.

I was frozen and miserable enough to wait. A few moments later, Charma opened the door, wearing a green bathrobe. I saw Wolfmother behind her, zipping up his jeans with difficulty. Apparently, my surprise entrance hadn't yet deflated his enthusiasm.

"I am so sorry!" I repeated as I stepped back into the apartment.

Charma laughed. "Why don't you have a coat? Change clothes, and I'll make tea." I went into the bathroom and dug out my other Century 21 outfit from my backpack, thankful it was dry, but depressed as hell to be putting it on. I laid my clothes over the shower-curtain pole.

"Much better," Charma approved when I came back out. She gave me a big hug. "Welcome home! Megan, this is Gary Carner. Gary, this is my roommate, Megan."

He grinned and pointed at me. "You're the one who calls me Wolfmother, right? Because of the T-shirt I was wearing the day I met Charma."

"Guilty," I admitted. "I called and said I'd be early," I told Charma. "I guess I should have—"

"No big deal," Wolfmother cut in. "Just doin' what comes naturally."

Charma smiled lovingly at Wolfmother and put on a tea-kettle in the kitchen. I wandered through an apartment whose four walls were familiar but whose contents were entirely new to me. Gone was the ruined found-on-the-street gear, replaced by the sixties Levittown-chic furniture that had once belonged to Charma's grandmother. There was one other surprise—what had been Charma's bedroom before the fire was now subdivided into two smaller spaces by a removable dividing wall. There was a single platform bed in each little room. It was clear which of these was mine—the one that wasn't strewn with clothing and massage oil.

"You like?" Charma asked, handing me a mug.

After my suite at the twins' manse, these looked like jail cells. No, wait. Coffins.

"It's great," I replied, trying to hide my dismay.

"Charma's really loud when we fuck," Wolfmother told me. "I don't think those dividers will do much. So maybe you can just crank your iPod."

"Don't you guys ever go to your place?" I asked him, sipping my tea and trying to sound casual.

"I used to be in a thing with my roommate," Wolfmother explained. "So we mostly chill here."

We went back to the kitchen and sat at the new—to me, anyway—pea-green Formica table.

"How come you're home early?" Charma wondered. "I thought you weren't coming until tomorrow."

"I thought I wasn't coming until tomorrow, either," I confessed.

"So?"

Maybe I would have filled Charma in if Wolfmother aka Gary aka Oversharing Guy hadn't been scratching his crotch that I was already much too familiar with.

"There was a problem. I came home. That's it."

Charma looked closely at me. "What do you mean, 'a problem'? Do you still get the money if the twins get in to Duke?"

"Like that's gonna happen!" Wolfmother interjected, chuckling. "Charma told me all about your gig, and I saw their thing in *Vanity Fair*. Laughed my ass off."

"Actually," I said, warming my hands on the mug, "they might just get in."

"I'm pretty sure an IQ is mandatory," Wolfmother opined.

"Megs, you didn't answer my question," Charma said. "Will you still get the money or not?"

I shook my head.

"Wait, *what?*" Charma exclaimed. "They got all that work out of you, and then they fucked you?"

"No, babe, I fucked *you*." Wolfmother leaned over to kiss Charma, then smiled at me. "Charma found her G-spot yesterday. Isn't that a killer?"

Killer? I was going to have to kill him.

"Wow," I ventured.

"Did you have any idea it was coming?" Charma asked. She pointed at Wolfmother. "And don't say *I'm* coming!" She giggled.

"Not a clue. I mean..." I sipped my tea. "It was terrible at first. All they did was insult me. I did this whole makeover thing just so I'd fit in. In Palm Beach, you're either a hair-makeup-designer-clothes diva, or you're the hired help. It's a whole subculture I'd never seen before."

"Gotta love that elitist shit!" Wolfmother crowed. "Tell us more."

"You name a vice, Palm Beach kids have it," I offered.

"You partied with those guys?" Wolfmother queried.

"I've been to three charity balls in the last six weeks, and I missed twice that many." I shook my head at the insanity of it all.

"And you got to know a lot of those kids personally?" he asked.

"Better than I ever thought I would."

Wolfmother scratched the stubble on his chin and looked at me intently. "Charma told me you worked for *Scoop* before you went to Florida."

"Uh-huh."

"You've done more serious writing than that?"

"When I was at Yale." I yawned and realized how tired I was.

"Did Charma tell you what I do for a living?"

I drained my tea and rose to set the cup in the sink. "Nope."

"I'm a magazine editor. At *Rockit*. Funny, I never saw you in the building."

My exhaustion evaporated in an instant. Wolfmother was an editor at *the* magazine where I wanted to write? He and Charma could do it all night, every night, and I'd be their one-woman cheering section if he'd give me a chance to show him my clips.

I tried to remain cool. On the surface, at least. "That's a great magazine."

"I'd love to see what you have to say about your experience down there," he suggested. "If you're interested."

Oh my God. *Was I interested?* I had enough material for five articles. "Definitely."

"You know our editorial stance, right? Don't hold back. Tell it all. The juicier the better—sex, drugs, rock and roll. If it's good, I can make it a feature. Say, ten to twelve thousand words?"

Ten to twelve thousand words? That was major. Career-making major.

"Sounds interesting," I mused, as if it were no big thing and I got offered to do a major feature for *Rockit* every day.

"Go for it, Megan," Charma urged. "That's exactly the kind of story you always said you wanted to write."

Wolfmother and Charma decided to have breakfast at San Loco on Tenth and A, but I declined the offer to join them. All I wanted was a hot bath. Natch, there was no hot water. So I tried to go to sleep, but even as exhausted as I was, it was a lost cause. I had grown used to the sound of the ocean and the birds in the palm trees, not the roar and rumble of the Department of Sanitation trucks and ambulances screaming north on First Avenue every few minutes.

But mostly, it was the roar in my head that kept me awake. I had no job and no money. Wolfmother had offered me a lifeline. What kind of a fool wouldn't grab hold?

I got out my iBook, propped myself up on two pillows, and booted it up. I didn't have my flash drive anymore, but I knew I wouldn't need it. Everything I needed to remember was inside my head. I opened a new document and started to type:

HOW TO TEACH FILTHY RICH GIRLS
by Megan Smith

If a waitress works a 6-hour shift, at a pay rate of $2.10 per hour plus tips, and if her tips average out to $11.00 per hour, how much will she earn on an average night?

(a) $78.60
(b) $67.80
(c) $76.80
(d) $68.70
(e) What difference does it make? She'll never afford her rent, anyway.

chapter thirty-seven

*W*ould you like gravy on your kasha varnishkes?" I asked the guy with the blue Mohawk. He wore a woolly black sweater with holes in it over a fishnet shirt. I noticed a small skull tattooed on his Adam's apple. With him was a girl with a shaved head and large discs inserted into her earlobes that stretched them to the size of dessert plates.

"Yeah, sure," Mohawk replied, sipping the black coffee I'd already brought him and Earlobe Girl.

"And two shots of vodka," Earlobe Girl added. "For both of us."

They were seated at one of the eight two-seat booths that had been my section ever since I'd started waitressing at Tver, the low-budget Russian restaurant and bar on East Tenth Street near Avenue B, two days after I got back from Florida. This was my third day on the job, and I was hoping that Vadim, the owner, would push me up to the bigger tables soon. Waitresses live on their tips. More bodies equaled more money, which I—sans Laurel's ATM card—needed badly.

Broke didn't begin to cover my present state of affairs. I had arrived with a couple of hundred dollars in cash from my expense money. I'd used some to buy cheap makeup at Duane Reade and almost as cheap clothes at the Sacred Threads consignment shop down the block from my apartment. You'd be surprised at the gems some people will throw away.

I was able to convince Vadim that I wasn't your typical East Village twentysomething hipster who would flake out and not show up to work, so he offered me a job the same day I applied. Sadly, the sartorial standards of his establishment were stuck in the Soviet era—we were forced to wear the world's ugliest black-with-white-apron waitress uniforms. If you had anything approaching womanly hips, which, thanks to Marco's everything, I certainly did, the shiny material only magnified them.

"Stoli?" I asked Earlobe Girl, pen poised over my order pad. Vadim had instructed his waitresses to always ask if the customers wanted the most expensive brand of alcohol. They never did.

Mohawk looked at me like I was crazy. "If we wanted Stoli, do you think we'd be eating *here?*"

"Bar pour," I confirmed, writing it on my order pad. "I'll have your drinks in a minute."

"Bring extra pickles," Mohawk added, then started to dig for gold in his left nostril.

I stifled the urge to puke. "Will do."

I knew I was lucky to have the gig, since I'd applied without any experience. My shift ran from four P.M. to midnight, and it was almost always busy. Being one of the few places left in the East Village where you could have dinner and drink for under twenty bucks, Tver was very popular. Over the general noise and the vintage Blondie blaring from the sound system, I had to shout my drink order to Vitaly, who was Vadim's eldest son. Then I went to the kitchen and put in my food order with Sergei, the owner's cousin. Tver was very much a family affair.

I held a glass under the Diet Coke dispenser, half-filled it, and drained it quickly before I hit the floor again. My feet pulsed with pain, and I felt as if someone were applying a hot poker to my lower back. Who knew waitressing was such hard work? I rued my decision not to work out while I'd been in Palm Beach; I was probably carrying around ten extra pounds.

I placed my palm on my lower back and pushed, then bent over to touch the floor with my palms. Boris gave me a dirty look. He was only ever nice to the Russian waitresses who worked three times as fast and four times as efficiently as I did.

So, back to it. This would probably be my last table before James arrived. I'd called him earlier in the day and asked him to meet me in the bar at twelve-thirty. Though my shift ended at midnight, I was responsible for refilling the pickle bowls, salt, pepper, ketchup, and mustard containers, as well as restocking the bar with lemon and lime slices and olives before I left. Usually, I was in a hurry to get through all of this so I could go home and collapse.

Tonight, though, I'd see James, whom I'd neither seen nor even talked to since coming back to New York four days ago.

I'd called him at his office. And to be honest, he hadn't sounded thrilled to hear from me. I had a sneaking suspicion that James-and-Megan had run its course, and not just from my side of the equation. I didn't have many regrets about it. He'd been good for me, and I hoped I'd been good for him, at a certain time and place in our lives. It's hard to move on, though, even when you know it's the right thing to do.

I brought Mohawk and Earlobe Girl their shots and their pickles, followed by their food. Then I took a slice of poppy-seed cake and coffee to a leather-clad elderly gay couple who'd apparently gotten lost on the way uptown from West Street. They had matching foreheads frozen in the perpetual surprise that I now knew, thanks to Marco, was the sign of a bad brow lift.

As I moved into my side work, I kept one eye out for James. Life is so funny. A year earlier, I would have been watching for him with excitement—joy, even. Now all I felt was trepidation.

I was finishing with the olives at the bar when James stepped through the front door. He was dressed for the weather—hat, gloves, heavy cashmere topcoat. For a moment I felt the rush of loving him. But it was like pain in a phantom limb, something that was no longer there.

"Damn, it's freezing out there," he greeted me.

"Hey. I just have to deliver checks on my last two tables and bring them their bills," I told him. "It won't take long."

He went to the bar, ordered a Scotch on the rocks, and watched me finish my work. Okay, so I have an ego—I hated that I was wearing the god-awful uniform. Even if I was no longer in love with him, I still wanted his last image of me to be "Damn, she looks good," and not, "Damn, she's got way too much junk in that trunk."

Finally, I was done, and I slipped onto the bar stool next to James's. Vitaly glanced my way. "Usual, Megan?" he asked.

I nodded. At the end of my shift on my first night of work, I'd asked for a flirtini, and Vitaly had looked at me blankly. Not only was his English still dicey after just two years in America, but no one in the history of the restaurant had ever ordered a flirtini, and probably—barring me—no one else ever would. I'd told him the ingredients, and he'd made an extra-big one, pouring some of the overflow into a second cocktail glass. He'd taken a sip and decided it was something that sounded like *taxi-bien*, which, I would learn the next day, means *so-so* in Russian. In Russian, *so-so* is quite a compliment.

"So . . . Yale to waitressing," James said, remarking on the obvious.

"And my back is killing me. Who knew downward mobility would be so painful?"

He didn't laugh. He just looked sad.

I drank half my flirtini in one swallow. It reminded me of the first one I'd ever had, at the Red and White ball. "I know we parted badly in Palm Beach," I began, "and I've been thinking a lot about—"

"Wait . . ." He finished his scotch. "I don't know how to say this except to just say it. There's someone else."

Wait, *someone* else? *Heather* else? "Heather?" I asked, not even trying to hide my distaste at the thought. "I knew she was still after you—"

"It's not Heather." He smiled. "Although you're right. After she got back from Turks and Caicos, she told me she thought there was something between you and that Will guy—that she had to tell me as a friend."

I shrank back in my seat. It would have been so much easier if I could have worked up some self-righteous indignation.

"And then she tried to kiss me."

Oh. I felt my indignation inflating. How dare she try to kiss my kind-of boyfriend!

"But I'd already met someone else. At the *East Coast* party on New Year's Eve," James explained.

"She's a writer," I said, and felt my body deflate again. A more accomplished writer than I and undoubtedly a Heather clone—tall, blond, athletic, and curvy, holding the PEN/Faulkner award. The kind of writer whose publisher hires Annie Leibovitz to do the jacket photo and then blows the photo up to the whole back cover of her novel. The kind of writer who would make James's parents weep with joy to be rid of me.

"Actually, she was bartending at the New Year's Eve party."

Vitaly put another round of drinks in front of us. I took a serious swallow of flirtini number two.

"While she's working on her very literary novel?" I asked.

"Shoe-Shoe isn't a writer. She just graduated from massage therapy school."

"Painter?" I guessed. "Actress? Musician?"

"No."

James had fallen for a massage therapist. "What did you say her name was, again?"

"Shoe-Shoe." He took a swallow of his second Scotch. "Spelled *X-I-U X-I-U*. Her real name is Emily, but she took the name after a really life-changing trip to Taiwan last year. It came to her in a dream. She's so *authentic*, Megan."

Just when you think you know a person. Merely picturing Xiu-Xiu, the authentic bartender-slash-massage-therapist, getting introduced to James's snob of a mother filled me with a helium-light kind of joy.

Once, in a rare heart-to-heart, my own brilliant mother had told me that many—possibly most—men who are very smart give lip service to wanting a very smart woman. In the end, they choose someone less threatening. My father, she believed, was one of the rare brilliant guys who really did want a brilliant woman.

Possibly, James was not.

I smiled at him. "I wish you and Xiu-Xiu all the best."

"Hey, thanks for being so great about this." He squeezed my hand. "How about you?"

I shrugged. "I'm making it up as I go along."

"No guy? Not that guy Will? Heather wasn't on to something?" he joked.

I thought about Will way too often. It was like wiggling your tongue in a cavity when you couldn't afford to go to the dentist. It hurt to do it, I knew I shouldn't do it, and yet I kept doing it anyway. "Not a chance," I told him.

"That's too bad." James finished his Scotch and wiped his lips with a cocktail napkin. "I hate to see you working in a place like this, though. You really should reconsider the article."

"Oh, I have," I assured him.

"You have?" He looked surprised and proud at the same time.

"It's for *Rockit*. An editor wants to see it. I should have a draft done by the end of next week. Twelve thousand words."

"Twelve thou?" He whistled softly. "That's great. Hey, if you want me to give it a read before you send it in—"

"I got it covered."

He smiled sadly, as if realizing that our reading and editing each other's work was a thing of the past. "Walk me out?"

Vitaly told us the drinks were on the house. I thanked him, went into the kitchen to clock out, and then stuffed my arms into a puffy down jacket too small to zip that I'd borrowed from Charma. It made me look like the Pillsbury Doughboy. James and I walked together along Avenue A toward East Seventh Street and then to my building. I looked up at the fire escape and remembered how I'd flashed half the neighborhood only nine weeks before. It seemed like a lifetime ago.

"So. Your place is okay now?" he asked.

"All fixed up."

"Well..." He opened his arms, and I went into them. Briefly, I wanted to stay there, in a place that had been good and safe for so long. But things change. I longed for that comfort, but I knew I didn't belong there anymore.

"Good luck with Xiu-Xiu. With everything," I told him, and meant it.

"You, too, Megan. I'll be looking for your story in *Rockit*."

I smiled. "So will I."

It was cold, and it was dark. But I stood on the front stoop and watched him walk away.

chapter thirty-eight

The next day, in a brief but significant lapse in sanity, I agreed to meet my sister at her hot-shit gym on the Upper West Side. I had considered sending a postcard claiming a spiritual awakening and a sojourn at an ashram in Kathmandu, but what with the Manhattan postmark and our having the same parents and all, I felt certain she'd figure out that I was back in New York.

Where was I supposed to begin with her? "I got fired from my job in Palm Beach." Now, *there's* a conversation starter. Or how about: "Just curious, did that guy you met on New Year's Eve kiss anything besides your lips?" I mean, I might as well settle down in my coffin and hand over the nails and the hammer.

In too many ways, it felt like the same-old, same-old. Lily had gotten acting and modeling work right out of Brown. She got whatever guy she wanted. And then there was me. Even with a Yale degree, the best job I'd been able to get was at *Scoop*, and I'd gotten fired from that. Job number two in Palm Beach? Fired from that. First guy whose kisses made my toes curl—that would be Will—essentially, I'd been fired from that, too.

Talk about exacerbating the old sister-rivalry thing.

Lily's daily routine was to go to Power Play, a small but exceedingly hip gym on the Upper West Side, specifically designed for those who didn't want to deal with the public during their morning workout. Then she'd have a late lunch with friends at a health food restaurant where mung beans were considered a main course. After that, she'd go either to acting class or to a movie; then there was her evening's performance, often followed by drinks or a light meal with whichever famous person happened to come that night to witness her breathtaking performance.

Since my shift at Tver started at four, I figured an eleven A.M. rendezvous at her gym would give me sufficient time to bitch through twenty minutes of light torture and then take off to enjoy a lunch heavy on the two main food groups—fat and sugar—and don my Waitress Woman costume for my evening's performance.

I beat Lily to Power Play and waited for her in the overpriced snack bar. Most people don't make an effort when dressing for the gym. But hey, I was meeting Lily, so I'd found the perfect leave-in conditioner to tame and render glossy my long curls. I'd done the twins' routine with my drugstore cosmetics. They weren't Stila and NARS, but it turns out L'Oreal and Maybelline aren't bad. I wore Ralph Lauren gray trousers that sat just below my waist (twelve bucks at Sacred Threads, due to an uneven thread in the right cuff) and a very fitted white T-shirt (men's Fruit of the Loom) under a shrunken plaid wool jacket with oversize velvet buttons (designer tag ripped out but probably Chanel, eighteen bucks at Housing Works).

When Lily arrived, she looked at me strangely, then grinned and hugged me. She got me a guest pass, and we changed in the surprisingly Spartan locker room. She asked me about Palm Beach, of course. I didn't offer much and left out the minor detail that I'd been fired. She wondered when the twins would know their SAT results. I said in a week. She said she was pulling for us.

Power Play was just two rooms—one for cardio, the other for weight training. No fancy step classes, no hatha yoga, no Billy Blanks kickboxing. In return, members got exclusivity, a nonexistent gawk factor, and no lines to use the machines. We started on a couple of treadmills. I watched Lily set hers so that the speed and the incline would increase gradually from a gentle warm-up to a really challenging workout.

If she could do it, I could do it.

Ten minutes later, she was beginning to hit her stride, and I was sucking wind like a beached blowfish.

"Slow it down a little," she suggested over the techno-pop blaring through the sound system.

"I'm fine!" It was difficult to form actual words.

After about twelve minutes, the inclines kicked up to Mont Blanc height, while the rubber ripped under my sneakers at approximately the speed of Lance Armstrong doing a time trial. I grabbed the sidebars and held on for dear life. I felt like I was going one-on-one with a giant metal sumo wrestler.

"Megan, slow it down!"

"I'm fine!" I insisted.

"But you're not in shape!" she protested.

That pretty much guaranteed I wouldn't slow down. I soldiered on like an insane woman.

Suddenly, a guy with biceps the size of Suzanne de Grouchy's breasts was in front of my machine, bellowing at me through cupped hands. "Miss! You are outside your fitness range!" He wore an official Power Play trainer's muscle shirt and a little name tag that introduced him as GERALD. Without waiting for my approval, he leaned over my machine and jabbed his finger at the emergency stop button. The button did what it was supposed to. The treadmill stopped.

"If you'd like to make an appointment with one of our trainers, you can do so at the front desk," Gerald suggested. "I'd recommend it."

"I need some water," I muttered to Lily. Red-faced from both exertion and embarrassment, I made a beeline back to the locker room.

"Megan!" Lily was at my heels.

"I don't want to hear it." I pushed through the locker room door to the drinking fountain right inside and guzzled thirstily.

It was all too much: leaving Palm Beach, being poor, breaking up with James, working as a waitress, having sex on the beach with the guy I was crazy about—a guy Lily had kissed on New Year's Eve—only to have him reject me afterward. More proof, obviously, that I could never, ever compete with my sister. Even as I drank, I felt my eyes fill with tears.

Then my sister's hand was on my shoulder. "What?" she asked. "What's wrong?"

"Everything." I stood up and wiped the tears from my cheeks with the bottom of my T-shirt.

She put her arm around me. "Come on."

We went to the very back of the locker room, where there were a few modern-looking sofas along with a table of complimentary refreshments—juices, bottled water, baked goods. Lily poured us glasses of caffeine-free iced mint tea, but we took a pass on the sugar-free vegan cookies.

"Okay, tell me," Lily commanded as we took over one of the couches.

Keeping it all bottled up inside was too much work. So the truth came spilling out—partially, anyway. I told her about the exposé I'd planned to write and how the twins had found out about it. And how the twins had come to think I was someone I wasn't. When I was done, I almost smiled. I sipped the mint tea, which I'd have preferred surrounded by some really good dark chocolate.

"You know what's funny, as in ironic, not ha-ha?" I asked, bringing the conversation back to what had happened in the gym. "In some weird way, living with the twins made me feel like I was the plainer, plumper little sister all over again."

"Is that how you see yourself?"

"No, I'm downplaying my perfection in the hopes that it won't bruise your ego too badly," I said sarcastically, since the truth was too obvious. "You can't imagine how much it sucked to grow up in the shadow of beautiful, sweet, talented you."

Lily looked uncomfortable and pushed some hair behind her ear. "I hid behind that, you know."

"Behind what?"

"Being the pretty one," she said, her voice low. "You were the brainy one. I was the pretty one."

Oh, no, I was *not* letting her get away with that.

"Lily, you went to Brown—"

"And I worked my ass off for it, too, because just once I wanted Mom and Dad to talk about my brain the way they talked about yours."

"In other words, being prettier, nicer, and more talented than me wasn't enough for you," I translated. "You had to beat me at *everything*?"

"Right back atcha, sis," Lily said.

God, was that true? It was. Brains were the only category I'd won. "Well, aren't we the walking cliché?" I mused.

"Sitting clichés," she corrected. "But Megan, have you looked in the mirror lately? I mean really looked?" She set her iced-tea glass on an end table next to fanned copies of *Fitness* magazine. "When I walked in today and saw you in the snack bar, it hit me how gorgeous you are."

I cocked a brow. "Are we playing nice Lily now?"

"No, we are playing honest Lily now. Something happened while you were in Palm Beach. In addition to the bad stuff, I mean. You're beautiful, Megan. You've always been, you just never noticed. And I'm not saying it to be nice. You are the whole package—smart, talented, *and gorgeous*."

I nearly laughed. "Do you know how many times I wished you were a bitch so I could hate you?"

"That's funny. I forgot to add funny. Smart, talented, gorgeous, and funny."

"And broke. Don't forget broke. And a waitress. A broke waitress."

"You never want to take anything from me, Megan, I know that," Lily began. "But I'm your sister. Please let me loan you some money? I've got it, I'll never miss it, and you need it."

She was right. Taking a loan from her would mean I was beholden in some way. But wasn't it about time for me to grow up and admit that love carried with it certain responsibilities? Like accepting help when you needed it, the same way you would give it if it were needed from you? Like being completely honest?

God. Maturity sucks.

I cleared my throat. "There's something else I didn't tell you about Palm Beach."

"What?"

This was the hardest thing of all. "That guy I introduced you to on New Year's Eve? Will Phillips, who lives next door to the twins? We kind of ... sort of almost had a thing."

The equivocation queen strikes again. Oh, fuck it.

"I fell for him so hard," I blurted out. "And then at New Year's, I saw him kissing you, but he didn't know you were my sister, and you didn't know I cared about him because I was lying to everyone about everything. Will and I hooked up that last night I was in Palm Beach. He was with me when the twins confronted me, so now he hates me as much as they do." I drained the last of my iced tea. "And that is that end of my sordid little confessional."

"Relax. It was one kiss at midnight," Lily assured me. "Besides, he's all wrong for me."

"Yeah, gorgeous and rich—there's a romantic deal-breaker," I quipped.

"The truth is, I kind of wanted more to happen, but then ..."

She smiled. "He said he was still kind of holding out for some-one else."

Me? He'd been holding out for me all that time? I rubbed my chest as if touching the place that was breaking inside of me would somehow help.

The pain would fade with time, I knew that. But I also knew a scar would remain, a ragged place inside of me, yearning for what might have been.

chapter thirty-nine

An intern stuck in her multiple-face-piercings-means-I'm-so-hip phase ushered me into *Rockit*'s conference room and told me to wait. I pulled off Charma's puffy jacket and took a seat. It was eerie being there, an exact replica of *Scoop*'s conference room seven floors below: same standard-issue black table, same Office Depot leatherette chairs. The only difference was that here, someone in charge had a whiteboard fetish. There were three of them on the walls, and one had somehow been attached to the picture window, destroying a perfectly lovely view of the Metropolitan Life clock tower across the street.

So many times at *Scoop*, when I'd been creating photo captions about the stars and their diets, the stars and their boyfriends, and the stars and their anorexia, I'd dreamed of seeing my byline in *Rockit*. Now, at long last, I was just an editor's okay away from having my dream come true. I'd uploaded my article to Gary—now that we were on professional terms, I willed myself not to think of him as Wolfmother—on Wednesday and asked for a meeting on Friday to discuss it with him. I knew I was being pushy, but this was my chance.

"Morning, Megan." Gary loped into the room. He wore a blue shirt with frayed cuffs and jeans with the baggy butt that comes from too much wearing and not enough washing.

"Hi, Gary," I greeted him hopefully.

He tossed my manuscript on the conference table and dropped into a seat. "I don't get it, Megan. You know what we publish here at *Rockit*. We talked about what I wanted, so you must know that this isn't it."

I'd known that what I'd turned in wasn't the story he'd wanted. But I'd hoped that what I'd written was so good, so compelling, that he'd publish it anyway. That was why I'd asked for the meeting.

It was the story of a recent Yale graduate up to her eyeballs in debt who goes to Florida to transform two filthy-rich girls into people who could pass for scholars, but in the process gets transformed herself in ways that she never could have imagined. Turns out the filthy-rich girls have brains and heart; they were just waiting for someone to come along and nurture it. The tutor, who spent so many years resenting her sister for being the beautiful one, has something to learn, too. The twins and the people around them, especially the estate cook and his lover, show the tutor how beautiful she really is.

I'd even put in the romantic angle—me still with J. but pretending to be single. Falling for W., the Palm Beach version of the boy next door. I'd assumed he was a shallow player because he was so rich and handsome, and then it turned out the only one playing was me.

I told Gary all that.

He listened intently. "Go on," he said with a wave of his hand. "I'm with you."

"Of course there's wretched excess," I explained. "And I wrote about it—you saw that. But there are also hundreds of women in Africa who have started businesses because of Laurel's foundation, kids in hospitals who got Christmas presents, tens of millions raised by those wretchedly excessive balls. People should know that, too."

I knew I hadn't submitted a typical *Rockit* story about the seamy underbelly of life in these United States. But I was confident his readers would eat it up. They'd be inside the soul of a girl from small-town New Hampshire who had taken advantage of the assumptions of the people around her to fool one of the country's most exclusive societies into believing she was one of them. While she was doing it, she'd possibly—maybe—preserved the fortune of two Palm Beach party girls.

"They'll see it how I saw it," I told Gary. "They'll have their assumptions rocked and their prejudices exploded, just like I did. We can add a sidebar in a couple of weeks, depending on whether the twins get in to Duke or not."

I'll say this for Charma's squeeze. He really listened. Now I took a deep breath, and awaited his verdict.

"Strong pitch," he told me.

Please-please-please . . .

"You're a really good writer, Megan. But it's just not for us."

No. I'd given it my best, most impassioned shot, and he'd said no.

"Good luck placing it." Gary stood and offered his hand. I stood and shook it, then slid my rejected article into a folder and put on that fucking puffy down jacket.

He walked me to the elevator, then said goodbye. And that, as they say, was that.

I pressed the down button and let my forehead rest against the cool wall. I'd been close. *So* close.

The door opened. I got in and pressed the "L" button, realizing I had no idea what to do with the rest of the day. Since I'd come back from Palm Beach, I'd been tooling and retooling this article. Never had twelve thousand words been so carefully rewritten and self-edited. My shift at Tver didn't start until four. It was far too cold to go for a walk. I didn't want to spend the money on a movie.

The elevator stopped on eight—one of the two floors occupied by *Scoop*.

The door opened. Debra Wurtzel, the last person on the planet I wanted to see at that particular moment, stepped on.

And the fun kept on coming.

She eyed me coldly. "Nice makeover, Megan. Maybe you should also consider a new set of ethics."

Fuck. She knew. Well, that made sense. Laurel Limoges was her friend.

"You heard." My voice was hollow.

"Of *course* I heard. It took me an hour to convince Laurel that I had nothing to do with your 'research.'"

We rode in silence the rest of the way down.

"I wasn't going to write it, " I told her as we got out of the elevator. I knew it sounded as empty as it had that last night at Les Anges.

"Uh-huh." It was obvious she didn't believe me. "What brings you to the building?" she asked as she pulled on a pair of leather gloves.

"I had a meeting at *Rockit*."

That got her attention.

"They're interviewing you?"

"No, I...I wrote a story. Freelance."

"About Palm Beach?" She narrowed her eyes at me. "You're a disgrace, Megan."

Everyone reaches her limit. Even me. "Think whatever you want, Debra," I said wearily. "I killed the Palm Beach exposé because while it *was* completely true, it wasn't a completely honest picture. What I gave to *Rockit* was a story about me and how being in Palm Beach changed me. It's a hundred percent true *and* a hundred percent honest. But you'll be happy to know *Rockit* had about as much interest in it as you have in me."

I was on my way to the door when Debra called to me. "Hold on, Megan."

I turned back to her cautiously. "What?"

"You have that story with you?"

"Yeah."

"I want to read it." She held out a hand.

I shook my head. "I don't think—"

"Megan." Debra deadeyed me. "I would say that after all of this, you owe me."

What the hell. It wasn't like I needed it anymore. I pulled out my story and slapped it into her palm. She curled it into the same oversize moss-green Fendi bag I'd seen Sage carry once. Then we stepped through the revolving door and into the biting wind of late January.

Debra tightened her ivory-colored cashmere scarf around her neck and started toward her waiting black Town Car.

"Debra?" I called after her. "I just want to say...if I let you down, I'm sorry."

She stopped and turned. "Did you meet anyone interesting down there?"

"Actually, I did," I admitted, despite it being a very strange moment for her to become interested in my personal life. "But it didn't work out. It's all in the article."

"That's too bad." She sounded oddly disappointed. The she reached for the door handle of the car. "What do you want me to do with the story when I'm done?"

"Chuck it, I guess."

"Take care, Megan." She ducked into the backseat of the car before the driver could get out and open the door.

I turned toward Broadway and the downtown R train, just another unemployed New Yorker trying to fight the cold and get through the day.

chapter forty

*Y*ou want flirtini?" Vitaly asked as I finished filling his
olive tray.

It was the Monday night after my ill-fated double-dip en-
counter with Gary and Debra. I'd been working and spending
more time with Lily since our session of True Confessions at
her gym. I was even going to let her buy me a new winter coat
tomorrow, but for tonight my bed was calling.

"No drink tonight," I told Vitaly. "I'm going home to change
into my spare feet."

He looked at me blankly, confirmation that appreciation for
my sense of humor is something acquired late in the English
learning curve.

My feet were throbbing, and even though Tver had been

busy for my entire shift, I'd made only twenty-five bucks in tips. Every lowlife in New York had decided to sit in my section. There'd been the drunk at booth one who had grabbed my ass as I set his rice pudding in front of him, and the lesbian couple in booth four who changed their order three times without ever actually making eye contact with me. Late in my shift, ten girls from New Jersey took booths two, three, and four, ordered half the menu, wolfed it down, and then pointed to a dead roach under the lettuce leaf of one girl's cheeseburger special. Her snicker led me to believe they'd provided said bug themselves to get out of paying. The Tver surveillance camera backed up my hunch. Vitaly and Vadim made them pay up, but there was no tip for me.

I said good night to my coworkers and stepped out into a crisp, fresh evening. The walk home featured the usual sights and sounds—sirens wailing in the distance, a junkie peeing between two trash cans at the corner of A and Tenth, a couple screaming at each other in front of my stoop. They were still going at it when I let myself into my building and made the five-flight trek up the stairs. I'd called ahead, since the last few nights I'd walked in on Charma and Gary doing the do on their side of the partition.

I undid the three locks and stepped into our Levittown kitchen. If Charma's grandmother had been visiting us, there would have been homemade chicken soup on the stove instead of what I saw: champagne flutes and an unopened bottle of Taittinger.

Either Charma had just gotten cast in something major, or Gary had gotten a huge raise, or—

"Surprise!"

Out jumped the Baker twins. They were beaming at me. As in not mad. As in they threw their arms around me in a group hug.

"What are you doing here? When—how did you get here?" I babbled.

"Not you, *we*," Rose corrected. "What are *we* doing here? That would be first-person plural. I should know, since I'm going to Duke next fall. I had to come tell you in person."

"Oh my God, you did it!" I hugged the girls again. The implications were not lost on me. If Rose got in, the twins were halfway—

"I got in, too," Sage said laconically, then assessed my waitress uniform. "Have we taught you *nothing*?"

"You got in! You're going! You got your money!" I found myself dancing around the kitchen. "I'm so happy for you guys!" And I was, I really, truly was. "You're rich!"

"And you know who else is happy for me?" Rose was beaming. "Thom!" she yelled before I could even ask.

Sage smiled. "They're madly in luh-luh-love," she informed me. "And I'm not even being bitchy about it. At least not to their faces. Joking."

Rose stuck her tongue out at her sister before turning back to me. "Hey, don't you want to know how we found you?" she asked eagerly.

"Fuck that. Tell her later. Let's open the champagne," Sage ordered. She popped the cork and filled four glasses. "To our tutor, Megan Smith, who did the impossible: got us in to Duke and got a fashion sense, even though she seems to have lost it."

We clinked glasses and drank. The champagne was heady,

but even more heady was the knowledge that it seemed I'd been forgiven. The question was, how?

Before I could even ask, Rose explained. "We read your article," she said softly.

"What art—"

Then I understood. The one I'd written for *Rockit*. That I'd given to Debra Wurtzel. Debra knew Laurel. Debra must have read it and then sent it to Laurel. The kindness of that overwhelmed me.

"We came off great, I might add," Sage said.

"So . . . you forgive me?" I asked tentatively.

Rather than answer, Rose reached into her jeans pocket and took out an envelope. "For you."

Heart hammering, I tore it open. It was from the Sage and Rose Baker Trust, payable to Megan Smith. For one hundred and fifty thousand dollars.

"We asked Grandma how much you were supposed to get. Then we doubled it. We figured we were each worth seventy-five thou, easy," Sage explained.

It's not often that I am at a loss for words, but at that moment I was rendered speechless.

"It's because you were so generous with us," Rose said simply.

Holy shit. A hundred and fifty grand. I could pay off my Yale loans. I could quit the restaurant, write freelance, and hold out for a job at a great magazine.

"I'm not poor, and the Baker twins are going to college," I marveled.

Sage looked horrified. "College?" She shuddered. "God, no. How boring would *that* be?"

"But the money? How do you get the—"

"Megan, Megan, Megan," Sage intoned with a long-suffering sigh. "I would have thought a Yale grad would pay attention to the fine print. The deal was, Rose and I got the money if we both got *into* Duke. Not if we both *attended* Duke."

It was hilarious. She was right. "You mean you outsmarted your grandmother?"

"It's a thing of beauty," she agreed, and lifted her champagne glass. "Another toast. Here's to us. And especially to *Sage Baker's Season.*"

"What's that?" I asked.

She spread her hands wide. "It's winter in Palm Beach, and the island's It Girl has been doing The Season since she was in sixth grade—galas, balls, ten-thou-a-plate charity dinners. But this year she has to put on one of her own." She placed her hands on my shoulders. "I'm calling it the Sage Stage." Sage mimed a headline with her hands. "It's to benefit women who are out of work, just finished drug rehab, whatever."

"Like a halfway house?" I asked skeptically.

"More like the ultimate makeover," Sage decreed. "It'll be on E! next winter."

Rose set her champagne glass on the table. "So are you going to show us your apartment?"

"What there is of it," I said, motioning for them to follow me around the apartment. "Addison Mizner designed the tasteful eight-by-ten living room, and the partition that makes up the cell-like bedrooms is Mizner's homage to Riker's Island, where—"

I stopped. On my bed were the suitcase and garment bag Marco had given me that first day he'd helped me with my wardrobe. They were bulging. Clearly, the girls had already given themselves the tour.

"Marco read what you wrote, too," Sage explained. "And he said you left him a note. He wants to play himself in the movie."

"He also said he couldn't bear to think of these on anyone but you. So go ahead," Rose urged. "Open one."

I unzipped the garment bag. It was full of Chloé and Zac Posen, Vera Wang and Pucci, Gucci and Alaia. Some I recognized, but some I didn't.

"One of Marco's friends opened a store called When Good Clothes Go Drag," Rose explained. "He cherry-picked these for you."

I was stunned.

"Don't gush yet," Sage cautioned. She tugged on my left shoulder so I'd pivot toward the wall, a wall that had been bare ever since I'd sold my parents' framed Woodstock T-shirt. Now an exquisite painting hung there.

It was Will and me in Hanan's garden, done in Hanan's inimitable style. She must have painted it from one of the photographs she'd taken of the two of us.

"Will wanted you to have that," Rose said quietly.

Something twisted in my heart.

"Did he...read the article, too?" I asked.

"That's why he sent this up here with us," Sage reported. She took a look at her Hermès Medor watch. "It's one-thirty. If we don't leave now, we'll miss the last set."

"Then we gotta go," Rose agreed.

"Whose last set?" I asked as they headed back to the kitchen and took their coats off the hook on the back of the door.

"Brain Freeze," Rose explained. "Thom knows the bass player from high school. They're at the Pyramid Club tonight."

"That's just around the corner," I told them. "Let me change out of this hideous uniform first." I was already on my way when Rose stopped me.

"Megan...I'm sorry, but it's kind of a double-date thing. I'm fixing Sage up with Thom's friend."

"I decided that having a musician as a boyfriend makes a statement," Sage explained.

Oh. Okay. I felt a little let down, but I shook that feeling off.

"We're staying at the Gansevoort," Rose told me. "I take it you're not waitressing tomorrow?"

We decided to meet for a very late lunch at Fatty Crab, the Malaysian place in the West Village. I hugged the girls goodbye and sat back down at the green Formica table. Then I took a chug straight from the bottle of Cristal. Hey, I deserved it. What an impossible, fantastic turn of events.

Feeling giddy from good fortune and champagne, I padded into the bathroom, turned on the shower, and was about to shed that uniform for the very last time, when I heard the fire alarm clang in the hallway.

The fire alarm. Again. I'm totally serious. Dammit. I was moving out of this fucking East Village firetrap tenement as soon as I cashed that check.

Being no fool, I ran to get the check, then pulled open my front door and bolted for the stairs. But my Serbian landlord was on the fourth-floor landing, calling up to me. "Stairs are blocked! Go to roof, quickly, Megan! Cross to next building!"

Fuck! I changed direction, ran up the steep steps two at a time, and rammed my upper arm into the heavy metal door to shove it open. It took three strong pushes, and then I was out, stepping onto the—

Sand.

Not concrete. *Sand.*

There was a *beach* covering my roof. It was dotted with beach umbrellas and chaise longues and a half-dozen of those portable gas heating units that can keep outdoor cafés toasty in the coldest weather.

On one of the chaises, clad in surfer jams and sunglasses, tall drink in hand, was Will.

"Flirtini?" He offered me the drink. "Since you couldn't come to Palm Beach, I decided that Palm Beach should come to you."

I stepped toward him, trying to find words. "Umm...no fire?" was the best I could do.

"It was pathetically easy to bribe your landlord into assisting us, I'm afraid. He didn't blink about letting us into your apartment, or about the team of burly guys we hired to haul up the sand. I'd think about moving if I were you."

I leaned over and pinched him.

"Ow!" He pulled his arm away.

"Just wanted to make sure this was real."

He rubbed his arm. "Was my manly yelp enough confirmation?"

I grinned, sitting down on the chaise in front of him. "I love Hanan's painting."

"It's great, huh?" he agreed, placing the flirtini in my hand. "That was the day I fell for you, you know."

I looked at Will, at his freckled arms and tapered fingers. He was so handsome. I still couldn't quite believe he'd like someone like...me. "Why?" I heard myself ask.

He took off his sunglasses. "Because you were so much yourself. Frizzy hair, dirt on your face, kind of goofy."

"Goofy?" I laughed. "Fair enough. Well, that was when it changed for me, too, you know. The way you talked about Hanan's paintings, even though your father would never show them. I still hope you will. Someday."

"Step one is moving here," he said.

Wait, had he just said... "Could you repeat that?"

"Here," he repeated. "To New York. Where I'm going to open my gallery. Hanan will be the first artist I show."

I must have looked as thrilled as I felt, because he held up a hand of caution.

"It won't be easy. My father is less than delighted. He's putting his money where his mouth is, meaning he's not investing in me. The twins are, though. And I've already talked with some of my frat brothers from Northwestern."

"And here I thought being in a fraternity was a waste of time," I teased. I took a sip of my flirtini. It was as good as in Palm Beach. Maybe better. "This..." I gestured wide. "All of this. It's amazing."

"Funny, that's the word I used about what you wrote." He looked down at the sand-colored roof. "Everything you did made sense in a bizarre sort of way."

"I'm so glad the twins gave you the article."

He looked up at me. "Oh, I read it before they did. My mom FedExed it to me, actually."

"Your...what?"

"Not a what, a who. Debra Wurtzel is my mother." He smiled

wide at what was surely my very shocked-looking face. "Believe me, I had no idea she'd sent you to Palm Beach until I read what you wrote. It was all her doing."

I was bewildered. "But... why?"

"Apparently, she thought you'd make a great tutor for the fabulous Baker twins of Palm Beach... and she wanted to give fate a little nudge. Basically, she thinks you're perfect for me."

"Parents are always wrong about that kind of thing," I pointed out.

"Maybe we'd better change that to 'usually wrong.'"

He stood up and walked over to a small makeshift bar near the edge of the roof. He pushed the button on a CD player. Bob Marley's "One Love" filled the night air. I laughed as Will helped me to my feet.

And then, in the middle of the East Village on a chilly New York winter night, on a white sand beach that was formerly the roof of my apartment building, we danced.

Acknowledgments

Thanks to Sara Shandler, Josh Bank, and their team; to Amy Einhorn, Emily Griffin, Frances Jalet-Miller, and *their* team; and especially to super-special-agent-in-charge Lydia dah-link Wills. Thanks also to my many friends in Palm Beach, and especially to my favorite mixologist, Pablo. Without Pablo, life itself would be impossible.